RESIMERCIAL REVOLUTION

FOR COMMERCIAL REAL ESTATE MASTERY

Tony Hardy J.D.

TABLE OF CONTENTS

From Residential Roots to Towering Transactions

Welcome to the "Resimercial Revolution!" *resimercial*, a portmanteau of *residential* and *commercial*, artfully encapsulates the dynamic fusion of two real estate realms traditionally siloed. This blending signifies more than a market niche; it heralds a transformative era where the rigid lines between residential and commercial business environments become beautifully blurred. This is the world of the Resimercial Revolution—a bold rejection of the "we've always done it this way" mindset and an embracing of a holistic approach over industry tradition.

Revolution speaks to radical change, an upheaval that redefines the very fabric of an industry. *Resimercial Revolution* embodies this spirit of transformation, seamlessly merging the residential and commercial realms of real estate. This indispensable guide is tailored for top-performing residential agents poised to transition into commercial real estate, as well as commercial brokers seeking to elevate their careers to unprecedented heights. It bridges the traditional divides, offering a playbook that distills nuance from over two hundred successful commercial transactions to provide a comprehensive exploration of everything from crafting initial letters of intent to navigating complex escrow processes. Here, residential agents find a clear path to expand into commercial ventures, while seasoned commercial agents discover innovative strategies to shatter their career ceilings. This resource not only illuminates the diverse perspectives of buyers, sellers, and stakeholders but also empowers real estate professionals to manage sophisticated deals with newfound confidence and creativity. Embrace the Resimercial Revolution, where breaking through the old barriers paves the way for mastering the art of commercial real estate.

At a bustling local real estate conference, filled with eager faces looking for insights into the ever-evolving real estate landscape, I found myself in a unique position. As a fireside chat commenced, the room buzzed with anticipation. The speakers, a managing broker of a prominent realty housing over four hundred agents and a high-profile real estate attorney, were poised to tackle the seismic shifts shaking the industry due to the recent NAR antitrust lawsuit.

As the discussion unfolded, the focus sharpened on the storm of changes—mandatory disclosures, buyer and tenant agreements, and the relentless push toward transparency and compliance stirred by the NAR settlement. Each point punctuated the room's air, drawing nods and scribbles from an audience clinging to every word.

I, as the sole commercial broker among the crowd, found myself with a unique vantage point. This viewpoint offered me a striking realization: the upheaval meant to standardize residential practices was nudging them closer to the modalities long upheld in commercial real estate. In our world, the preliminaries of touring properties, sharing information, or engaging with other brokers and off-market opportunities are often preceded by strategic agreements and meticulous planning—practices not as common on the residential side until now.

This evolution is not merely a shift but a significant elevation of industry standards, compelling residential agents to adopt a more methodical and rigorous approach akin to their commercial counterparts. The conversation at the conference, while rooted in the immediate effects of legal changes, inadvertently highlighted a broader transformation: the blurring lines between residential and commercial real estate practitioners.

As the room absorbed the weight of these changes, the palpable sense of urgency underscored a pivotal shift within the industry. This convergence of residential and commercial practices is not merely a trend but a fundamental evolution that demands adaptation. Those who choose to embrace this shift will find themselves at the forefront, enhancing their professionalism and deepening their service of offerings. However, for those reluctant to adapt, the risk of obsolescence grows ever more real.

Resimercial Revolution is crafted as your indispensable guide through this transformative landscape. It equips you with the integrated skills and strategies essential for thriving in this new era of real estate. By mastering these concepts, you position yourself not just to survive but to excel in steering through the complexities with confidence and foresight. Herein lies the opportunity to not only continue in the industry but to lead it, shaping your legacy through innovative practices and visionary transactions.

Over the past fifteen years, my career in real estate has been intensely focused on the commercial sector. In September 2020, I ascended to the role of Executive Director at KW Commercial, Keller Williams ONEChicago, initially guiding three offices and forty agents. My role has since expanded to Regional Director for KW Commercial where I now influence strategic commercial deployment across thirty-four offices in various states within the region.

Parallel to my leadership journey, I've cultivated a diverse team of twelve commercial brokers—some entirely new to the industry, others transitioning from residential sectors. I've introduced them to the methodologies outlined in this book, emphasizing that establishing a robust commercial practice usually requires three to five years of concerted effort. This team has exceeded expectations, successfully closing over $100 million in transactions. They have garnered significant recognition, including a Rookie of the Year award at Keller Williams—bestowed upon the highest achiever among more than a hundred new agents—and several gold and platinum awards from the Chicago Association of Realtors across office, retail, and multifamily asset classes. Notably, in 2022, they facilitated a headline-making $10.35 million mixed-use deal in Hyde Park.

Furthermore, their influence stretches beyond mere transactions. They actively participate on various commercial committees and hold seats on several influential boards within the industry. This exceptional team exemplifies the impact of the strategies presented in this playbook. By merging residential and commercial realms, they are not only advancing their careers but also significantly shaping the future of the real estate industry through effective mentorship and leadership.

This playbook arms you with strategic tools to compete, win, and dominate, especially in today's landscape where controlling inventory and maintaining sharp market intelligence are critical. Against the backdrop of unprecedented interest rate hikes and shifting market trends, mastering these key elements will position you for success.

Here are the four essential pillars you'll master in this book:

1. Mindset: Develop a mental game akin to elite athletes, staying focused and resilient during high-stakes transactions.

2. Team Building: Learn to assemble your own team of specialists, just like a sports team, where every role is critical to the overall success of a deal.

3. Dedication and Strategy: Commit to continuous learning and deliberate preparation, much like athletes train rigorously for game day. This ensures you can capitalize on every opportunity.

4. Vision: Go beyond the transaction and see the long-term impact of your work on communities, mirroring the legacy-focused mindset of visionary coaches.

These pillars will help you turn market headwinds into tailwinds, enabling you to win more listings, engage with buyers meaningfully, and tackle challenges with the confidence of a commercial real estate expert.

At the end of each chapter, workshops will encourage you to apply what you've learned, pushing you to handle real-world scenarios through role-playing to ensure you're prepared to lead clients through complex transactions.

Are you ready to join the revolution?

Let's GO!

Opening Play: Understanding the Resimercial Landscape

Success is no accident. It is hard work, perseverance,
learning, studying, sacrifice, and most of all, love of what
you are doing or learning to do.
—Pele

Over two decades ago, in the echoing chambers of a university assembly hall bustling with potential and promise, a pivotal scene unfolded. Here, amid the maze of recruiting booths draped in corporate colors, a young African American man stood on the brink of his professional life. He was mere months from graduation, his future rippling out in front of him like the pages of an unopened book.

Before stepping into the fair, Professor Sanders of the agribusiness management and finance class had lined up the young man and his peers for a preliminary drill. Known for his insistence on professionalism, Sanders had a simple yet crucial test for them: the perfect handshake.

It was more than a formality; it was a lesson in making enduring first impressions. With a firm grip and a direct gaze, the young man earned a nod of approval, setting a confident tone for the day.

As he navigated the fair, he interacted with representatives from various fields, collecting brochures and engaging in conversations. Yet, it wasn't until he approached a modest booth highlighting the world of commercial real estate that his curiosity peaked. The company, Transwestern, was not the flashiest presenter, but its focus on impactful urban development and strategic investments caught his attention.

A dialogue with a Transwestern vice president revealed the high stakes and intense rhythms of real estate transactions. Her words laid out a path of rigorous hours: "Start your day at seven a.m. and wrap at seven p.m.; show us your dedication, and you'll fast-track your way to success." This proposition, though filled with promise, sparked a deeper realization in him. He sought not just a job but a career—one that would offer not only financial rewards but also opportunities for significant professional growth through strategic and meaningful contributions.

Politely declining the offer, he left Transwestern's booth enriched with a clearer vision of his professional aspirations. This encounter, though brief, was profound, steering him away from a path of routine and toward one where his ambitions could thrive.

With renewed purpose, he exited the fair, not with a job offer in hand but with a conviction to carve a niche in an industry that shaped entire communities. This experience marked not the conclusion of a simple job search but the commencement of a formidable journey into the realms of commercial real estate—a journey destined to reshape skylines and redefine his role in the tapestry of urban life.

Embracing autonomy in his career, the young broker transitioned to Century 21 Enterprise Realty, determined to carve his own path and committed to working each day from seven a.m. to seven p.m. for himself. His dedication quickly shone through, earning him office keys in mere weeks due to his habit of arriving first and leaving last. This unwavering commitment reaped immediate rewards; within six months, he outearned what two years that the previous corporate role would have provided.

His journey, though, was fraught with the typical vicissitudes of real estate—unpredictable first-time buyers who often compromised deals with their whimsical decisions or poor financial management. Despite these challenges, he closed his first year on a high note, surpassing his corporate salary.

The following year, his efforts were recognized with a promotion to team leader, but the highs of leadership came with new lows. Deals fell through for reasons as whimsical as they were frustrating: one buyer squandered his down payment on a spontaneous safari in Australia; another, buoyed by a surprising credit score boost, indulged in a new Cadillac, thus ruining his loan approval. Yet another gambled away his earnest money during a reckless weekend in Vegas. Each setback was a stern lesson in the unpredictable ways personal lives could derail professional successes.

The tide turned in the second quarter with a door-to-door campaign that led him to Mr. Jenkins, an esteemed resident not initially interested in selling. Instead, Mr. Jenkins was curious about the market value of his four-unit apartment building. This opportunity to handle a modest yet strategic property would mark a turning point in his career. The building, with two one-bedroom and two two-bedroom units, provided a tangible asset to manage. Mr. Jenkins provided the rent roll, a central document detailing the income each unit generated, pivotal for evaluating the property's worth and investment potential.

After thorough market comparisons, they settled on a listing price of $400,000 with a win-win compensation amount. The property quickly drew interest once listed on the MLS and featured in a local newspaper. A buyer from the Chicago Transit Authority, enticed by the advertisement, presented a full-price offer. The deal was poised for a smooth close until a last-minute complication at the closing table tested all parties involved.

Facing his first major closing at just twenty-two, the young agent was both excited and daunted by the prospect of earning the largest payday of his career. The tension peaked during the closing proceedings when Mr. Jenkins's attorney, perhaps to assert dominance or unsettle the young agent, dismissively called him a "young punk" in front of everyone. He questioned Mr. Jenkins pointedly, "Do you realize you're paying this 'young punk' a sizable amount of money to sell your building?"

Mr. Jenkins, unwavering in his support, responded with confidence and trust that had been built over their dealings. "Yes, I'm fully aware," he declared, his tone firm and composed. "I agreed to pay him that amount because he's earned it, just as I'm paying you to manage the legal aspects of this transaction." His endorsement not only sealed the deal but also fortified the young agent's commitment to a career defined by integrity and diligence. This incident wasn't merely a transaction concluded; it was a profound validation of his professional path in the demanding yet fulfilling world of real estate.

This pivotal experience marked his first significant foray into "resimercial" real estate—a blend of residential and commercial where transactions involve properties meant for investment rather than personal occupancy. It was a moment of realization about the impact of meticulous preparation, the necessity of trust between client and broker, and the delicate balance of handling the numerical and human facets of real estate deals. These formative experiences laid the foundational principles he would carry into his evolving career, aiming to transform not just properties, but lives and communities.

Returning to his apartment, he walked back to a modest multiunit property that marked one of his earliest forays into real estate investment. Living in the first-floor unit and renting out the others was his initial venture into what's known as house hacking. This strategy didn't just teach him property management basics; it also provided a financial buffer against the unpredictable income flow typical in early real estate careers. Owner-occupants of multiunit properties could qualify for substantially lower down payments, a situation increasingly accessible due to revised lending guidelines by entities like Fannie Mae and the Federal Housing Administration (FHA). Recently, these organizations adjusted their requirements to allow as little as 5 percent down for two-to-four-unit properties—a sharp decrease from the traditional 10–20 percent. This change is a game changer for new investors or those guiding clients to start their portfolios in real estate.

This adjustment underscores a vital investment strategy: leveraging owneroccupied financing advantages to build an initial portfolio. Alongside this, Community Reinvestment Act programs can provide additional down payment assistance, paving the way for a robust entry into property investment. He employed a strategy dubbed "4-3-2-1": beginning with a four-unit property, an investor can systematically move to smaller properties, eventually funding a single-family home entirely through cash flow from previous investments. Each step not only builds equity but also prepares an investor for the larger down payments required in commercial real estate.

As he settled back into the quiet of his multiunit, his curiosity about the neighboring twenty-five-story tower building undergoing transformation—couldn't be quenched. The commotion of its redevelopment had disrupted his rest, but it also reignited his deeper interest in commercial real estate ventures on a larger scale. He took it upon himself to research who the new owners were and what their plans entailed, realizing that projects of such magnitude were where he wanted to direct his future efforts. This was more than mere curiosity; it was a strategic move to align his career trajectory with the high stakes and high rewards of commercial real estate.

This 4-3-2-1 investment strategy is not just about acquiring properties: it's about strategically positioning oneself for exponential growth. This method involves purchasing multiunit residential properties in descending order—starting with a fourplex, then a triplex, followed by a duplex, and finally a single-family home. The magic of this strategy lies in the accumulation and utilization of equity.

Building Equity Through Sequential Sales

Each property serves as a stepping stone. As you live in and manage each unit, not only do you gain invaluable experience, but you also pay down the mortgage, thereby building equity. Over the years, this equity accumulates, and when you sell the four-unit building, the return on your initial investment can be substantial. This capital, once released, can be the key to unlocking more significant investments.

The Power of Stacking with 1031 Exchanges

Here's where "stacking" comes into play, layering opportunities to magnify your investment potential. By using a 1031 exchange, you can defer paying capital gains tax on the sale of your investment property, as long as you reinvest the proceeds into another like-kind property. This strategy allows you to leverage the full power of your investment capital to move up to larger properties, such as an eight-to-twelve-unit complex, effectively doubling your unit count and potential cash flow.

Leveraging Rental Income for Bigger Loans

Lenders play a pivotal role in this strategy by allowing you to use a portion of your rental income to qualify for larger loans. This aspect is particularly beneficial as it considers the income-generating potential of the properties, not just your income, thereby enhancing your borrowing capacity.

Family Investment Dynamics

This strategy isn't just for individual investors; it's a powerful tool for generational wealth building. Seasoned investors often use this approach to introduce younger family members, like nieces or nephews, to the world of real estate investing. By guiding them through this process, they help the next generation leverage existing assets to climb the property ladder faster and more efficiently.

Every clang and beep of construction next door served as a reminder of the possibilities that lay in mastering commercial deals. It wasn't just about owning properties; it was about transforming them, about contributing to the skyline and, by extension, to the community. This reaffirmed a commitment to not just participate in real estate but to shape its future, steering his career toward larger, more impactful projects.

From College Fair to Career Clarity: The journey began at a bustling college job fair, where a young African American student discovered his passion not just for real estate, but for the intricate dance of negotiation and strategic investment. This moment of clarity was more than just a career choice; it was the first step toward a profound understanding of the market's potential. Professor Sanders's lessons on professionalism, particularly the importance of a firm handshake and direct eye contact, laid the foundational skills necessary for successful interactions in the world of real estate.

Early Career Choices and Lessons: Turning down a corporate job offer with rigid hours and a guaranteed salary, the young man chose instead to dive headfirst into the field of real estate, valuing flexibility, the potential for growth, and direct control over his success. This decision highlighted a crucial lesson in weighing opportunity costs and understanding the time value of money—concepts first introduced in his finance classes.

Implementation of the 4-3-2-1 Strategy: As his career progressed, the implementation of the 4-3-2-1 investment strategy underscored the practical applications of his academic insights. Starting with a fourplex and advancing through to a single-family home, each step was not just a purchase but a strategic move that built equity and expanded his portfolio. This strategy showcased the practical side of residential real estate as a gateway to larger commercial deals.

Leveraging Financial Tools and Real Estate Programs: The narrative also touched on leveraging various financial tools and real estate programs to minimize upfront costs and maximize investment returns. The use of owner-occupant financing options like FHA loans highlighted how entry-level investors could reduce down payment requirements, while the Community Reinvestment Act and bank down payment assistance programs further eased the financial burden.

Stacking and Scaling Investments: The concept of "stacking" through 1031 exchanges was introduced as a method to preserve capital gains and reinvest in ever-larger properties. This strategic use of real estate laws not only optimized financial growth but also encouraged a long-term vision for real estate investing, demonstrating the scalability of this approach.

This chapter encapsulates a fundamental transformation from a novice, influenced by early lessons and opportunities, into a seasoned investor harnessing sophisticated strategies like the 4-3-2-1 method and 1031 exchanges. It celebrates the journey of growth, learning, and strategic foresight in real estate, emphasizing that success in this field is as much about smart financial decisions as it is about understanding and navigating the human elements of business and community impact.

Workshop: Full-Court Press—Foundations of a Real Estate Playbook

1. **Kickoff: Reflecting on Your Position in the Field**

   ○ Participants reflect on their career trajectory—weighing the flexibility and growth potential of real estate against the stability of a corporate structure.

   ○ Each participant writes down what aspects of real estate are most appealing and explains why.

2. **Financial Fitness Drill: Time Value of Money**

   ○ Calculate and compare potential earnings over two years in a corporate setting versus initiating a real estate venture.

   ○ Engage in a discussion on personal interpretations of the "time value of money" and its significance in career planning.

3. **Scrimmage: Perfecting Your Professional Game**

   ○ Engage in a role-playing exercise to practice introductions and firm handshakes, receiving direct feedback on presentation skills.

   ○ Identify and discuss three critical aspects of professional appearance and plan their implementation at the next networking opportunity.

4. **Strategic Playmaking: Investment Strategy Planning**

   ○ Using the 4-3-2-1 strategy model, outline a personal real estate investment plan:

      ● 4 Units: Start with choosing a property type and location. Justify your selection based on market research.

      ● 3 Units: Plan the next investment following.

      ● 2 Units and 1 Unit: Continue refining your investment strategy, detailing how each transaction moves you closer to your goals.

      ● Discuss potential exit strategies.

         ○ Keeping the property for more than ten years is not an option in these discussions.

5. **Financial Endzone: Calculating Financial Advantages**

   ○ Workshop on financial calculations for owner-occupied financing, including different schemes like FHA and Fannie Mae.

   ○ Discuss how leveraging such financing options can be a game changer in real estate investment growth.

6. **Legal Playbook: Real Estate Laws in Action**

   ○ Explain the mechanics of a 1031 exchange and simulate its application in future real estate transactions to optimize capital preservation.

   ○ Describe and discuss "stacking" as a strategy to amplify real estate holdings.

7. **Victory Lap: Reflecting on Scaling Your Investments**

- O Reflect on the journey from starting small to scaling up through strategic investments and its impact on long-term financial objectives.

- O Write a reflective piece on applying these strategies to not only enhance personal wealth but also contribute positively to the community.

CHAPTER 2

The Transition—Focusing on Investors

Success is not an accident, success is actually a choice.
—Steph Curry

The next morning, the cacophony of construction jolted me awake. The beeping of bulldozers backing up and the clatter of materials being unloaded were unmistakable. Glancing at the clock, it read 7:05 a.m.—I was already late. In a rush, I hurried to the office, the adrenaline from yesterday's big deal still buzzing in my veins.

As I burst through the office doors, Mr. Lucas, the managing broker, was there waiting, an amused smirk playing on his face. Tall, dark, and undeniably charismatic, he was not just a broker but a prominent real estate developer and a serial entrepreneur who insisted on punctuality. "I thought you committed to seven a.m. starts," he teased his tone light but pointed. "Looks like someone was celebrating a bit too hard last night. Remember, if you're on time, you're late, and if you're early, you're on time. Today, you missed the mark."

Despite the gentle chiding, his next words were of congratulations. He extended his hand, the pride in his eyes evident. "Job well done on that closing yesterday," he said, clasping my shoulder with a firm grip that spoke of respect and expectation. It was a brief conversation that steered toward the future.

In his office, surrounded by the tangible successes of his career—awards, model buildings, and photos of notable properties—we discussed my next steps.

Seizing the moment, I shared the resolve that had been forming since the previous day's success. "Mr. Lucas, I've been doing some thinking," I began, my voice steady despite the morning's rocky start. "From now on, I want to focus exclusively on investors. No more first-time homebuyers for me."

Mr. Lucas raised an eyebrow, his interest piqued. "That's a bold shift," he remarked. "Tell me more."

I explained my new direction, fueled not just by the allure of bigger deals but by the repetitive business model that investors offered. The steady flow of transactions, even if they were not headline-grabbing, promised a more consistent and potentially lucrative pipeline.

As our conversation deepened, Mr. Lucas supported my decision, providing guidance on how to refine my approach. He understood the challenges of pivoting in real estate but also recognized the potential for significant growth.

The journey from residential to what I would come to call "resimercial" real estate was set into motion that morning, spurred by the relentless noise of construction next door—a daily reminder of the opportunities that lay just beyond the traditional path.

This change was not just a shift in focus; it was an evolution in my career, marking the beginning of a deeper engagement with real estate investment and development. Each transaction, each day at the office became a step toward becoming a pivotal figure in the real estate market, transforming properties and my professional trajectory.

Understanding one's strengths and recognizing when to delegate is critical. My practice has long adhered to the philosophy of placing the best team on the field, a strategy that ensures both client satisfaction and optimal outcomes. This approach was put to the test recently during a particularly memorable listing presentation for a one-hundred-unit apartment complex.

The seller, an experienced investor, expressed his intention to sell the large complex. During our discussion, he revealed a broader ambition: he also owned a portfolio of eighteen two- and three-flats valued at over $7 million. While these properties were generating significant cash flow, managing them across multiple locations had become a distraction as he scaled his operations. He was ready to streamline his portfolio, starting with these smaller units.

The prospect of securing a $7 million listing was enticing. However, having shifted my focus exclusively to larger commercial transactions over the years, I recognized that managing the sale of two- and three-flats would not play to my strengths. Commitment to my client's best interests led me to seek the right agent for this task.

After thorough research and consultations within and outside my office, I identified Antonio, a referral partner with a stellar track record in handling such properties. I facilitated an introduction, and Antonio took over the sale of the portfolio. His dedication was evident as he navigated numerous challenges, including over a dozen open houses, an encounter with an unleashed dog, and even a sprained ankle from an unexpected leap over a fence to escape.

Antonio's efforts paid off—within six months, he sold all the properties at 98 percent of the list price. The client was thrilled with the outcome, which spoke volumes about the effectiveness of choosing the right team for the right task. As a result of this successful partnership and the excellent results Antonio delivered, the client was confident in listing the one-hundred-unit complex with me, viewing my ability to orchestrate the right team as a unique advantage.

In a poignant reminder of the gritty realities of real estate, our initial meeting about the one-hundred-unit complex took place in its boiler room. The setting was reminiscent of a scene straight out of a "Mystery Thriller"—a musky, cobweb-filled basement room where the hum of the boilers and the mix of moisture in the air set a dramatic backdrop for our discussions.

This experience reinforced a valuable lesson: sometimes, slowing down to strategically delegate is the fastest way to accelerate success. It also underscored my commitment to providing tailored solutions, ensuring each client feels understood and expertly served, no matter the complexity or scale of their real estate endeavors.

Finding Your Sweet Spot: The Resimercial Agent Model

The decision to shift from serving first-time homebuyers to focusing on investors was driven by a simple yet powerful economic principle: opportunity cost. As a real estate agent, saying "no" to potential business is never easy, especially when the budget is tight. However, specializing in investment properties rather than residential sales opened a new realm of financial and professional growth.

Optimizing Income as a Resimercial Agent: A Mathematical Breakdown

When considering the financial dynamics between handling residential versus investment properties, the distinction in client interaction and transaction frequency becomes starkly apparent. This difference is not merely in the nature of the transactions but also in the potential for increased earnings and continuous client engagement offered by focusing on investors.

Here's how the numbers typically play out:

Initial Investment Opportunities

Imagine an investor who purchases several distressed two-flats over the course of a year—properties that need vision, creativity, and a solid team to bring them back to life. On the front end, you're representing that investor through each acquisition, guiding them through due diligence, valuation, and closing. Each purchase adds momentum to your pipeline and builds a relationship rooted in trust and performance.

Months later, those same properties are transformed—renovated, stabilized, and ready for market. Now you're back in the driver's seat, this time helping your client list and sell the completed projects. Each successful resale not only strengthens your client's portfolio but also your own reputation as a broker who can manage the full life cycle of an investment—from acquisition to disposition. We call these homeruns.

If you partner with another agent—perhaps one who specializes in marketing or managing open houses—you can split the responsibilities while doubling your bandwidth. Together, your team could handle two, three, or even four investor clients at once, each cycling through multiple projects a year.

Some brokers hesitate to share the spotlight, believing they can handle everything themselves. But scaling a business isn't about holding onto every piece of the pie—it's about creating a system that can multiply results. By collaborating strategically, you build capacity, consistency, and sustainability—turning one investor into a stream of repeat opportunities.

Over time, that single investor can evolve into a network of clients who trust your process and rely on your results. What began as a handful of acquisitions in one year can quickly become a rhythm of multiple projects in motion at once—each one feeding into the next. That's how a resimercial broker transitions from chasing transactions to building momentum, and from working deals to building a business.

The Shift into Resimercial Mastery: Tony's Journey Begins

Tony leaned back in his office chair, his mind buzzing with excitement. The real estate market was shifting, and he knew this was his opportunity to rise above the rest. He had spent his first two years in the business building a solid career in residential real estate, closing deals on single-family homes and small multifamily properties. But something was changing—more of his clients were asking about investment properties, and he could sense that the commercial side of the business held the real potential for growth.

On a chilly afternoon, Tony received a call from Mr. Jenkins, a client who had recently sold a four-unit building through Tony's guidance. "I've got something bigger for you," Jenkins said. "A six-unit building that I've owned for quite some time, I'm thinking of selling. Come by, I need your advice." Tony immediately saw the opportunity. This was his chance to step up from residential to resimercial—a bridge between residential and commercial real estate that could lead to repeat business.

When Tony arrived at the property, he was greeted by Mr. Jenkins, who took him on a tour of the center entrance six-flat. As they walked through the property, Tony could see the potential. Each unit was spacious—three bedrooms, two baths—and equipped with individual heating systems, making it ideal for future condominium conversions. Jenkins had started making upgrades, with HVAC, in-unit laundry, and dishwashers in each unit already in place, but much of the renovation work was dated. "It's a diamond in the rough," Jenkins explained. "I made these updates a little over ten years ago and it's getting close to the time where I may need to renovate again. But I'm not sure if I want to invest more time and money in it or let it go."

Tony knew this was his moment. "Jenkins, this place has serious potential," he said. "If you're up for it, I'd like to handle the listing and work with you on this project. But we'll need a strategy—this isn't just a simple sale." Jenkins agreed, and Tony knew he was stepping into a more complex, dynamic side of real estate that would demand his full attention.

Tony knew that if he wanted to make a mark in this part of the market, he couldn't do it alone. As he walked through the property with Jenkins, his mind raced with ideas. The building had potential—but he wasn't sure how to analyze the value, determine the market rent and what to make of all the repairs needed. That's when he thought of Linda, one of the more experienced agents at his office. Her family had owned apartment buildings for years, and she was well-versed in the ins and outs of multifamily properties. If anyone could help him navigate this, it was her.

Back at the office, Tony wasted no time. He approached Linda and laid out the situation. "I've got this client, Mr. Jenkins, who's thinking of selling his six-unit building, but I'm not sure where to start with the numbers. I know you've worked on similar deals before—would you be willing to help me with this one?" Linda, always eager to lend a hand, agreed right away. "I'd be happy to help, Tony. Let's take a closer look at the building and do some analysis together."

Linda and Tony spent the next few days reviewing the rent roll and comparing the property to other similar buildings in the area. It didn't take long for them to realize that the rents were well below market rate. The current tenants were paying between $1,100 and $1,200 per month, but comparable units in the neighborhood were renting for around $1,500. "This building has a lot of untapped potential," Linda pointed out. "If Jenkins invests in some updates, he could either raise the rents significantly or sell it as a value-add opportunity for another investor."

Together, Tony and Linda prepared a proposal for Jenkins. They walked him through the numbers, showing him how bringing the rents up to market rate could increase the value of the property. Jenkins was impressed with their analysis and decided he didn't want to go through the trouble of shuffling the tenants and making repairs. So, he agreed to list the property for sale. "You've convinced me," he said. "Let's put it on the market."

Collaboration in Action: Closing the Deal

With the listing agreement signed, Tony and Linda moved quickly. They knew time was of the essence in getting the property on the market before potential buyers snapped up other opportunities in the area. Linda, with her family's background in operating apartment buildings, had valuable connections. One of those connections happened to be a family friend who was always on the lookout for properties with value-add potential.

"I might have the perfect buyer for this," Linda told Tony one afternoon as they worked on the marketing strategy for the building. "My family friend, Mike, has been looking for a solid investment like this. He's got experience with renovations and isn't afraid of a project."

Tony felt a wave of relief. He knew the power of networking, but this was his first time seeing it work so quickly in the commercial world. Linda reached out to Mike, and within days, they had arranged a tour of the property. Mike was impressed with what he saw. While the building needed some cosmetic updates, the infrastructure Jenkins had put in—like individual heating units, upgraded plumbing and electric—was a huge selling point.

By the end of the week, Mike had made a full-price offer. Tony could hardly believe how smoothly things were moving. This was his first commercial listing, and within a matter of days, they had a serious buyer on the hook. "This is the power of collaboration," Tony thought to himself. Working with Linda hadn't only helped him understand the numbers, but it had also fast-tracked the sale.

The next step was to sit down with Jenkins and present the offer. Tony and Linda met with him at the property to go over the details. Jenkins was pleased. The offer was fair, and it was exactly what he had hoped for—a smooth sale without the hassle of waiting for months or dealing with multiple showings and lowball offers. "You two really came through," Jenkins said, shaking Tony's hand. "I knew I made the right call when I asked you to handle this."

Mike's Vision: Renovations and a Long-Term Strategy

With the full-price offer in hand, Tony and Linda sat down with Mike to discuss his plans for the building. Mike was the kind of investor who saw potential where others might see work. He wasn't interested in flipping the property for a quick profit—he was in it for the long haul, and he had a clear vision of how to maximize the building's value over time.

"The bones of this building are solid," Mike said, flipping through the inspection report as they sat at a local café after finalizing the offer. "What I want to do is update each unit as the tenants turn over. New appliances, modernized kitchens, and baths—nothing too fancy, but enough to bring the units up to market standards. It'll increase the rent roll, and over time, we'll have a much more valuable asset on our hands."

Tony nodded, taking it all in. This was the kind of long-term strategy he had read about but hadn't yet seen in action. Mike's plan wasn't just about increasing the rent roll—it was about creating a property that could serve as a solid rental investment for years, but also be positioned for a potential condominium conversion down the line.

"If the market conditions are right in a few years," Mike continued, "I could look at converting these units into condos. The individual heating systems that Jenkins put in already set the stage for that. Once the units are renovated and the neighborhood continues to grow with more businesses moving in, the demand for condo ownership might take off. It's always good to have that exit strategy in the back pocket."

This was a huge learning experience for Tony. Not only was he seeing how value could be added incrementally with each renovation, but Mike's foresight in considering a future condo exit was eye-opening. Commercial real estate wasn't just about immediate gains—it was about planning for future opportunities and understanding the cycles of the market. Tony's confidence grew as he realized that this wasn't the last time he would work with an investor like Mike, who saw the big picture.

A Seamless Transaction and the
Start of a New Partnership

The next few weeks flew by. Tony and Linda coordinated with Jenkins to ensure a seamless transition. With everything in place, they closed the deal without a hitch, and Mike officially became the owner of the six-unit property.

As they wrapped up the paperwork, Mike turned to Tony. "You've been great to work with on this, Tony. I'll need your help when I start turning these units over and looking for new tenants, and if I decide to move forward with the condo conversion down the line, I want you to handle the sales."

Tony couldn't believe his luck. Not only had he successfully closed his first commercial deal, but he had also earned the trust of an investor with long-term plans. This wasn't just a one-off sale—this was the start of a partnership. Tony had learned so much from working with Linda, and now he was starting to see the bigger picture of what a career in resimercial real estate could look like.

Building Long-Term Relationships
and Strategic Partnerships

Tony understood that real estate was about more than just buying and selling properties—it was about relationships. But it wasn't until he worked with Mike, the investor, that he saw how valuable long-term partnerships could be. Unlike his experience in residential real estate, where closing a deal often meant the end of the relationship, working with investors meant there was always something more on the horizon.

When Tony and Linda helped Mike renovate the first two units, they did more than just complete a task—they set the stage for future business. Mike's plan was clear: update the kitchens, baths, and appliances, raise the rents to match market standards, and position the property for future success. Within weeks, the building's rent roll had jumped, just as Tony and Linda had predicted. This wasn't just about selling properties—it was about creating long-term value. And with every uptick in the rent roll, Tony saw the tangible results of their efforts.

What really struck Tony was the return on effort. With residential clients, you might work months to close a deal, only to wait years before they need your services again. But with investors like Mike, the work never really stopped. There was always a new project, a new tenant, or a new property to consider. The opportunities multiplied, offering Tony a more predictable and scalable path to success. Mike's follow-up call confirmed it: "I've got another property, Tony. This one's a bit bigger, and I'd like to get your thoughts before I make an offer. Let's walk through it next week."

For Tony, this was validation. His decision to shift focus from traditional residential sales to commercial real estate wasn't just a good idea—it was the smartest move he could have made. The opportunity cost of sticking with residential deals became clear: by choosing to work with investors, Tony unlocked a steady stream of transactions, each one building on the last. His collaboration with Linda had been the catalyst that set everything in motion.

The Power of Teamwork and Expertise

Reflecting on the success of the Jenkins deal, Tony realized how crucial it was to build strategic partnerships. He could have attempted to tackle the sale on his own, but bringing Linda in had made all the difference. Her background, growing up around apartment buildings, gave her an edge that Tony didn't yet have. Together, they had combined their expertise to present a compelling proposal to Jenkins, which eventually led to a fullprice offer from Mike.

This wasn't just about knowing how to sell a property—it was about knowing when to call on others for help. Linda had brought insights into apartment management, pricing, and renovations that Tony hadn't yet developed. By leveraging her experience, they not only closed the deal but also demonstrated to Jenkins and Mike that they were a powerful team capable of handling complex transactions. This was Tony's first real lesson in the value of collaboration in commercial real estate.

Recognizing Potential in Every Property

One of the most significant lessons Tony took away from the sale was the importance of recognizing and communicating a property's potential. The Jenkins building wasn't perfect—there were aesthetic issues, and the tenants were paying well below market rent. But where some might see problems, Tony and Linda saw opportunity.

Their ability to show Mike the hidden value in the building—structurally sound units, individual heating systems, and untapped rental income— was key to securing the sale. Mike could envision how a few strategic upgrades could significantly boost the building's value over time. This insight wasn't just about closing a deal; it was about helping Mike realize the long-term potential of his investment.

Thinking Ahead: Long-Term Strategies for Success

Mike's plan didn't stop at renovating a few units—he was thinking five, ten years down the line. His strategy involved more than just increasing the rent roll. If market conditions were favorable, Mike was already considering converting the units into condos, thanks to the infrastructure Jenkins had put in place. Tony saw firsthand how investors think beyond the immediate gains—they consider how each move sets them up for future opportunities.

This was a crucial lesson for Tony. Working with investors wasn't just about handling the deal at hand—it was about thinking strategically, understanding market trends, and aligning current actions with longterm financial goals. Mike's ability to see the big picture opened Tony's eyes to the level of sophistication required to succeed in commercial real estate.

Conclusion: Return on Effort and Opportunity Cost

The journey from walking into Mr. Lucas's office to closing the deal on the six-flat was a pivotal experience for Tony. It taught him the importance of focusing on investors, building strategic partnerships, and recognizing the hidden potential in every property. Working with investors like Mike offered a return on effort that residential real estate couldn't match. With every deal, Tony wasn't just completing a transaction—he was building a long-term, scalable business model.

Looking back, Tony knew that the opportunity cost of sticking with residential sales would have been high. By shifting his focus to investors and collaborating with experts like Linda, he had created a pathway for success that would continue to yield results for years to come. This was the real power of resimercial real estate—the ability to blend residential and commercial deals into a sustainable, profitable business.

Workshop: Turning Opportunity into Wins

Welcome to "The Resimercial Game Plan" workshop, where agents will learn to balance their schedules, focus on key activities, and apply the lessons from the chapter to build sustainable careers in real estate. This workshop will include fun sports-themed activities to reinforce the importance of strategy, teamwork, and execution. Remember, this isn't just about working harder—it's about working smarter!

Warm-Up Drill: Setting Your Schedule for Success

Activity: The Pregame Routine

Objective: Get agents thinking about their daily routines and time management, ensuring they dedicate focused time to their career.

Instructions:

1. Discussion: Kick off the session with a brief conversation about how successful athletes prepare for game day. Just like a professional athlete must wake up early for practice, agents need to schedule their day to ensure they're maximizing their time.

2. Challenge: Ask agents to create their Game-Day Schedule. This doesn't need to be a seven a.m. to seven p.m. grind, but it should reflect time dedicated to prospecting, client follow-ups, research, and networking.

3. Time Blocking: Introduce the concept of time-blocking. Have agents map out a daily plan with at least three dedicated blocks of time for prospecting, meetings, and professional development.

4. Quick Sharing: Have each agent share one or two nonnegotiable blocks of time they plan to schedule each day (e.g., morning prospecting, afternoon client calls, or time for research). This will help reinforce accountability and give ideas for scheduling priorities.

Drill 1: The Opportunity Cost Playbook

Activity: The Play-Calling Huddle

Objective: Get agents to think critically about opportunity cost—how saying "yes" to one task means saying "no" to another—and to focus their time and efforts on high-impact activities.

Instructions:

1. Scenario Setup: Divide agents into small groups and present them with a series of fictional scenarios. Each scenario presents two opportunities, but agents can only choose one. For example:

   ○ Scenario 1: You've been asked to list a luxury home by a one-time seller, but at the same time, you have a chance to meet with an investor who wants to buy a portfolio of small multifamily buildings.

   ○ Scenario 2: You have a morning full of meetings scheduled, but a high-value investor just called and invited you to see a property they are considering buying in the afternoon.

2. Playbook Decision: In their groups, agents must decide which opportunity to pursue and explain why. They should weigh factors like long-term potential, repeat business, and return on effort.

3. Group Discussion: Bring everyone back together and have each group explain their decision. The goal is to help agents realize the importance of prioritizing opportunities that can provide longterm gains, even if it means passing on short-term wins.

Drill 2: Building Your Dream Team

Activity: Draft Day

Objective: Teach agents the importance of collaboration and building a network of experts who can help them succeed, just like Tony partnered with Linda.

Instructions:

1. Team Draft: Agents will each "draft" a team of experts they would rely on for a commercial deal. They need to think of:

   - A property manager or expert in multifamily buildings (like Linda)

   - A marketing guru to help present the property

   - An analyst who can handle numbers and pro forma analysis

   - An attorney to handle legal aspects of transactions

   - Any other key player (e.g., contractors, inspectors, etc.)

2. Role Assignment: Each agent writes down who they would draft for each role, considering the strengths and skills needed. Encourage them to think of real people in their network or roles they still need to fill.

3. Team Building Discussion: After each agent drafts their dream team, have a group discussion about the power of collaboration. Ask:

   ○ Why did you choose these individuals for your team?

   ○ How can collaboration save time and lead to better results?

4. Takeaway: Reinforce that agents don't have to do everything themselves—having a strong team in place allows them to focus on what they do best while relying on experts to handle other areas.

Drill 3: Identifying Hidden

Value on the Field

Activity: The Playmaker's Vision

Objective: Help agents learn how to spot hidden value in a property, just as Tony and Linda did with the six-unit building.

Instructions:

1. Game Setup: Present agents with fictional property listings that have potential but require strategic vision to see it. For example:

   ○ A multifamily property with outdated kitchens but prime location.

   ○ An office building with below-market rents but long-term leases in place.

   ○ A retail center with several vacancies but surrounded by new developments.

2. Spotting the Potential: Have agents work individually or in small groups to "analyze" the property and identify at least two hidden opportunities (e.g., increasing rents through renovations, converting units to condos, or repositioning the asset for a higher value use).

3. Playmaker Discussion: After reviewing the properties, agents should share their analysis with the group. What hidden value did they find, and how would they advise their client to proceed? This will encourage agents to think creatively and see beyond surface-level details.

Drill 4: The Follow-Up Touchdown

Activity: 4th Quarter Follow-Up

Objective: Reinforce the importance of follow-up and nurturing long-term relationships, much like Tony did with Mike.

Instructions:

1. The Game Situation: Each agent must think of a client or prospect they haven't followed up with in a while. It could be an investor, a residential client considering an investment, or a commercial owner who might want to sell.

2. The 4th Quarter Call: Give each agent five minutes to craft a quick follow-up message. It can be a check-in, an offer to meet for coffee, or simply sharing market insights.

3. Live Practice: Agents share their messages with the group and get feedback. Then, challenge them to actually send the message by the end of the workshop.

4. Takeaway: Following up and staying top-of-mind with clients is how you build long-term relationships and create repeat business. Just like in football, the game isn't won in the first quarter—success comes from persistence and finishing strong.

Final Drill: The Postgame Review

Wrap up the workshop with a brief discussion on the importance of balancing short-term wins with long-term planning. Revisit the themes of opportunity cost, teamwork, and return on effort. Ask agents to share one key takeaway they'll implement in their business.

Encourage agents to commit to a consistent game plan for their careers. By focusing on collaboration, recognizing potential, and prioritizing long-term client relationships, they'll continue to score big wins in their real estate practice.

Conclusion

Just like in sports, winning in real estate isn't about doing everything on your own. It's about having the right game plan, working with a team, and staying focused on the long game. The lessons learned in this chapter will help agents turn every opportunity into a win, driving them toward long-term success in resimercial real estate.

This workshop is designed to be fun, interactive, and actionable reinforcing the lessons from the chapter while engaging agents in a meaningful and enjoyable way!

Post–NAR Settlement Realities: Demystifying the New Realities in Buyer Representation

Success is no accident. It is hard work, perseverance, and most of all, love of what you are doing.
—Pele

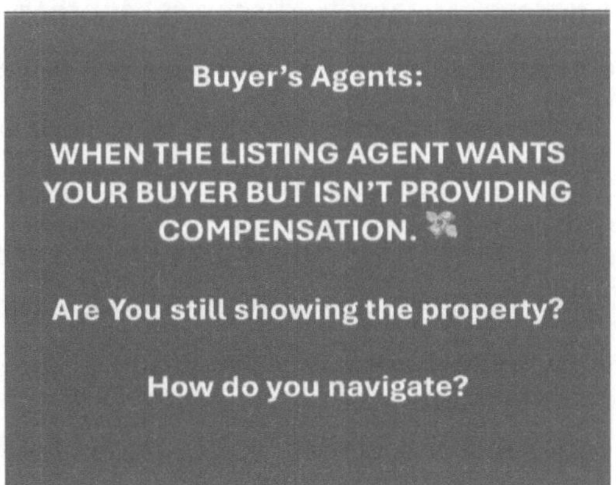

In a bustling downtown real estate office, the atmosphere is thick with anticipation and a hint of anxiety. Sarah, a seasoned residential real estate agent, is preparing her materials for an important client meeting.

Today's agenda is critical: explaining the new National Association of Realtors (NAR) rules to her client, Jack, a prospective homebuyer eager to dive into the market but wary of the complexities involved.

Jack, a diligent saver, and first-time buyer faces a new hurdle. Following the recent NAR settlement, a significant change has swept through the industry, altering how buyers and agents interact. From this day forward, agents like Sarah must secure a buyer agreement before showing properties, a pact that starkly outlines that buyers might need to directly contribute to the agent's payment for services out of pocket if the seller doesn't cover these costs. For Jack, who has been meticulously saving for a down payment, this could mean an unexpected strain on his budget.

Sarah's office, usually a hub of lively conversation and ringing phones, today feels more like a strategic planning room. She is set to explain to Jack that residential agents are now expected to operate with the precision and upfront clarity more typical of commercial brokers—a shift pushing the "Resimercial Revolution" into full throttle.

The narrative thickens as Sarah discusses another pivotal change: buyer-side cooperating brokerage fee splits are no longer a given in any transaction, nor advertised. Agents like her now need to contact listing brokers directly to negotiate and ascertain details, requiring upfront negotiation and written confirmation. This practice, a routine checkbox in a commercial deal's lengthy checklist, now adds a layer of complexity and potential risk to every residential transaction.

Later that afternoon, Sarah meets with Jack in a quiet coffee shop, a neutral ground to demystify these daunting new rules. She begins by addressing the elephant in the room—the potential for her pay as a buyers agent to come directly from his pocket. Jack listens intently, his brow furrowing as he absorbs the impact of this new buying landscape. Sarah reassures him, explaining that this transparency is designed to align their interests closely and ensures that he receives the dedicated service he deserves, irrespective of the seller's stance on agent payment arrangements.

As their meeting progresses, Sarah illustrates how these changes are part of a broader industry shift. She explains cryptic messages in listings, and other desperate attempts by agents to signal payment arrangements subtly, is a practice now fraught with legal risks, confusion, hefty fines, and penalties.

This chapter will provide a comprehensive guide for both agents and buyers to effectively navigate the post–NAR settlement realities of buyer representation. We'll explore the new landscape of real estate, where clear communication and transparency have become even more critical. From outlining the value agents provide to buyers, to clarifying disclosure and payment structures, this chapter offers a playbook to succeed in this evolving environment.

Specifically, we will focus on key areas such as:

- **Clear Communication:** Ensuring all parties—agent, buyer, and seller—are aligned through precise and transparent dialogue.

- **Value Articulation:** How agents can present the true value of their services, backed by a track record of success and expertise.

- **Disclosure and Agreements:** Clarifying the scope of services and managing buyer expectations from the outset.

- **Fee Structures:** Explaining new scenarios where buyers may be responsible for costs and how to address these shifts proactively.

- **Aligning with Buyer Needs:** Crafting tailored strategies for matching active listings and off-market opportunities with a buyer's specific goals.

This chapter will also highlight how these regulatory changes, while challenging, present an opportunity to build stronger, trust-based relationships. By adapting to these new realities, agents can elevate their service delivery, leading to more successful transactions and enduring client relationships.

As we transition into the next chapter, we will deepen the exploration of these themes within the commercial real estate sector. With more complex transactions and higher stakes, the need for transparency, strategic communication, and delivering value is even greater. This next chapter will equip you with the tools to navigate the unique dynamics of commercial buyer representation and broker collaboration, ensuring your success in this competitive field.

Disclaimer: Please note that specific policies, procedures, and requirements may vary by office, MLS, and state. It's essential to consult with your local regulations and governing bodies to ensure compliance.

By the end of their meeting, Jack feels more confident, equipped with knowledge, and ready to make informed decisions. Sarah, in turn, realizes that while the road ahead is more structured, it's also filled with opportunities for those willing to adapt and lead in this new era of real estate.

Navigating Real Estate Commitments

Jack's eyes swept over the bustling streets of Hyde Park as he pondered the weight of his decision. Preapproved for an $800,000 loan, he was diving into one of Chicago's most storied neighborhoods, a decision that came with significant financial implications. Known for its vibrant community and prestigious landmarks, Hyde Park wasn't just a location; it was a statement. Nestled between the intellectual hub of the University of Chicago and the serene stretches of Lake Michigan, with cultural treasures like the Obama Library and the Museum of Science and Industry nearby, the neighborhood promised more than just a home; it offered a lifestyle.

However, the potential payout for Sarah, based on the property's anticipated sale price, was a hard pill to swallow for Jack. His savings were earmarked for a 20 percent down payment to reduce his mortgage costs, not for representation costs. But Sarah, ever the consummate professional, anticipated his hesitation and came prepared to ease his concerns. Before the meeting, Sarah had diligently researched available properties within Jack's budget. She scoured the listings on various reputable online sites including MidwestInvestmentAdvisors.com, and negotiated and confirmed in writing buyer-side splits with other agents—all of which were agreeable to a reasonable cooperating brokerage rate. Yet, it was the expired listing of a small apartment building that caught her attention. After a direct discussion with the owner, who expressed dissatisfaction with his previous agent, an opportunity arose. The owner was willing to offer an incentivized payment structure if Sarah could bring a buyer. With this in hand, Sarah included the property in the lineup for Jack and shared the appropriate agency disclosures and a buyer representation agreement that would not impact Jack financially.

At their meeting, Sarah presented agency disclosures and the buyer agreement, which clearly outlined Jack's obligations—specifically, that he wouldn't be responsible for any broker related out-of-pocket expenses if he purchased one of these assets. The agreement also disclosed the exact amounts the sellers had agreed to pay her, ensuring full transparency.

This clear communication helped build Jack's trust and confidence, encouraging him to move forward.

With a cautious nod, Jack agreed to view the properties, starting with the townhome that, while ideally located, required significant renovations—more than Jack was prepared to undertake. The other properties also failed to meet his expectations, leading Sarah to suggest the small apartment building that had recently reentered the market.

As they approached the six-flat, they were greeted by a charming scene. The owner, a gentleman named Henri Dupont, was tending to the lush garden that adorned the front of the majestic red stone building. Its intricate architectural details captured the essence of Hyde Park's historical elegance.

Henri, spotting Sarah and Jack from the sidewalk, wiped his hands on a cloth and walked over with a welcoming smile. "Bonjour," he began, his accent coloring the greeting with a touch of authenticity. "I'm Henri. Welcome to my little piece of Hyde Park. I hope it impresses as much as it has charmed me over the years."

The introductions were warm and polite, with Sarah skillfully bridging the gap between Jack's cautious intrigue and Henri's evident pride in his property. As they prepared to tour the building, the air was filled with a mix of anticipation and the crisp scent of autumn leaves—a perfect backdrop for what could be a defining moment in Jack's journey into real estate investment.

Property Tour and Beyond

As Sarah and Jack followed Henri through the grand entrance of the building, they were immediately struck by the elegant common areas that blended modern security features with classic architectural elements.

The marble floors shone under the light filtering down from a skylight that ran the length of the stairwell, illuminating the antique-styled white railings and the lush greenery of strategically placed plants.

Their tour began with Mary's apartment. Since she was a traveling nurse and is currently away, her apartment served almost as a showpiece, everything neatly arranged, exuding a calm and inviting atmosphere. The sprawling two thousand square feet included a grand room that doubled as a library with built-in shelving, a large wood-burning fireplace, and high ceilings adorned with stained glass transoms that scattered colorful light across the polished wooden floors.

Henri detailed the recent renovations, noting the individual heating and air conditioning zones for each unit, the modern laundry rooms, and the spacious decks that offered outdoor living space. As they moved through the building, each apartment unveiled its own charm and story. When they reached the apartment of the Jameses, two university professors, they were greeted warmly and the sweet aroma of freshly baked cookies filled the air, enhancing the homely feel of the meticulously kept residence.

The tour continued with Henri showing off his unit, which was a testament to his life as a sculptor and an artist. The four-thousand-sq'uare foot duplex was a masterpiece of luxury living, well-appointed with a sauna, Jacuzzi, smart toilets, and a kitchen equipped with Guggenheim appliances that any chef would dream of. The lower level, which Henri used as his studio, was lined with his artworks, transforming the space into a private gallery.

Henri shared his plans for moving to the Maldives for a prestigious commission that would require his presence for over two years. This move motivated his decision to sell the building, providing a unique opportunity for someone like Jack, who could appreciate the property's value both as a home and an investment.

Despite the allure of the building and its potential as a prime real estate investment, Jack had reservations due to the $1.2 million asking price, which stretched his budget considerably. Sarah, understanding his concerns, suggested they visit Jack's loan officer at the local bank to explore financing options that could make the purchase feasible.

Walking into the bank, they were greeted by the warm smiles of the staff. Jack's loan officer, a meticulous man with a keen understanding of real estate investments, welcomed them into his office. The walls were adorned with plaques and certificates, signaling his expertise and success in helping clients navigate complex financial waters. One of the banks financial planners, who everyone fondly called "The Professor" for his depth of knowledge, waved them over. "I'm headed to the local café— can I grab you two some coffee or tea?" he asked with a friendly grin. Sarah smiled back, "A coffee would be great, thank you." Jack nodded, "I'll take a tea."

As they sat down, the loan officer pulled up Jack's file on his computer and began discussing various financing scenarios that could work for Jack. He mentioned possibilities like adjusting the loan term, exploring different types of mortgages, or even looking into special programs for buyers investing in properties like the one Henri was selling.

As they continued discussing Jack's financing options, the loan officer leaned forward, ready to dive deeper into the distinctions of commercial financing.

"Now, since we're looking at a commercial loan, it's important to remember that it's structured a bit differently than the thirty-year fixed residential loans you might be familiar with, Jack. Commercial loans are typically amortized over thirty years, but the actual term will usually be much shorter—five, seven, or ten years at most."

Jack's brow furrowed slightly, and Sarah leaned in, sensing this was where things got more complex.

The loan officer continued, "That means, even if we amortize the loan over thirty years to keep your monthly payments manageable, the term of the loan will require a balloon payment or a refinancing after that five, seven, or ten-year period. So, you'll need to think ahead. For instance, even if you choose the ten-year term, most lenders will require the interest rate to reset at the five-year mark. At that point, the new rate will be tied to either the 10-year Treasury yield or SOFR (Secured Overnight Financing Rate), depending on the loan structure you choose."

Sarah nodded in understanding and turned to Jack. "In other words, the rate you lock in today won't last for the full duration of the loan. You need to plan for a possible rate adjustment in five years, which could significantly affect your payments."

Jack leaned back, processing. "So, if interest rates climb in the next five years, I could be looking at a much higher rate when it resets?"

"Exactly," the loan officer confirmed. "That's why understanding how both the 10-year Treasury and SOFR work is critical here. The 10-year Treasury reflects long-term interest rate expectations and inflation. If inflation rises, so does the yield, which in turn can push up your rates. SOFR, on the other hand, is more tied to short-term borrowing between banks, but since it replaced LIBOR (London Interbank Offered Rate), it's become a key reference for adjustable-rate loans in the commercial space. If SOFR rises sharply in the future, your adjustable-rate loan could spike when it resets."

Jack's expression remained serious. "So, what's the risk? Could we really see that much movement in these rates?"

"Well, the 10-year Treasury tends to move slowly," the loan officer explained, "but it's still influenced by inflation, economic growth, and global events. SOFR can fluctuate more depending on liquidity and short-term financial stress. Right now, we're in a relatively stable-interest environment, but if rates rise significantly over the next few years, your payments could increase when your loan resets. However, if you lock in a fixed rate now, you can avoid that risk at least for the first five years."

Sarah jumped in, smiling. "But the flip side is, if the rates don't move up much, or if they dip, an adjustable loan could actually save you money. It's all about your risk tolerance and your ability to weather potential rate hikes."

Jack took a deep breath. "It's a lot to consider. I can see why locking in a rate might make sense, but it sounds like I need to be ready for whatever happens in five years."

"Exactly," the loan officer agreed. "That's where smart financial planning comes in. You'll need to think ahead about your refinancing options or even selling the property before the reset. But with a solid strategy, you'll be in a good position to take advantage of the property's appreciation and market conditions by that time."

A short while later, as they dove deep into the intricacies of SOFR and the 10-year Treasury, The Professor returned with not only their drinks but also sweet treats from Marcel's bakery, adding a moment of lightness to their detailed conversation.

Finalizing the Deal: The Mechanics of a Successful Real Estate Investment

As they nibbled on the delicious pastries, the discussion took a promising turn. The loan officer explained that the bank offered a special credit for properties purchased by owner-occupants in the Hyde Park neighborhood—a $7,500 incentive aimed at encouraging more loans in the area. This was a significant boost to Jack, who was grappling with the idea of a sizable down payment.

Moreover, it was revealed that a seller could offer a credit of up to 6 percent of the purchase price toward decorating or closing costs, which in this case could amount to $72,000. This would significantly reduce the upfront financial burden on Jack. Encouraged by this news, Sarah drafted a full-price offer of $1.2 million with a stipulation for the $72,000 seller's credit. This effectively lowered Henri's net from the sale to 94 percent of his asking price, a concession he was willing to accept considering the simplicity and speed of the transaction it promised.

Henri, appreciating Jack's earnestness and commitment, agreed to the terms. Henri countersigned the purchase and sale agreement and dual agency disclosure. They moved forward with the deal, setting the stage for a life-altering investment for Jack. The final down payment, now adjusted after the seller's credit and bank incentive, was precisely $160,500—aligning perfectly with Jack's initial budget.

Let's break down the financial mechanics of this investment:

- **Purchase Price**: $1.2 million

- **Down Payment**: $160,500 (after credits and incentives)

- **Remaining Mortgage**: $960,000

- Ο **Interest Rate**: 6.25 percent amortized over thirty years

- Ο **Monthly Mortgage Payment**: Approximately $5,911

- Ο **Ten-Year Term to reset in year five at then-current interest rate**

The income from the property, primarily from the rent of $20,000 per month, comfortably covered the monthly mortgage and all associated expenses. Here's a detailed look at the monthly costs:

- Ο **Property Taxes**: $1,500

- Ο **Insurance**: $350

- Ο **Water and Utilities**: $350

- Ο **Landscaping**: $200

- Ο **Janitorial Services**: $300

After all expenses, including the mortgage, Jack's net cash flow came to about $12,889 per month. Living in the building rent-free added to the attractiveness of the deal, effectively increasing his disposable income.

The Closing and Beyond

The day of the closing was filled with anticipation and excitement. Jack, accompanied by Sarah, signed the papers that would transfer ownership of the iconic Redstone building into his hands. The moment was a culmination of strategic planning, sharp negotiation, and financial acumen. Henri handed over the keys to Jack, confident in his decision to pass on the stewardship of his beloved building to someone as dedicated as Jack.

Before the final handshake, the loan officer handed Jack a valuable tool for his future planning—an interest rate sensitivity analysis. The report showed Jack exactly how different interest rates could impact his mortgage balance in five years, depending on various rate adjustments. This breakdown took much of the guesswork out of managing future payments. "Now you have a clear sense of how to prepare," the loan officer said, smiling. "You'll know exactly what to expect as your loan resets." Sarah reminded Jack that he could always view a sample of this analysis at ChargingTheStorm.com for future reference.

Afterward, Sarah received a well-earned payday for her role in facilitating the transaction. Recognizing the effort and dedication Jack had put into this investment, she also presented him with a thoughtful closing gift—a framed photograph of the Redstone building. The image symbolized new beginnings and all the achievements yet to come.

As they stepped out of the closing, Jack shared with Sarah his newfound enthusiasm for real estate investment. His cryptocurrency investments had recently seen a significant increase in value, and he was eager to diversify his portfolio further into real estate. Energized by his successful entry into the market, he requested Sarah to keep him informed of any new investment opportunities, particularly those that could offer similar returns.

Sarah, pleased with the outcome and excited about the prospect of continuing her professional relationship with Jack, assured him that she would be on the lookout for properties that matched his investment criteria. As they parted ways outside the title company, it was clear that this transaction was just the beginning of a promising investment journey for Jack, guided by Sarah's expert hand.

Summary: Navigating a Buyer's Journey in the Resimercial Revolution

The journey that unfolded between Sarah and Jack serves as an exemplary scenario of how residential real estate practices are evolving in alignment with commercial standards, especially in the wake of regulatory changes like the NAR settlement. This transition is pushing the industry toward what has been termed the "Resimercial Revolution," where residential agents adopt strategies traditionally used in commercial transactions.

Initial Preparation and Meeting: Sarah's approach to her first meeting with Jack underscored the necessity of meticulous preparation and understanding of new regulations affecting buyer-agent relationships. Before meeting Jack, she thoroughly researched the local property inventory and confirmed pay structures directly with listing agents, ensuring compliance with NAR's new guidelines that restrict public disclosure of pay related to buyer agent representation. Her proactiveness allowed her to reassure Jack that his financial responsibility would be minimal and managed through seller contributions.

Property Selection and Viewing: Sarah's knowledge of the Hyde Park area and its significant landmarks, combined with her strategic selection of properties, positioned her well to cater to Jack's interests. Her efforts to secure a representation agreement directly from a seller for an expired listing not only maximized her earnings potential but also highlighted a key commercial practice—direct negotiation.

Financial Structuring and Negotiation: The transaction showcased Sarah's adeptness at structuring deals beneficial to all parties involved. By integrating a bank-offered credit and a substantial seller concession into the deal structure, Sarah effectively reduced the financial strain on Jack while ensuring the seller's quick closure of the sale. Her ability to negotiate these terms exemplifies a skill set that is highly prized in commercial real estate dealings.

Closing the Deal: The closing process highlighted the culmination of all preparatory and negotiation strategies Sarah employed. It was not just a transaction but a transformational event for Jack, who moved from being a traditional homebuyer to an investor, thanks to Sarah's guidance. Her comprehensive service didn't end at the closing; it extended to postsale engagement and planning for future investments, emphasizing the ongoing client management typical in commercial transactions.

Transition to Resimercial Brokerage: This transaction was a pivotal moment for Sarah, marking her transition into a Resimercial brokerage. She adeptly navigated the complexities of the deal by applying commercial brokerage tactics, such as detailed financial analyses and strategic client education, which are less common in residential settings but critical in commercial deals. Her success with Jack not only solidified a long-term client relationship but also positioned her to handle more sophisticated real estate investments, reflecting the broader industry shift toward a Resimercial model.

This case encapsulates the essence of the Resimercial Revolution: a move toward blending the best practices of residential and commercial real estate to better serve clients navigating complex transactions. Sarah's journey with Jack is a blueprint for residential agents aspiring to elevate their practice in an increasingly competitive and regulated market.

Conveying Your Value in Buyer Representation

Navigating the intricacies of representing buyers in commercial real estate requires a blend of tact, foresight, and strategic documentation. The process involves more than just finding properties—it's about defining your role, clarifying expectations, and ensuring your efforts are properly acknowledged. Here's a structured approach to help you not only formalize your representation but also lay the groundwork for long-term client relationships and future collaborations.

1. **Request Comprehensive Property Details:** Initiate your interaction by requesting detailed information about the property. This should include owner financials, additional property photos, actual financials, utility bills, and a list of recent capital improvements. These details provide deeper insights into the property and test the listing broker's transparency and reliability in sharing necessary information.

2. **Discuss Cooperation Early**: It's essential to clarify cooperation and representation terms at the very beginning of your discussions with the listing broker. With recent policy updates, automatic or pre-published compensation offers are no longer permitted— everything must now be discussed and documented directly between the parties.

   Consider framing your outreach in a professional, transparent way, such as:

   "Our team would like to confirm the buyer representation terms for this opportunity. Can you share how your brokerage is handling cooperating broker arrangements on this listing?"

   This approach opens the door for a constructive conversation about structure and expectations without referencing specific percentages or dollar figures. It reinforces professionalism and helps ensure that everyone is aligned before presenting offers.

3. **Evaluate the Response Carefully**

A clear and direct reply—such as, *"Our team is open to collaborating under mutually agreeable terms"*—reflects a cooperative and professional broker. When another party communicates transparently, it sets the tone for a smooth transaction and future collaboration.

However, if the response is vague, hesitant, or avoids confirming participation details, that may be a sign to proceed with caution. Ambiguity early in the process can foreshadow challenges later, especially when it comes to formalizing terms of cooperation or recognizing each party's role. Addressing these details upfront helps protect everyone's efforts and establishes accountability before deeper negotiations begin.

4. **Document Every Interaction:** After each discussion, send an email summarizing the conversation. This email serves as a record and helps maintain clarity about the terms throughout the deal's progression. It's important to note that most disputes in commercial real estate are not about disagreements per se, but about remembering details over the long span of complex transactions that have many moving parts. Keeping a written record ensures that all parties remember their commitments, helping to refresh memories at the closing of what can sometimes be marathon deals. Get signed agreements from all parties to facilitate transparency and have conversations as early in the process as possible.

5. **Reference Fee expectations in Offers:** When submitting an offer, explicitly mention the agreed co-op to ensure all parties are aware and have formally acknowledged the payout expectations.

This step is vital in securing your fees and provides a clear reference in the transaction documentation, minimizing disputes at closing. It may also help fulfill the agent's duty of disclosure.

6. **Leverage Past Successful Collaborations:** Strong relationships in the industry and a track record of successful deals can be powerful assets, especially in competitive offer situations. When facing multiple offers, emphasizing past successful collaborations with brokers, buyers, or lenders can set your team apart. In a recent negotiation where the listing agent indicated there were higher offers on the table, we provided a list of our client's real estate holdings to demonstrate their experience and reliable history of closing deals.

   Additionally, when the agent shared a half dozen sales comparables to justify their pricing, we responded by sharing interior photos of those properties, pointing out that they were superior in finishes, features, and amenities. We also highlighted our substantial market share in the neighborhood, evidenced by the fact that we represented the buyers or sellers in three of the six comparables provided. This approach reassured the sellers of our insight and experience, positioning our offer as credible and well-informed despite the competitive environment.

7. **Prepare for and Manage Pushback:** Be prepared for any changes in stance from the listing broker regarding the buyer agent coop. Having all agreements well-documented is key. Moreover, the way a listing broker handles these initial discussions often mirrors how they will behave at closing. If a broker shows reluctance or changes terms last minute, it reflects on their overall professionalism and reliability.

By implementing these steps, brokers can foster professional relationships characterized by transparency and mutual respect. This approach not only secures immediate transactions but also paves the way for future dealings, creating a network of trusted professionals who value integrity and clear communication.

The aftermath of the NAR settlement introduces rules that could inadvertently aid in refining buyer selection processes. These new regulations mandate that buyers sign a representation agreement that clearly outlines the potential for unremunerated agent services. This requirement acts as a natural filter; only truly committed buyers will likely agree to such terms. This self-selection process ensures that agents invest their time and resources into clients who are not just browsing but are serious about purchasing property. While this might necessitate more upfront work in terms of client education and contractual agreements, the long-term benefits are substantial. Agents can focus their efforts on buyers who have demonstrated a commitment to the process, thereby enhancing the efficiency of their practice and increasing the quality of their transactions. This streamlined approach optimizes an agent's workload and fosters a more focused and dedicated client-agent relationship, ultimately leading to more successful real estate outcomes.

Navigating the New Norms in Buyer Representation

In the ever-evolving landscape of real estate, the aftermath of the NAR settlement introduces a pivotal shift that could inadvertently streamline buyer selection processes. With the implementation of rules mandating that buyers sign a representation agreement; a new layer of transparency is introduced. This agreement must explicitly disclose the potential for agents to go unrewarded for their services unless compensated directly by the buyer, particularly in instances where the seller does not cover the buyer's agent. Such a stipulation serves as a natural filter, sifting out those merely browsing from those genuinely committed to purchasing.

This requirement for a formal commitment may deter the casually interested, thereby ensuring that real estate professionals invest their resources in clients who are serious and prepared to engage fully in the process. While this shift necessitates a greater initial investment in client education and contractual clarity, the payoff is substantial. Agents can allocate their efforts more efficiently, focusing on buyers who have demonstrated a clear intent to proceed. This refined focus not only optimizes the agent's workload but also enhances the overall quality of transactions by fostering more dedicated client-agent relationships.

Workshop: Huddle Up—Strategies and Plays for Navigating Buyer Representation in the Resimercial Revolution

Welcome to "Huddle Up," where we'll employ a dynamic sports-themed workshop to dive deep into the evolving playbook of buyer representation. This workshop, mirroring a strategic game-day huddle, is designed to arm real estate professionals with advanced tactics for navigating the Resimercial Revolution—a blend of residential precision and commercial expertise.

Agenda:

1. **Pregame: Understanding the Field**

   - Quick icebreaker activity where participants introduce themselves with a sports-related fun fact.

   - Overview of recent changes in the NAR rules and their impact on buyer-agent dynamics.

2. **First Quarter: Strategic Positioning**

   - Role-playing activity: Participants split into groups, with each member assuming a distinct role (buyer, seller's agent, buyer's agent). The scenario involves negotiating buyer-side cooperating broker's payout under the new rules. For instance a listing agent hiding the ball, perhaps saying send me the agreement we can figure that out later.

   - Interactive discussion on the importance of securing buyer agreements upfront and ideas for creative payout structures.

3. **Second Quarter: Running the Plays**

   ○ Teams engage in a timed challenge, creating quick pitch presentations on how to explain and negotiate and communicate buyer agent's value proposition effectively, ensuring compliance with NAR guidelines. (How do you add value to the transaction as a buyers agent? A buyer can find their own properties online these days.

   ○ Discuss the 10-year Treasury and SOFR what are they today? Discuss today's thirty-year fixed rate three-, five-, and seven-year adjustable rate.

   ○ Feedback session where other groups provide constructive criticism and alternative strategies.

4. **Halftime: Review and Regroup**

   ○ Break for refreshments with a sports trivia quiz on famous coaching strategies that have changed the face of sports—drawing parallels to changing real estate practices.

5. **Third Quarter: Defensive Strategies**

   ○ A case study review of a complex buyer representation scenario, where unexpected challenges arise, such as undisclosed fees.

   ○ Groups collaborate to develop contingency plans and preventive measures, emphasizing clear communication and detailed agreements.

6. **Fourth Quarter: Scoring the Winning Touchdown**

   ○ Role-play activity transitions into a competition where each group must handle a live negotiation scenario with actors playing difficult clients or agents.

   ○ Points are awarded for professionalism, creativity in overcoming objections, and adherence to the new NAR regulations.

7. **Overtime: Building Endurance**

   ○ An interactive panel discussion featuring experienced brokers who share real-life stories about transitioning to the new buyer representation model.

   ○ A Q&A session where participants can ask detailed questions about specific challenges they've faced in their practices.

Postgame Analysis:

   ○ Wrap-up session with key takeaways, emphasizing the importance of adapting to new industry standards while maintaining a high level of service.

   ○ Distribution of resource materials, including a playbook of strategies discussed during the workshop, to help agents implement these tactics in their daily practice.

Workshop Benefits: Participants will leave "Huddle Up" with a solid understanding of the new buyer representation landscape, equipped with practical tools and strategies to enhance their client relationships and navigate complex transactions effectively. This hands-on approach ensures that agents can tackle any challenges in the Resimercial real estate market with confidence and precision.

CHAPTER 4

Negotiating the Buyside After the NAR Settlement—Reading the Defense

A good hockey player plays where the puck is. A great hockey player plays where the puck is going to be.
—Wayne Gretzky

Are Listing Agents Greedy When They keep the lion's share? At first glance, it might seem unfair when a listing agent retains a larger share, offering the buyer's agent less than half. However, the reality in commercial real estate is far more nuanced.

Listing agents often invest years nurturing relationships with sellers, securing trust, and negotiating terms, which is why they may justify taking a larger share. These relationships often go beyond mere transactions—they're built on repeat interactions, strategic advice, and long-term partnerships. For example, a listing agent may have represented the seller when they purchased the property years ago, possibly taking a reduction back then to secure the deal. Now, part of the current closing might reflect the value of ongoing advisory services.

Additionally, sellers specifically select brokers they trust to represent them, agreeing to a pay that reflects the agent's expertise, market knowledge, and ability to deliver results. The seller may value the listing agent's representation, irrespective of how it's ultimately split with a buyer's agent.

Sometimes, listing agents may over-negotiate a lower split with a buyer's representative, believing they have the upper hand or relying on their in-network buyer to close the deal. While this might seem like a strategic move, it can backfire. If a buyer's representative perceives it as a signal that the listing agent doesn't value their involvement, they may prioritize other investment opportunities with their qualified buyers. This approach can result in the seller missing out on offers from serious investors who might have been brought in through broader collaboration.

Even when listing agents calculate that they don't need as much collaboration from a buyer's agent, this strategy doesn't always succeed. If their network fails to deliver qualified buyers, the property can sit on the market for months. Ultimately, this often forces price reductions that may outweigh the percentage the listing agent was trying to retain. In such cases, both the seller and the listing agent lose— highlighting the importance of maintaining balance and collaboration in negotiations.

For buyer's agents, focusing on how much the listing agent is earning shouldn't be the driving factor. Instead, it's about delivering value to the buyer. In many cases, investor-buyers have no issue stepping up to compensate a buyer's agent where they see value—especially if that agent can effectively navigate the complexities of the deal and mitigate risks.

Understanding how to navigate these situations will be critical for agents transitioning into the resimercial space. The dynamics of payout structures are evolving, and success will depend on an agent's ability to adapt and find creative solutions to align interests.

In commercial real estate, split share often reflect the level of responsibility, effort, and expertise required to close the deal. For instance, we recently collaborated with a seller's attorney on a $30 million, 120-unit apartment complex. The property had fallen out of contract three times with another brokerage, and the attorney reached out to us to bring a qualified buyer. When we inquired about the payout structure, the attorney candidly responded, "We're not paying a dime—get your money from the buyer."

This kind of arrangement, where the buyer assumes responsibility for covering the costs, is becoming increasingly common as the industry adjusts to new norms brought on by regulatory changes like the NAR settlement. For agents, this underscores the importance of demonstrating the value of your representation—not just to sellers but also to buyers who recognize the expertise and guidance necessary to navigate these often-complex transactions.

Navigating this evolving landscape requires resimercial agents to approach each deal with a strategic mindset, balancing the expectations of all parties while maintaining professionalism and focus. By mastering these scenarios, agents can position themselves as indispensable advisors in an ever-changing marketplace.

A buyer's agent's track record and the quality of their buyer may ultimately influence the split sharing arrangements. Listing agents may be cautious about sharing equally if the buyer or agent is less experienced, as these scenarios often require additional guidance and effort. For new agents, the path to earning larger shares in future deals lies in consistently building a strong reputation and demonstrating value.

Seasoned brokers understand the importance of deal flow and proven performance, often prioritizing relationships with agents who can navigate the complexities of commercial transactions with confidence. If you're just starting out, approach each opportunity as a learning experience. Take the time to build rapport, establish credibility, and refine your skills. While equal splits may not come immediately, every transaction contributes to your growth and lays the foundation for future success.

Ultimately, patience, professionalism, and consistent performance are your greatest tools. As you develop a proven track record of closing deals, you'll naturally gain leverage to negotiate more favorable terms. Until then, focus on adding value, proving your ability to execute, and treating every deal as an opportunity to move closer to your long-term goals in commercial real estate. The path to success in commercial real estate is through building relationships with key players in the industry. For example, Emma, a top-producing luxury residential agent known for her meticulous attention to detail and prowess in securing prime properties, realized that many of her high-net-worth clients were also seasoned investors. This insight led her to explore the "resimercial" space, blending her residential expertise with commercial investments, thus broadening her skillset and growing her business in the wake of evolving industry dynamics post the National Association of Realtors (NAR) settlement.

This strategic shift requires adapting to new rules and effectively merging residential and commercial real estate practices, leveraging existing relationships to navigate a transforming landscape.

Offers of Compensation

Emma's journey into commercial real estate is not about leaving her roots but expanding her horizons. By collaborating with the right commercial broker, she sees an opportunity to offer her clients, who value her honesty and expertise, a more comprehensive suite of services. This strategic shift positions her perfectly for the Resimercial Revolution, allowing her to utilize her residential acumen in a more complex, commercially focused market. The new NAR rules, demanding upfront negotiation of all offers of compensation and in some respects eliminate the simplicity of MLS listings with predetermined share amounts. Emma embraces these changes, recognizing the potential to redefine her professional trajectory and enhance the value she provides to her clients.

One bright Monday morning, Emma stumbles upon a listing that catches her eye—a promising commercial property located at 333 Main Street. The listing, nestled in a bustling district known for its rapid growth and high investor demand, could be the perfect opportunity to make her mark in the commercial arena. With a blend of excitement and a dose of newfound caution, Emma crafts an email to the listing agent, Mark. She requests additional information about the property's financials, lease agreements, and any other relevant details that could help her assess the deal's viability for her clients. But then, recalling the new rules, she adds a crucial line to her email: "Oh, and by the way, is there an X percentage amount for the cooperating broker representing the buyer on this deal?"

Days pass, and Emma receives a comprehensive response from Mark. Attached is a link to a folder brimming with detailed financial statements, high-resolution photos, and meticulously documented lease agreements. The information is gold, but it's Mark's note on the compensation that causes Emma to pause. It reads:

"Seller has given me permission to inform all Buyers and Buyer's Agents that the seller invites all offers that will be evaluated based on Purchase Price and all terms, including any Buyer request for Buyer's Agent Compensation."

The ambiguity of Mark's statement puzzles Emma. It's a far cry from the straightforward residential deals where sharing structures were clear and often generous. Here, in the commercial territory, the rules of engagement are different, and every term is up for negotiation—including her pay.

Emma sits back, her fingers hovering over the keyboard, contemplating her next move. She knows this could be a significant deal, but how should she approach the negotiation to ensure she is fairly compensated without jeopardizing the potential transaction? The challenge is daunting but also exhilarating. She realizes that navigating these negotiations will require a blend of diplomacy, strategy, and a deep understanding of commercial real estate dynamics.

Reading the Defense

Emma perched at her desk, found herself at a pivotal moment, the glow of the computer screen casting a soft light on her focused expression. Mark's email, punctuated with details of the listing and a vague note on compensation, sat open before her. His prompt reply, rich with property specifics yet vagueness on the splits, spoke volumes.

The email subtext suggested that Mark and his client probably hadn't initially anticipated needing another agent's help to sell, but the detailed information indicated that they could probably now use help with the lifting. There was no prearranged amount for a buyer's agent. This omission of a broker co-op was not just a minor detail; it was a strategic pivot point. Emma couldn't simply blast this listing to her top ten investors. The lack of clarity around payout meant each introduction carried a potential cost—her unpaid time and effort. Instead, she needed a direct, more calculated approach.

Among Emma's contacts was Tom, a seasoned investor urgently seeking a property due to the time constraints of his 1031 exchange. With a significant amount of capital at his disposal and a pressing deadline, Tom was an excellent match for the $7 million listing. This noteworthy opportunity aligned perfectly with his needs, making him the ideal candidate for the property. Before crafting her response to Mark, Emma arranged a private meeting with Tom.

Emma strategized her approach, considering how best to present this complex situation as an opportunity rather than a constraint. "Tom, there's an off-market listing that might fit your exchange criteria," Emma began, setting the stage for a candid discussion. "However, the listing doesn't specify a buyer's agent payment arrangement. They've asked for my involvement, which suggests there's some potential flexibility, but I need to know if you'd be willing to bridge any gap in the amount should the seller not fully cover my fee."

Her transparency about the situation helped transform Tom from a passive client into an active participant in the negotiation process.

Together, they crafted a tactical response to Mark's vague terms.

> Subject: Coordination Request for Potential 1031
>
> Exchange Acquisition Discussion
>
> Dear Mark,
>
> Thank you for your prompt and comprehensive response regarding the listing at 333 Main Street. The detailed information you

provided has been invaluable in our assessment, and we believe this property could significantly align with the investment strategy of our client, Tom, who is currently navigating a critical phase of a 1031 exchange.

Tom, a seasoned investor with substantial capital ready for deployment, has prioritized your listing as a top consideration for his portfolio expansion. Given the stringent timeline imposed by his 1031 exchange requirements, he is poised to act swiftly, provided certain conditions are met. We propose an initial discussion to explore this opportunity further and to outline Tom's specific requirements. While we understand the sensitivities involved in direct seller interactions, we believe a collaborative approach could facilitate a more informed and efficient negotiation process. To this end, we suggest arranging a Zoom call where we can discuss the finer details and address any preliminary concerns.

Seller Contribution: Tom is fully prepared to delve deeper into the due diligence required for such a substantial investment. However, he respectfully requests acknowledgment of a potential payment arrangement where, should the transaction proceed to a successful close, the seller considers contributing X percent of the final sales price to the buyer's broker at closing. This would not only streamline the financial aspects of the deal but also reinforce the collaborative spirit of this potential transaction.

Scheduling a Meeting: Could we schedule a meeting at your earliest convenience? A direct conversation could help clarify any outstanding questions and expedite the decision-making process. We are flexible with timings and would appreciate any suitable slots you could provide.

Attached is the letter from Tom's 1031 exchange intermediary and proof of liquidity, highlighting his readiness and serious intent.

We look forward to your feedback and hope to facilitate a meeting that leads to a mutually beneficial arrangement.

Best regards,

Emma

Follow-Up:

After sending the email, Emma prepared for various outcomes. To her strategic advantage, Mark, appreciating the seriousness and readiness of Tom as highlighted in the attachments, discussed the proposal directly with the seller. The seller, recognizing the potential of engaging directly with a well-capitalized buyer, suggested that he join the forthcoming Zoom meeting to address the proposal comprehensively.

This move, initiated by the seller, positioned the upcoming discussion as a pivotal moment. It allowed for direct engagement, potentially speeding up the negotiation process and aligning all parties toward a favorable outcome. Emma's tactful approach not only respected the professional boundaries but also opened the door for a high-level conversation that could streamline the transaction for Tom's significant investment.

Tom valued Emma's expertise and insisted that any negotiations include a clear acknowledgment of her role and rightful compensation. This wasn't just about securing a property; it was about setting a precedent for how Emma's work was valued.

Backed by Tom's confidence, Emma approached the meeting strategically. She communicated his readiness to proceed while clearly outlining the expectation that her role and contribution be formally recognized in the terms of the deal. The clarity of her position not only highlighted her professionalism but also deepened trust between her and Tom, setting the tone for a productive partnership.

The meeting was a delicate dance of diplomacy and strategy. Emma's adept reading of the situation, her preparation, and her ability to turn a potential oversight into an opportunity for clear communication underscored her transition into a formidable force in commercial real estate. Her approach reshaped a potential conflict into a collaborative dialogue, opening the door for future dealings where her expertise and contributions would be unmistakably recognized and compensated.

During the Zoom call, Emma was both forthright and diplomatic. She shared Tom's credentials, emphasizing his readiness and financial strength, underscored by his active 1031 exchange. With tact and precision, she introduced a proposal that recognized her role in facilitating the transaction and illustrated how aligning terms through the seller's cooperation could ultimately support Tom's decision to move forward.

Tour and Unexpected Turn: The seller and Mark agreed to Emma's terms, intrigued by Tom's profile and the promise of a straightforward transaction. They scheduled a property tour. During the visit, however, Tom discovered issues that dampened his interest—specifically, deferred maintenance and a potential environmental hazard linked to the property's past as a dry cleaner.

Emma's quick thinking turned what could have been a deal-breaker into another opportunity. After discussing the situation with Tom, she reached out to another client, a construction company owner looking for offseason projects. She communicated this new prospect to Mark and the seller, who was impressed by her proactive approach and agreed to honor the same payment arrangement.

Closing the Deal

The closing of the deal with the construction company owner marks a significant milestone in Emma's resimercial venture. Her adept handling of the transaction not only brought her the largest payday of her career but also cements her reputation as a resourceful and reliable broker, straddling the residential and commercial realms with ease. Mark and the seller invite Emma to the post closing celebratory dinner. The dinner becomes a pivotal moment for Emma, Mark, and the seller, as they discuss the benefits of a continued partnership. Acknowledging the synergy between them, they invite Emma to colist his next two properties and to assist in finding a replacement property reinvesting his gains from the sale, as he now faces his own 1031 exchange challenge.

This scenario highlights the evolving dynamics within the real estate brokerage industry post–NAR settlement. Emma's adaptability and proactive communication prove instrumental in navigating these changes, illustrating that the initial challenges of adapting to new regulations can also pave the way for innovative business models and richer professional relationships. Her story is a beacon for other agents facing similar transitions, showing that with resilience and strategic thinking, challenges can indeed be transformed into substantial victories, redefining the essence of what it means to be a successful real estate broker in today's market.

Reflection: This scenario exemplified the new dynamics in real estate brokerage post–NAR settlement. Emma's experience highlighted the importance of being prepared, adaptable, and communicative. It demonstrated that while the initial phases of adapting to new rules might be fraught with challenges, they also presented opportunities to innovate and redefine professional relationships. Emma's story served as a beacon for other agents navigating similar transitions, showing that with the right approach, challenges could be transformed into victories.

Working with Commercial Brokers: Establishing Deal Flow

As a top-producing luxury residential realtor, Emma realized the vast potential in leveraging her client relationships to branch into commercial real estate, embracing the **resimercial revolution** stirred by the latest NAR settlement. This shift demanded more than just expertise in high-end residential properties; it required a solid foundation in commercial deal flow to truly service her investor clients effectively.

Understanding that deal flow is the lifeblood of commercial real estate, Emma embarked on a strategic partnership with Mark, a seasoned commercial broker. Initially, Emma subscribed to a commercial listing service, immersing herself in the commercial market and familiarizing herself with new opportunities as they surfaced. This proactive approach was helpful, but Emma quickly recognized the importance of direct relationships in the commercial sector.

Building Relationships and Gaining Trust

Emma began by reaching out to brokers like Mark, checking in to discover overlooked opportunities or listings that hadn't yet attracted the right investor. She respected Mark's space, allowing him the first chance to connect his listings with potential buyers. However, she also made herself available as a secondary option, providing a fresh network of investors through her luxury residential contacts.

Her respect for Mark's initial efforts to sell his hottest listings paid off. As they closed a few deals together, Mark's confidence in Emma's abilities grew. He began to see her not just as a luxury residential realtor but as a valuable partner in the commercial realm.

Establishing a Reciprocal Relationship

This growing trust led Mark to invite Emma to directly market some of his listings to her network, providing her with the necessary deal flow to establish herself in the commercial market. Emma's ability to deliver commercial opportunities to her clients enhanced her reputation as a comprehensive real estate professional, bridging the gap between residential luxury and commercial investment.

Moreover, whenever Emma's clients decided to sell their commercial assets, she and Mark collaborated by colisting these properties. This arrangement allowed Emma to integrate seamlessly into the commercial sector without needing to overhaul her existing business model. It also enabled her to maintain her status as a top luxury realtor while simultaneously building a robust income stream through commercial real estate.

A Symbiotic Partnership Flourishes

The partnership between Emma and Mark exemplifies how residential agents can successfully transition into the commercial market by leveraging relationships and establishing reliable deal flows. Their collaboration not only broadened Emma's professional offerings but also enriched Mark's business with high-caliber clients from Emma's network.

As they celebrated their success at a post-closing dinner, they realized the potential for a long-term mutually beneficial business relationship. The seller, impressed by their teamwork, proposed that they team up to find his next investment, further cementing their partnership. Emma and Mark's story is a testament to the power of strategic alliances in navigating the complexities of today's real estate market, highlighting how adaptability and collaboration can lead to unprecedented professional growth and success.

That may seem counterintuitive, but an agent who just landed a new $7 million listing may not want help selling that one. However, that same listing broker may appreciate an agent making a few calls and sharing the stale $3 million listing they landed a hundred days ago that has minimal traction. Use this opportunity to show the senior agent that you are coachable and can get a commercial deal over the finish line. You might even learn a thing or two in the process. Commercial brokers may even delegate tasks to you because they have a captive audience. Some newer agents may ask, is it my job to do x? A savvy resimercial agent will look at it as an opportunity to create a win-win. Remember: to win, you need a track record of a couple dozen, or more commercial deals closed. To get deals closed with your buyers, you need access to deal flow.

Deal flow in commercial real estate refers to the consistent stream of investment opportunities that a broker can present to potential buyers. This concept is crucial for several reasons, especially in the dynamic and competitive landscape of commercial real estate. Let us consider a typical client meeting and how it might play out.

Marcus Montgomery, a seasoned commercial real estate broker at Sky's the Limit Commercial sat by a panoramic window across from Mr. Thompson, a representative from a large institutional investment firm, in the quiet corner of a bustling downtown cafe. The afternoon light filtered through the windows, casting a warm glow over the array of property executive summaries and market analysis reports spread between them.

"Mr. Thompson," Marcus began, his tone reflecting his years of experience, "it's important to us that we're in a position to share a steady flow of diverse investment opportunities with you. The deal flow keeps you engaged and also ensures that we have a comprehensive understanding of your strategic investment objectives."

Mr. Thompson nodded; his attention fixed on the documents. Marcus continued, "The more information and feedback you share even about the deals you decide to pass on gives us the data points needed to get more opportunities inf front of you that align with your 'strike zone'— the specific conditions under which you are prepared to invest. It's my job to understand these criteria deeply and to present deals that you want to swing the bat at"

Marcus slid a well-prepared offering memorandum across the table. "Here's an opportunity that I believe aligns perfectly with your goals," he said. The document detailed a mixed-use development that promised high returns in a burgeoning area of the city.

"By regularly bringing relevant opportunities to your attention, I aim to build a robust trust between us, demonstrating my understanding of the market and more importantly, my commitment to your success," Marcus explained, pointing to the projections of market growth and tenant demographics.

Mr. Thompson seemed impressed but cautious. "And what about the broader market conditions?" he asked, a hint of concern in his voice.

Marcus was prepared for this. "Navigating market shifts is part of why consistent deal flow is so important," he replied confidently. "It allows us to adapt quickly, ensuring that we capitalize on opportunities at the right moment and adjust our strategies when needed to avoid downturns."

He leaned back, allowing Mr. Thompson to absorb the information. "Think of it as having diversified opportunities that mitigate risks and also enhance potential returns through timely investments."

Marcus then outlined how he managed his deal flow. "Through continuous market research and expanding our network, we keep our finger on the pulse of the market. We utilize cutting-edge technology to streamline our processes, ensuring that we can act swiftly when the right opportunity presents itself."

"As for communication," Marcus added, picking up his coffee, "keeping the lines open with our clients ensures that we are always aligned with your changing needs and preferences, making every transaction as smooth as possible."

Mr. Thompson looked reassured. "And the cost?" he inquired.

"I like to call it a success fee and we only collect when al deal that checks all of your boxes, survives a thorough due diligence review and reaches the finish line. Only then does it translate into revenue for our brokerage, which sustains our operations and fuels our ability to bring you additional opportunities," Marcus answered. "Not to mention, satisfied clients like yourself often lead to referrals, which expands our client base and, by extension, our market reach and capabilities."

As the meeting drew to a close, Marcus summarized, "Our proactive approach in managing deal flow doesn't just enhance our service; it cements our role as indispensable partners in your investment journey."

Mr. Thompson closed the offering memorandum, a smile breaking over his face. "Marcus, it's clear you know your craft. Let's proceed with this deal and see where it takes us."

As they shook hands, Marcus felt the satisfaction of another potential deal moving toward a close, his strategy once again proving its worth in the complex world of commercial real estate.

The next thing you need is *access to capital.* Knowing the lenders that are regularly closing commercial deals in your airspace and finding out their sweet spot and down payment requirements can get you in the game.

They may have qualified buyers looking for inventory, and they may send them your way from time to time. Moreover, it will probably not work out if you can't find your buyer the money they need to get the deal over the finish line. Commercial lenders typically require the buyer to access 20–30 percent of the purchase price in liquid, readily accessible funds, meaning you'll need a buyer with roughly $250,000 in the bank, plus some reserves, to do a million-dollar transaction.

Commercial property managers, attorneys, and inspectors are also in the lineup. A home inspector may tell you that an inspector is an inspector, but you're typically not inspecting a commercial deal the same way you'd check a residential or two-to-four-unit. Alex's venture into commercial real estate was both educational and fraught with the complexities typical of large-scale transactions. Under the guidance of his mentor, a seasoned commercial broker with decades of experience, Alex was poised to navigate these intricacies with a level of professionalism that belied his relative inexperience in the field.

Drafting and Negotiating the Letter of Intent (LOI)

The first critical step in any commercial real estate transaction is the drafting of the letter of intent. This document outlines the major deal points such as the purchase price, timelines for inspections, financing details, and deposit requirements. Alex and his mentor spent considerable time crafting an LOI that was clear, and concise and left no room for ambiguity in laying out the major business points between the parties— all important factors in commercial negotiations.

Their LOI detailed a twenty-one-day inspection period, running concurrently with a seventy-five-day window for securing financing, and earnest money deposits that were substantial enough to demonstrate serious intent but also protected their client should contingencies not be met.

When writing the offer, they also, included a list of relevant real estate holdings and track records for the buyer. Another valuable bit of information they shared was an email from the lender indicating that they've had preliminary discussions with the investor about the asset and that financing appears achievable.

Navigating the Inspection Process

The inspection phase revealed the first major challenge. The property, a mixed-use building with both commercial and residential units, had several issues that a less experienced investor might find daunting. The inspector discovered an old oil tank in the basement and identified a need for caulking around bathtubs and the installation of GFCI outlets in the kitchens—a mix of minor and potentially major concerns.

Alex's initial buyer, transitioning from residential investments, was overwhelmed. The prospect of dealing with what appeared to be significant issues, particularly the oil tank which hinted at potential environmental hazards, spooked them. They were also overly fixated on the smaller, more familiar residential-type issues like the caulking, which in the grand scheme of things, were trivial but emblematic of their inexperience in commercial settings.

Introducing a Seasoned Investor

After the first buyer backed out, Alex's mentor stepped in to redirect the deal's trajectory. He introduced another investor from his network, a contractor with extensive experience in commercial properties. This new investor was unfazed by the issues that deterred the first buyer.

Understanding the bigger picture and recognizing the value of the property beyond its immediate repairs, the new buyer focused on the oil tank. Contrary to initial fears, the tank was full, indicating no leaks. This was a significant relief as it meant there was no soil contamination—a potentially expensive and deal-breaking issue. The buyer saw an opportunity: he sold the oil for a profit and removed the tank at a minimal cost.

Financing and Closing the Deal

Financing for commercial properties often involves more substantial down payments and more rigorous scrutiny of the buyer's financial background. Alex and his mentor worked closely with a commercial lender who understood the property's value and the buyer's potential to improve it. With the lender's support, the deal moved smoothly to closing.

The property closed at a purchase price of $1.625 million, $100,000 more than the initial offer, reflecting the true value and potential of the property that the first buyer missed. This transaction not only provided a significant equity gain for the new owner but also payday for Alex and his mentor.

Conclusion

This scenario underscored the importance of understanding all aspects of commercial real estate, from the negotiation of initial terms to the complex due diligence process. For Alex, it was a profound learning experience that highlighted the necessity of having knowledgeable allies. His mentor's ability to leverage his network and expertise turned a potentially failed deal into a successful transaction, showcasing the invaluable role of experience in commercial real estate.

Drawing the curtain on the vibrant and challenging world of commercial brokerage, it's clear that transitioning from residential to commercial real estate is not just a step up—it's a leap into a complex, multifaceted arena.

The journey from identifying a viable commercial asset to closing the deal is intricate, laden with numerous moving parts that include, but are not limited to, sophisticated financial analyses, understanding nuanced market dynamics, and navigating complex financing scenarios. This is a domain where the stakes are higher, the deals are larger, and the players are more calculating.

Resimercial and the Path Forward

For those new to commercial real estate, the path forward is not about solo heroics or relying solely on one's burgeoning knowledge of the field. It's about recognizing when to leverage the expertise and experience of seasoned professionals. Teaming up with an experienced commercial broker isn't just a smart move—it's a strategic one. These veterans bring to the table a wealth of knowledge, from accurately valuing properties to structuring deals that align with both buyer and seller expectations, all the way to navigating the often-turbulent waters of commercial financing.

The essence of commercial real estate brokerage is collaboration. By moving your ego aside and embracing the guidance of a seasoned broker, you not only enhance your learning curve but also significantly increase the likelihood of success for your clients and yourself. In commercial real estate, "two heads are better than one" rings especially true, as these collaborations can lead to more strategic decision-making and innovative solutions to complex problems.

The move to resimercial and ultimately to commercial mastery is filled with challenges, but it also opens a world of opportunities for those willing to embrace it. For the new agent, understanding the intricacies of commercial deals, from the complexity of the transactions to the sophisticated nature of the financing, is paramount. Remember, in this high-stakes arena, the goal is not just to cross the finish line but to do so with the insight and expertise that only a collaborative approach can provide. By partnering with an experienced commercial broker, you're not just facilitating deals; you're building a foundation for a successful career in commercial real estate.

Getting into Commercial

If you want to get into commercial real estate, know why. Is it because you see large deals with massive broker payouts? Or do you feel a burning desire to do more? It may be a short-lived event, if only for the large and sexy sale. I say this because challenges in commercial real estate comes at you from all different kinds of angles some can be very complex and problematic. Sometimes these deals take a year or more to close, and you can't take your eye off the ball for even a second to focus on something else, like a side job or side hustle, because the deals will demand your undivided attention day after day eight out of ten folks who get into commercial real estate don't make it. One reason is that they run out of runway before the dollars start rolling in another is that they get overwhelmed are trying to go at it alone.

Also, all the clients are millionaires, and your need to make your car payment can't be what drives the transaction. Remember, commercial developers and investors are making these moves to preserve wealth and create legacies worth leaving.

Workshop: Game On—Mastering the Commercial Real Estate League

Objective: Equip real estate agents with the skills, knowledge, and strategies needed for successful entry and growth in commercial real estate.

Duration: Full-day workshop (6 hours) / 3 hours (Condensed version Available)

Materials Needed: chargingthestorm.com

- Case study handouts (Emma, Sarah, and Alex's stories)

- Projector and screen for presentations

- Whiteboards and markers

- Role-play cards and scenario descriptions

- Commercial real estate glossary handouts

- Feedback and scoring sheets

- Certificates of completion

Workshop Agenda:

1. **Kickoff Session: Pregame Warm-Up (30 minutes)**

   - Introduction: Brief overview of the commercial real estate landscape.

   - Icebreaker: Participants share their experiences and expectations.

○ Workshop Goals: Outline objectives and the day's schedule.

2. **First Quarter: Drafting Your Team—Emma's Story (1 hour)**

   ○ Presentation: Overview of Emma's transition to commercial real estate, focusing on building relationships and navigating new NAR rules.

   ○ Group Activity: Participants are divided into teams to analyze Emma's strategy for securing her first commercial client. Discuss what she did well and areas for improvement.

   ○ Role-Play: Teams role-play negotiations between a residential agent and a commercial broker to secure a partnership.

3. **Second Quarter: Scouting the Field—Sarah's Story (1 hour)**

   ○ Case Study Discussion: Detailed walk-through of Sarah's approach to leveraging her luxury residential expertise in commercial deals.

   ○ Interactive Quiz: Quick-fire questions about terminology and processes in commercial real estate based on Sarah's story.

   ○ Group Exercise: Teams create a plan to transition their residential skills to commercial deals, identifying key actions and potential challenges.

4. **Halftime: Strategy Huddle (30 minutes)** ① Break: Refreshments and networking.

   ○ Halftime Talk: The motivational speaker discusses resilience and adaptability in changing markets.

5. **Third Quarter: Playing the Long Game—Alex's Story (1 hour)**

   ○ Role-Play Setup: Introduction to Alex's mentorship experience and his first commercial deal.

   ○ Role-Play Activity: Teams act out Alex's first negotiation with a commercial seller, focusing on overcoming obstacles and securing a deal.

   ○ Review: Groups receive feedback on their negotiation tactics and learn from each other's approaches.

6. **Fourth Quarter: Winning Strategies (1 hour)**

   ○ Group Discussion: What does it take to succeed in commercial real estate? Discussion led by a seasoned commercial broker.

   ○ Strategy Workshop: Participants draft their personalized entry strategy into commercial real estate, incorporating lessons learned throughout the day.

   ○ Presentation: Each team presents its strategy and receives constructive feedback.

7. **Overtime: The Final Whistle (30 minutes)**

   ○ Q&A Session: Open floor for participants to ask questions to a panel of experienced commercial brokers.

   ○ Closing Remarks: Summary of key takeaways and encouragement to apply the strategies learned.

   ○ Award Ceremony: Certificates of completion are handed out, celebrating everyone's participation and effort.

Postworkshop Follow-Up:

- ○ Feedback Forms: Participants are asked to fill out feedback forms to improve future workshops.

- ○ Resource Sharing: Additional reading materials and resources are emailed to participants for further learning.

This workshop framework provides a comprehensive, engaging, and practical approach to helping residential agents transition to commercial real estate, using the sports-themed playbook format to make learning interactive and enjoyable.

CHAPTER 5

In the Paint—Analyzing Commercial Opportunities

*The most important thing is to try and inspire people so
that they can be great at whatever they want to do.*
—Kobe Bryant

To be an effective commercial agent representing investors on the buyer or seller side of a transaction, it's essential to become proficient in understanding and explaining the fundamental deal points and market analytics. Choosing the right investment opportunities to work on and selecting the right investors to work with is imperative. A commercial deal can take anywhere from three months to more than a year to close from the time it's placed under contract and that's irrespective of the time involved in identifying the right investor.

When qualifying investors, prioritize them based on their activity in the market over the past twelve to twenty-four months. Ask about their recent acquisitions, how they sourced those deals, and whether they used a broker. Inquire about the last property they purchased and the last one they passed on, and why. These questions will help you understand the types of deals they prefer, whether they lean toward turnkey assets or value-added opportunities that require more work.

Value-added investments involve purchasing an asset, such as a multifamily or retail space, that may have some vacancy or need improvements to bring the rents to market rates. It's important to qualify the amount of work the investor is willing to do, as some prefer light value-added or cosmetic improvements only, while others are open to more extensive renovations. Determine if the investor has a team or if they plan to outsource the work.

It's key to understanding the investor's decision-making process. Ask them directly what happens next if they see an investment opportunity they like today. Find out if they need to consult with other investors or a board of directors before presenting an offer and inquire about their preferred lenders and whether they have a property management team in place to ensure success after closing.

To enrich your approach in commercial property analysis, start with a site visit. For retail spaces, take note of the parking lot's condition and gauge customer engagement by observing the volume of cars and foot traffic. Consider the store's location, whether it's a bustling intersection or nestled mid-block, as this impacts potential for filling vacancies. For office buildings, delve into the tenant directory. Researching the tenants, especially those that aren't household names, provides insight into the building's business dynamics. With apartments, focus on the grounds' cleanliness and overall upkeep, documenting your observations with photos. This hands-on evaluation lays a solid foundation for understanding a property's real-world value and potential.

Please keep in mind that each commercial property is unique, and the analysis may require additional considerations, depending on the asset type, location, and market conditions. Adaptability and attention to detail are important for successfully navigating the complexities of commercial real estate investment and effectively guiding your clients through the analysis process.

When it comes to non-owner-occupied investments in commercial real estate, the lease is the star of the show. It's the foundation upon which your cash flow income is built. However, not all leases are created equal. There's a whole cast of characters, each with their own strengths and weaknesses, that can impact the value of your investment. Let's break it down. Three main factors account for a whopping 80 percent of a lease's value: tenant credit, income generated, and the length of the lease. These are the heavy hitters you need to pay attention to.

First up, tenant credit. Picture this: you have a tenant named Taylor who has a solid credit score, a stable job, and a history in their field. They're not overspending on rent, they've got some savings, and their expenses are manageable. In the world of market-rate apartments, Taylor is the ideal tenant. You want a building full of Taylors.

However, some owners prefer a mix of market-rate tenants and those with subsidies from organizations like Section 8 or Catholic Charities. While Taylor and her clones are generally reliable, life happens. Jobs are lost, health issues arise, and rent payments suddenly become inconsistent. On the other hand, subsidized tenants have their rent guaranteed by established organizations like the Department of Housing and Urban Development with track records of stability, even in tough economic times.

So, how does this play out in the numbers? It's all about the cap rate, which essentially is a measure of the risk. When analyzing commercial real estate investments, the annual income a property generates is only one factor in its overall valuation. Different types of properties on the same block, generating the same income can have drastically different values based on the nature of their tenancies, the creditworthiness of tenants, and the cap rate applied. Let's consider a broker and an international investor weighing, corporate credit to bring these options to bring the picture into focus.

A Call from Afar

Naomi's phone buzzed just as she was wrapping up a client meeting. The number on the screen was international, unfamiliar. Something told her this wasn't just a cold call. "Naomi Winters," she answered, her voice steady and professional.

"Ms. Winters, I'm Laurent Dufresne. I've been referred to you by a colleague of mine. I'm an investor, originally from France, but I've recently liquidated some assets in Europe and I'm looking to place capital in the US commercial real estate market. I've had a few brokers offer me what they call value-added opportunities, but I'm realizing those might require more attention than I can give, given the distance."

Naomi sat up a little straighter, her curiosity piqued. She had worked with international investors before, and they often faced this same dilemma. "Value-add sounds appealing at first glance," she replied, "but you're right—it often involves hands-on management, especially in the early stages. If you're not planning to be here to oversee things regularly, it might not be the best fit."

Laurent's tone shifted, his relief evident. "That's exactly what I'm concerned about. I'm based overseas, and while I don't mind rolling up my sleeves, managing something from thousands of miles away just isn't practical. I need an investment that's more… hands-off."

Naomi nodded, understanding the balance Laurent was after. "It sounds like you need something with more stability—something where you can rely on a steady income stream without having to worry about daily operational challenges. There are plenty of solid opportunities that offer that kind of return, without the need for constant attention."

Setting the Course

Laurent exhaled, as if a weight had been lifted. "I'm glad to hear that, Naomi. The last thing I want is to be stuck dealing with unexpected issues from across the Atlantic. The brokers I've spoken to so far seemed more interested in offloading projects that weren't quite right for me."

"That happens," Naomi agreed, "but it's all about finding the right fit for your goals. If you're looking for a more hands-off approach, we should focus on stabilized assets or properties with long-term, reliable tenants. It won't be a 'fixer-upper,' but it will give you peace of mind, knowing you've got something more predictable."

Laurent was quiet for a moment, then continued. "That makes sense. My previous investments in Europe were similar. I don't mind value creation, but I need the right balance—something where I can trust the asset to perform without me checking in daily."

Naomi could sense that this was going to be a rewarding relationship. "Let's start with a clear strategy, Laurent. We'll target properties that align with your long-term goals—something that offers a strong return

without the operational headaches. Maybe a triple net lease or an asset with a well-established tenant base."

1. **Fast-Food Restaurant (Corner Property with McDonald's as Tenant)**

○ Annual Income: $1 million

○ Cap Rate: 4.5 percent (reflecting McDonald's strong corporate guarantee and the stability of fast-food tenants)

○ Valuation: Using the 4.5 percent cap rate, the valuation of the McDonald's property would be approximately $22,222,222. This higher valuation reflects the premium investors are willing to pay for the low-risk, high-credit-quality tenant like

McDonald's that typically signs long-term, triple net leases where the tenant is responsible for all property expenses.

2. **Small Office Building (Occupied by Allstate Insurance)**

   ○ Annual Income: $1 million

   ○ Cap Rate: 6.5 percent (considering a moderate risk due to Allstate's good credit but higher landlord responsibilities compared to a triple net lease)

   ○ Valuation: At a 6.5 percent cap rate, the office building's valuation would be about $15,384,615. The cap rate is higher than that of the fast-food restaurant due to the generally greater landlord obligations in office leases and potentially shorter lease terms compared to prime retail leases.

3. **Apartment Building (Mixed Market-Rate and Subsidized Tenants)**

   ○ Annual Income: $1 million

   ○ Cap Rate: 8 percent (reflective of higher management intensity and potential variability in income due to a mix of market-rate and subsidized units)

   ○ Valuation: With an 8 percent cap rate, the apartment building would be valued at $12.5 million. Apartment buildings typically have higher cap rates due to factors like tenant turnover, more intensive management requirements, and, in this case, the mixed tenant base which could introduce more income variability and risk.

Setting the Course (Continued)

Laurent sat in front of his large oak desk in his estate on the French Riviera, the early afternoon sun spilling over the Mediterranean in the distance. Across the screen from him, Naomi greeted him warmly from her office in Chicago, the skyscrapers of the city reflecting the last light of day behind her. "Laurent, I know you're planning to visit the States soon, and I've already lined up some interviews with property management companies for when you're here," Naomi said, smiling as she adjusted her camera. "But in the meantime, I want to walk you through three properties that could be great additions to your portfolio. They all generate $1 million in annual net operating income, but the upfront capital investment varies based on tenant quality, the length of the leases, and your level of involvement."

Laurent leaned forward, intrigued. "Perfect. Let's dive into it."

Naomi shared her screen, bringing up the first property—a fast-food restaurant on a prime corner with McDonald's as the tenant. "This is a straightforward option. McDonald's has been here for two years, and there's eighteen years left on the original twenty-year lease, with two ten-year renewal options. The beauty of this lease is that it's triple net, so McDonald's takes care of everything—property taxes, insurance, and maintenance. You don't need to worry about repairs or negotiations, and they're responsible for their own upkeep. You just collect the rent, which is actually a direct deposit into your account every month. The yearly rent also increases by 3 percent, so it keeps up with inflation."

Laurent nodded as he reviewed the numbers on his end. "That's quite stable. What's the asking price on this one?"

Naomi smiled. "Because McDonald's is a high-credit tenant with longterm stability, the cap rate is low—4.5 percent. So, with $1 million in net operating income, the asking price is $22,222,222. It's a higher capital investment, but you're paying for security and minimal involvement. Essentially, you're buying peace of mind."

Laurent leaned back in his chair, thinking. "It sounds ideal, but I imagine there's a lot of competition for this kind of deal. What's next?"

Naomi swiped to the second property. "This one's an office building, currently leased to Allstate Insurance. They're a good, reliable tenant with solid credit, but the deal comes with a bit more responsibility. It's not a triple net lease, so you'll be responsible for the roof and structure, although the building is only a year old, so it should be maintenance-free for quite some time."

Laurent tilted his head. "How much longer is Allstate's lease?"

"They've got fourteen years left on a fifteen-year lease, with two seven-year renewal options," Naomi replied. "The rent also increases by 3 percent annually, just like McDonald's. But here's where it gets tricky. When Allstate's renewal comes up, they might not need the entire building, which happened a lot post-COVID. They could decide to downsize, and you'd have to find another tenant to fill the remaining space. That could mean more landlord responsibilities, like hiring someone to clean the common areas or shovel snow."

Laurent nodded. "So, what's the asking price?"

"With a 6.5 percent cap rate, you're looking at about $15,384,615," Naomi explained. "It's a bit more involvement than McDonald's, but you still have a stable tenant for at least fourteen more years. You'll need to be prepared for more maintenance down the line as the building ages, though."

Laurent tapped his fingers on his desk. "Interesting. What's the last option?"

Naomi swiped to the third property. "This is an apartment building with a mix of market-rate and subsidized tenants. It offers the highest return but also the most management. Apartment leases are typically renewed annually, so there's no automatic rent increase like with McDonald's or Allstate. You'll need to negotiate rent hikes with each tenant every year and handle repairs as needed. The property would require more handson management, which is why I've lined up some property management companies to meet with you when you visit."

Laurent frowned slightly. "I see. A bit more labor-intensive, then."

"Definitely," Naomi confirmed. "At an 8 percent cap rate, the asking price is $12.5 million. It's a significant discount compared to the other two properties, but that's because of the higher level of involvement. You'd need to stay on top of tenant relations, negotiate rent increases annually, and potentially deal with more repairs as tenants come and go."

Laurent rubbed his chin, contemplating. "So, to sum it up: McDonald's is the low-risk, stable option with almost no involvement. Allstate is in the middle, offering decent stability but with the potential for more work when their lease comes up for renewal. And the apartment building offers the highest return but demands the most management."

Naomi nodded. "Exactly. It really comes down to what kind of involvement you want. Do you prefer something hands-off, or are you willing to deal with more responsibility for a higher reward?"

Laurent chuckled. "I think I've made my decision. I'll take some time to review everything, but McDonald's seems like the winner here. I like the idea of stability without the extra work."

The Squeeze Play—Value Added

In commercial real estate investing, there are two primary approaches: passive investing and value-added investing. Passive investors prioritize steady income with minimal involvement. They invest, collect checks, and deal with occasional maintenance, like a new roof or parking lot repair, but largely remain hands-off.

On the other hand, value-add investors are more hands-on. They're willing to take on projects that need work—such as buying a vacant building, overhauling it, and spending eighteen to twenty-four months filling the space with tenants. While this path requires upfront effort and time before seeing income, it can yield substantial long-term rewards.

For example, a passive investor may earn an 8 percent return immediately. By the time a value-add investor earns their first dollar after two years, the passive investor has already earned 16 percent. However, the valueadd investor can target returns in the high teens by the third year, driving up the property's value and maximizing return on investment (ROI) over time.

ROI, or return on investment, is a measure of profitability that calculates the percentage gain or loss from an investment relative to its initial cost. For real estate investors, ROI reflects how effectively they're increasing the property's value and generating income from their investment.

There's also a middle ground: light value-add. In this scenario, the property is generally in good shape but could benefit from some updates—such as renovating kitchens and bathrooms as units become vacant. Suppose you invest $20,000 per unit and raise rent by $300 per month. For thirty units, that's a $600,000 investment that adds $108,000 to your annual net operating income (NOI).

New investors might think, "$600,000 for $108,000 in return? Is that worth it?" But the numbers tell a different story. That $108,000 in extra NOI represents an 18 percent return on your $600,000 investment. Plus, thanks to forced appreciation, the property value increases significantly—$108,000 in additional NOI equates to $1.44 million in added value at a 7.5 percent capitalization rate (cap rate). If you continue making improvements as 30 percent of your units turn over each year, you're potentially adding $4.32 million in property value over three years.

Another consideration for value-added opportunities is individual heating units vs. central boilers. While experienced investors often prefer boiler systems for easier management at scale, newer investors might resist paying for tenants' heat. But here's the reality: heat is already factored into the rent. A building with a central boiler will generally have rents one to two hundred dollars higher per unit compared to a building with individual heating, offsetting heating costs during cold winters.

Even with individual heating units, policies need to be in place to ensure tenants can afford their utilities. Otherwise, if a tenant fails to pay the gas bill, frozen pipes could lead to water damage across multiple floors—resulting in costly repairs and lost rent.

Savvy investors look for win-win scenarios. For example, a thirty-unit boiler building with rents $150 higher than the competition generates an extra $54,000 per year, which covers heating costs with room to spare. Or, installing solar panels could reduce energy costs for both tenants and common areas, enhancing the property's appeal.

Ultimately, value-add investing requires creative solutions. While newer investors might focus on cosmetic upgrades—like updating cabinets and appliances—seasoned investors recognize the opportunity in improving the overall living experience. Planting community gardens or adding amenities can create a better environment for tenants, which boosts retention and adds long-term value.

In real estate, "To whom much is given, much is required" holds true. Beyond profit, value-add investing has the power to transform communities. The key is to focus on win-win strategies that benefit both investors and tenants. When done right, the returns follow naturally.

Understanding the spectrum and continuum of real estate ownership and its cyclical nature is a fascinating proposition. The different lease types and asset classes often reflect the stage the investor is in. Are they in the wealth creation stage, willing to take on bigger risks for larger rewards, like the value-add investor tackling a two-year construction project or the developer with an even longer investment horizon? Or are they in the wealth preservation stage, like the absolute net lease owner who wants their principal to grow without the hassle of shuffling paperwork?

At the far end of the spectrum is the ground lease or absolute net lease, which is about legacy. These investors have the potential to make mistakes along the way, like the apartment owner who decided to run a large Bitcoin mining operation out of the basement, leading to skyrocketing electricity bills and making the asset harder to sell. But with the security of a long-term lease paying substantial monthly rent, there's room for recovery and the opportunity to find their footing over time.

As a commercial real estate broker, your role is to navigate these complexities and guide your clients toward the best opportunities for their goals in their stage of investment. It takes mastering the language, understanding the nuances, and diving deep into the details. But if you're willing to put in the work and get your hands dirty, the rewards can be substantial. With the right knowledge and tenacity, you can rise to the top of this challenging and dynamic field.

The meticulous nature of commercial real estate transactions, often involving leases with over 35,000 words, demands thorough review and understanding. Such complexity underscores the importance of not navigating these waters alone. Always ensure that you're consulting with a commercial broker who is deeply familiar with the intricacies of commercial leases and capable of guiding you effectively.

A Playbook for Navigating Commercial Real Estate

Misconceptions About Commercial Brokerage

As Warren Buffet aptly said, "People get very emotional about their money." Some agents, after losing a residential deal, come to commercial real estate thinking, "There's no emotion in commercial." That's another common misconception. In fact, the very reason they're making that shift is driven by emotion—whether it's frustration, anger, or a desire for something more stable. But commercial real estate can be equally, if not more, emotionally charged. Imagine losing a $10 million deal. The disappointment you feel, and the emotions your client goes through, are palpable.

The myth that commercial real estate is solely for the "ruthless" is not only outdated, but it can also lead newer agents astray. Some enter the field with a "cutthroat" mentality, believing it's the only way to succeed. However, seasoned brokers know better: commercial real estate is built on professionalism and long-term relationships, not aggressive, confrontational tactics. Ironically, it's often the novice agents who approach deals this way, thinking it's a shortcut to success.

Newer agents may also believe the reputation of commercial real estate as a shady business, and while it's true that some brokers engage in unethical behavior, these individuals tend to show clear warning signs. Painting all brokers with that broad brush can be counterproductive—especially if you're trying to establish yourself in the field. Relationships matter in commercial real estate, and so does understanding the nuance of deals. Sometimes, a newer agent's suspicion stems from a lack of knowledge. It's why working with an experienced agent who knows their way around deals is invaluable.

The Challenges of Transitioning Brokers

Residential brokers transitioning into the commercial sector often face a steep learning curve. Deals in commercial real estate are fundamentally different and tend to be more complex, leading to frustration when deals falter. In some cases, residential brokers may threaten to file complaints, misunderstanding strategic decisions as unfair practices. However, commercial transactions require a deep understanding of long-term strategies that extend beyond the immediate terms of the deal.

For example, commercial sellers may prioritize outright sales over leases to maximize returns, or they might prefer tenants who can elevate the property's profile, like publicly traded companies. These decisions aren't arbitrary—they're calculated strategies designed to enhance the long-term value of the property. A residential agent new to commercial real estate may hear that a landlord wants a particular tenant type and mistake it for a fair housing issue. However, it's essential to recognize that commercial real estate is focused on business, not housing.

Landlords are extending long-term credit through commercial leases, so they need to ensure the business leasing the property can meet its obligations. Questions like, "What type of business are you running?" or "Have you done this before?" are standard, and a business's viability plays a large role in the selection process. For instance, an owner might prefer to wait for a regional franchise rather than sign with a local mom-and-pop shop to boost the property's credibility and long-term value.

On the other hand, the way a mom-and-pop store is presented can make all the difference. A seasoned commercial broker may anticipate the landlord's concerns and come prepared with supporting documentation—a strong bank statement, a letter of endorsement from an elected official, a detailed menu, or credentials of a renowned chef. By presenting the mom-and-pop operation as a credible, sustainable tenant, the broker could very well secure the lease and win the owner's trust. In this way, even small, local businesses can get a chance if positioned correctly with a strategic approach.

Navigating Complexities in Commercial Deals

In commercial real estate, standard practices such as requiring proof of funds or detailed real estate holdings prior to property tours might unsettle those accustomed to the less stringent residential market. However, these practices are essential in a realm where the financial stakes are exceptionally high. They serve to ensure that all parties are credible and committed, thereby safeguarding the investments involved.

Building Collaborative Relationships

The path to success in commercial real estate is paved with collaboration, not competition. Establishing a good rapport with seasoned brokers can open doors to high-value listings and opportunities. For new agents like the hypothetical character in our narrative, understanding the importance of patience, thorough preparation, and respect for established protocols is key.

Thriving in Commercial Real Estate

Thriving in commercial real estate requires more than just understanding the numbers; it demands an appreciation for the sector's complexities and an ability to navigate its emotional terrain. By debunking myths, fostering professional relationships, and adhering to industry standards, agents can not only survive but thrive in the competitive world of commercial real estate.

By requiring buyers to acknowledge the financial obligations associated with their agent's efforts, the industry moves toward a model that emphasizes informed consent and commitment. This evolution in practice not only aligns with the meticulous nature of commercial real estate dealings but also promises to elevate the standards of residential transactions, pushing the industry toward a more professional and transparent future.

Workshop: Game-Day Strategies—Mastering Real Estate Transactions

Objective: Equip real estate agents with practical skills to navigate complex transactions using real-life scenarios and role-playing exercises.

Materials Needed:

- Book (for reference and scenario setups)

- Optional: Access to role cards and additional resources on ChargingTheStorm.com

Workshop Sections:

1. **Pregame Warm-Up: Understanding the Fundamentals**

   - Quick review of key concepts from the book (Cap rates, tenant credit analysis, etc.)

   - Group discussion on the importance of thorough lease review and detailed due diligence.

2. **First Quarter: Setting the Field**

   - Participants break into small groups.

   - Each group is given a brief on a property (from the book), including tenant details, financials, and lease summaries.

3. **Second Quarter: The Play Begins**

   - Role-playing exercise begins:

     - One participant plays the commercial broker.

- **◉** Another takes on the role of a potential investor.

- **◉** A third acts as the opposing broker.

- ○ ① Scenario: Negotiating a deal with complex lease terms and potential tenant issues.

4. **Halftime: Review and Revise**

- ○ Groups gather to discuss the outcomes of their negotiations.

- ○ Facilitator provides feedback and highlights effective strategies and common pitfalls.

5. **Third Quarter: Advanced Plays**

- ○ Introduction of more complex scenarios from the book involving higher stakes and more detailed financial calculations.

- ○ Groups rotate roles to gain different perspectives.

6. **Fourth Quarter: Closing the Deal**

- ○ Final role-play scenario where groups must close the deal considering new information that affects the property's value (e.g., sudden market changes, tenant bankruptcy).

- ○ Emphasis on adapting strategies and using advanced negotiation techniques.

7. **Overtime: Reflect and Learn**

- ○ Groups share their experiences and key takeaways.

- ○ Discussion on how to apply these strategies in real-world settings.

○ Optional: Guided access to ChargingTheStorm.com for further learning and role card usage.

8. **Postgame Analysis:**

   ○ Workshop wrap-up with Q&A session.

   ○ Distribution of certificates or acknowledgments for participation.

   ○ Encouragement to visit ChargingTheStorm.com for continued education and resources.

Extra Points:

   ○ Facilitators highlight the importance of consulting with knowledgeable brokers and using the right tools, as demonstrated in the workshop scenarios.

   ○ Participants are encouraged to regularly practice these scenarios to refine their skills, akin to athletes training for a game.

CHAPTER 6

Resimercial to Commercial

Excellence is not a singular act but a habit. You are what you do repeatedly.
—Shaquille O'Neal

Amid the ferocity of a Chicago blizzard, an ambitious real estate agent named Tony braved the elements to attend a career night that promised to pivot his path into the world of commercial real estate. The drive from Chicago to Naperville, typically a smooth half-hour journey, transformed into a grueling two-hour trek. Roads were choked with snow, and ice-slicked ramps, causing pileups that turned highways into parking lots. Tony, determined and unswayed by the chaos, took to the backstreets, navigating through the storm's fury.

Finally arriving at the headquarters of a national commercial real estate firm, Tony entered a room buzzing with the energy of possibility. The conference room, resembling a situation room from a high-stakes trading movie, was set for a career night that would change the trajectory of his career. Here, amid brokers known for sealing deals on properties as varied as shopping centers and hospital campuses, Tony felt the pulse of the big leagues.

At the front stood Vincent Marlowe, the managing director, whose presence commanded attention. He painted a vivid picture of the firm's global impact, noting transactions were completed every five minutes—a testament to its reach and influence.

Vincent Marlowe then delved into the essence of commercial real estate brokerage—a world far removed from the glitz of HGTV property shows, rooted in grit and persistence. He outlined the rigorous expectations, and the relentless pursuit required to succeed.

After the presentation, Tony and other attendees were handed stacks of documents—an initial test to assess their analytical prowess. Overwhelmed yet invigorated, Tony spent the entire night, blizzard howling outside, dissecting the material. By morning, he had composed a comprehensive report filled with analytics and narratives, which he promptly sent to Marlowe.

Persistence defined the following two weeks as Tony called daily, each attempt met with silence until one Monday morning when Marlowe answered, his voice carrying a mix of anticipation and respect. "Hi Tony, I've been expecting your call," he stated, acknowledging both Tony's tenacity and the substance of his report. "You have what it takes to succeed in this business. It's not just about knowledge but about persistence, using the phone as your lifeline."

Tony was invited to join the firm as a junior broker, a role that barred him from client interactions until he could fluently speak the language of investments. His days were filled with rigorous training; market research, understanding dynamics, and constructing strategic plans to engage top investors—each potential client's profile pinned meticulously across a strategic board resembling a detective's crime-solving map.

This boiler room-like environment, while daunting, was exactly where Tony needed to be. It provided him with the foundational skills and the relentless ethos required to thrive in the competitive arena of commercial real estate. Each call and each strategic plan laid the groundwork for what would become a lucrative and impactful career, steering Tony from an aspiring broker to a master of commercial transactions.

This period was akin to a high-stakes training camp. Tony was drilled on the time value of money calculations, crafting perfect letters of intent (LOIs), and mastering the art of overcoming objections to secure listing agreements. The role-plays and practice sessions were intense, honing his skills for the moment he'd finally step out on behalf of the firm.

Mastery Through Resistance

One crucial lesson learned was the importance of resistance in sealing deals. Objections were not hurdles but gateways to opportunities, a concept embraced wholeheartedly by the commercial brokerage community. Handling these objections was an art form, one that required listening intently, understanding the underlying concerns, and addressing them without being confrontational.

Practice Makes Perfect

Like Steph Curry, who shoots over five hundred practice shots a day, understanding the importance of repetition. Each objection handled, and every role-play conducted was akin to those practice shots—preparation for the game-time situations that would inevitably arise in real estate negotiations.

Real-Life Applications

Vincent often emphasized, "If you don't face resistance, you're not making real deals." Learning to navigate through this resistance was crucial. Numerous scenarios were simulated:

1. When a client indicates that they may want to sell a property however, hesitant enter into a formal listing agreement, brokers learned to collect the objection silently acknowledging it before diving deeper into understanding their reservations.

2. The objection to listing a property, often due to fears of market exposure or tenant reactions, was tackled by illustrating the control and strategic advantage of formal listings.

3. Discussing dual agency became a lesson in demonstrating value and commitment to both buyers and sellers, ensuring that all parties understood the burdens and benefits of representation.

Drumroll, please! Commercial brokerage is why we're here. Moving your practice from resimercial to commercial closings is pivotal in your real estate career. Disclaimer, this is going to be hard, VERY HARD!

The Art of the Pivot: Handling Objections Like a Seasoned Playmaker

The key to managing any objection is being aware of what the client is telling you. Also, it's important to unpack why they're saying what they're saying, and why it's important to them. These may sound very similar, but they can be very different in the field. Often, by getting clarification on the nature of the pushback, you'll be able to understand how to manage your client's "objection." Opportunities rarely come in a gift-wrapped box with a pretty red bow on top. They typically show up as challenges. Objections are typically opportunities that come in a box that stretches you just outside of your comfort zone.

Handling Objections:

Anticipate that objections simply are part of the deal. You don't get to pick and choose what an opportunity looks like. Opportunities often come in the form of pushback on your ideas and occasionally, may even show up initially as a flat-out "no," with some swear words followed by a hang-up of the phone. This scenario while somewhat extreme, happens regularly enough that we should be prepared for it. If a millionaire with a commercial portfolio is committed enough to shout at you, then there's probably an opportunity there if you're levelheaded and still standing when they're done with their diatribe. Be ready to listen to potential objections and have questions ready to unpack in certain situations. No matter what happens, leave the conversation on a positive note and remain cordial, so you can follow up.

Here are a few situations to consider:

1. **The client wants to sell but they don't sign an agreement:**

    When the client first mentions they're hesitant about signing a listing agreement, don't respond immediately. This is what I call *collecting the objection*—acknowledge it subtly perhaps with a nod, note it mentally and continue with the conversation. The second time they mention it, briefly acknowledge it by saying something like, "Understood," and keep moving forward. The key here is to not address it too soon.

    By the third time—or later in the conversation—circle back to it and address it directly but not in a confrontational way: "You've mentioned this a couple of times, so I can tell it's important to you. Let's unpack that a bit. What's holding you back from listing the property?"

This opens the door for the client to share their concerns while you focus on listening and asking open-ended questions. Avoid responding too quickly, either positively or negatively, to allow them to fully express their reasons. Your goal here is to gather more information, not to counter their concerns.

You might follow up with something like: "Mr. Seller, maybe now isn't the right time to list the property. Let's take a step back and focus on understanding the asset better. If we could walk through a couple of apartments and review the rent roll and financials, it would help us have a more productive conversation about the best strategy moving forward."

This approach gives the client space to share their objections while positioning yourself as a consultant, not just a salesperson, and guiding the conversation toward discovery and collaboration.

2. **"I'll sell the property if you bring me a buyer, but I don't want to list it":**

The challenge is that the property owner has issues with "listing the property." The opportunity here is that this property owner has separated himself from 90+ percent of other investors and has indicated that they are, in fact, a seller. If you can find out their motivations for wanting to sell, then maybe you can help. Their reluctance to list the property at this time is understandable. For most investors, listing a property is like going to the dentist. They must worry about tenants finding out that the property is for sale, and all the other brokers they've spoken with or worked with over the years will find out they picked you and not them.

It's inconvenient, too, because buyers will be showing up and noticing the projects they've put off and other things. Investors have all kinds of reasons in their heads why they should sell without listing. Sometimes they think, "I have so many brokers calling me regularly, I could just tell all five of them that the property is available, and one of them will bring a buyer, and we'll make the deal." It seems simple enough, but it's all made-up stuff because listing the property will bring the property owner out of their comfort zone. Unpacking the motivation and finding out the block could come down to a couple of great questions. "Mrs. Seller, if we did identify the right buyer that paid your price and closed quickly, what would you do with all the time you'd regain in your life with not having to manage the property anymore?" "A follow-up question could be, and what would you do with the money?" "What's holding you back from going to market with the property?"

3. **"I need to find my replacement property first because I need to replace the cash flow":**

That's completely understandable. The key here is to dive deeper into their motivation for selling. What type of cash flow are they looking to replace? And why go through the hassle if they already have a steady stream of income? For example, one investor mentioned that he was considering retiring and wanted a property that required less management so he could spend more time enjoying life.

In cases like this, it can make sense to show potential replacement properties and discuss the market conditions—such as how long assets like his, as well as the potential replacements, typically stay on the market when priced correctly. Considering the number of available replacement options, along with the time required for marketing, negotiating, and financing, it may be wiser to go to market and find the right buyer rather than rush into another deal.

Reassure them by pointing out that there are enough available deals in the current market for them to feel confident that at least one suitable replacement will be available when they're ready to make the move. This way, they can achieve their goal without feeling pressured or compromising their cash flow.

4. **"My niece or a family member has a real estate license, and I have to list with them because of x, y, or z":**

There are a few ways to go about this, but it typically comes down to the agent being able to show the value they bring because of specialization, the strength of their network, and their track record for handling similar deals. Also, if the opportunity presents itself, look up the family member's track record. If it isn't strong, remind the potential client that this is a potentially complex commercial real estate transaction, not a condominium sale and that it's important to have someone involved who cares and knows what they're doing. In this instance, I'd recommend doing something nice for the family member when the deal closes, like taking them out for a nice dinner or to a ballgame but giving them the assignment may not be the best business decision.

5. **From buyers, "If you think it's such an awesome deal, why don't you buy it?":**

I do think this is a good deal for these three reasons, and I may be willing to invest some capital into the deal with you for a percentage of the equity. I don't have the bandwidth to deal with day-to-day operations, but if you already have the infrastructure in place we can continue the conversation.

6. **"I've owned my property for many years and have very little debt on it. Why would I ever sell it?":**

One reason to sell is that these properties typically need a major capital infusion from time to time, and sometimes it makes sense for the next investor to deal with that. Also, have you considered the return on equity? The return on equity conversation goes something like this: We've performed an analysis on your property, and you're correct, it is performing well, and you have may have $3 million or more in equity in the property. Everyone isn't ready for this conversation, as sometimes it takes a bit of education for some investors. In any event, there is $3 million sitting there that isn't earning a return. Most savvy investors want to put their dollars to work. They may say something like, "What do you mean, no return? I'm cash flowing." The cash flow you're receiving is related to the initial down payment and capital you put into the property. The three million in equity you have would earn an additional $240,000 per year at an 8 percent cap and you wouldn't sacrifice the appreciation/depreciation you are befitting from now. That $240,000 cashflow number could be more substantial if it were leveraged using debt on an eight-cap deal. So, if you transferred a portion of that equity to another asset, it would continue to grow. It may also help to share other available investment opportunities.

7. **A seller may have a problem with an agent being a dual agent:**

Typically, a seller selects an agent to represent them in the sale of their property because they believe the agent will get the job done. In other words, "Mr. Seller, you liked my presentation and agree with our marketing strategy for the asset, and my track record is strong. At the end of the day, you're hiring me to sell the property, and that's exactly what I plan to do. I will call every owner and follow up on every opportunity until I find the buyer who will pay the highest price and get the deal over the finish line. The dual agency allows me to do just that." Another way to say it is, "You're not hiring me to put the deal in the computer and wait for someone else to sell it. "If another agent brings the buyer, that's perfectly fine. But when *qualified investors* respond directly to my marketing, I'm often in the best position to explain the property's strengths clearly and answer their questions immediately."

8. **Buyer and tenant representation sometimes gets tricky:**

It's common for buyers to respond directly after seeing a listing advertisement or sign on a building. They reached out directly because it's convenient. And once they call, they start asking questions, gathering details.

This is where the line on representation begins to blur.

It would be prudent here to ask for clarification here on whether they are reaching out as a principal or a broker?

A residential agent may ask if they are represented by a broker. The nuance is that a high percentage of commercial investors are also brokers.

Oftentimes they will indicate that they are the buyer or tenant and press for more details—asking whether the price is negotiable, how flexible the terms, or what the seller's expectations are.

Before long, they're requesting additional information and even scheduling an appointment for a viewing.

And still, no mention of a broker.

At this point, the interaction feels straightforward: they saw *your* marketing, contacted *you* directly, and are moving toward the next step because of the information and access you've provided. The momentum is building, the deal is taking shape, and it appears you're working directly with the principal.

But that's where things can shift.

Sometimes, just as the process advances, they reveal that they do in fact have a broker who will be writing the offer. Other times, the surprise comes on the day of the tour when the broker shows up alongside them—even though the appointment was scheduled directly with you.

And in both scenarios, you've already built the foundation: the exposure, the information, the clarity, the access, the interest. The heavy lifting has been done.

So where's the line?
What happens next?
And how do you protect your time, your value, and your professional boundaries without jeopardizing the deal?

What Happens Next

When a buyer suddenly introduces a broker after you've already provided information, scheduled a tour, or begun discussing terms, the key is to stay professional and keep the deal moving.

Your responsibility is to the **property owner**, and your focus remains on managing the process clearly and efficiently.

○ **Reset Communication—Professionally and Calmly**

A simple reset keeps everything clean:

"Great—thanks for letting me know. I'm more than happy to work with your agent. Going forward, I'll coordinate next steps directly with them so everything stays streamlined."

This restores proper protocol and prevents you from being placed in a position that looks or feels like dual agency.

○ **Clarify Roles Without Discussing Compensation**

This part is important:
agency and compensation don't always align.

Clarity Without Overstepping

To avoid confusion later, it's best to communicate directly with the buyer's agent or set up a conference call so that everyone is on the same page:

Just to keep everything clean, agency and compensation could be separate issues. Since the buyer/tenant reached out to the listing agent directly as a direct result of their marketing efforts. This could be a scenario where the parties to the transaction compensate their respective agents directly.

This keeps the responsibility where it belongs:
with the buyer/tenant and their broker, not you.

You're not telling the buyer they owe money.

You're not negotiating another broker's commission.

You're simply protecting the process.

The Bottom Line

Buyers often contact you because of *your* marketing and *your* information. When they later insert a broker, you simply reset communication, clarify expectations, and continue the process professionally.

Also remember in oftentimes this a seasoned millionaire real estate investor not a first time homebuyer.

Agency, representation, and compensation rules vary by state and brokerage. Always follow your local laws, MLS policies, and your managing broker's guidance.

Traditionally, in commercial real estate, working with a buyer's agent has never guaranteed that the seller will cover their share. The recent NAR settlement is highlighting this reality for residential agents as well, but it's a practice that commercial brokers have always been clear on.

9. **The other company or agent said they'd list the property some other lesser amount:**

Mindset: Consider the Mercedes versus Ford analogy as a compelling way to set the tone and reinforce the value of premium service. This analogy could be a compelling framework to structure the conversation.

Handling Objections Like a Pro: The Conundrum

Setting the Mindset

Navigating buyer and seller discussions about price and associated 5ns than just settling on numbers. Think of it this way: if you're in a Mercedes dealership you're not there to discuss the price of a Ford. You value the quality, the prestige, and the performance of a Mercedes. It's similar when you're engaging with clients about the cost associated with the transaction, such as the brokerage fee. By the time cost discussions come up, they've already recognized your potential value—they're not just looking for any broker, they're considering you.

This is a key moment to establish not just the value of your services, but also the unique benefits they stand to gain from your expertise. It's not merely about the fee; it's about the value you bring to their table. You're offering a comprehensive suite of services that go far beyond just listing their property. You're actively engaging in the market, leveraging deep industry knowledge and extensive networks not only to list their property but to ultimately sell it, for the highest price, in the shortest period and navigate the transaction to the goal line.

Effective representation in commercial real estate requires a nuanced understanding of the market, strategic positioning of the property, and a proactive approach to finding the right buyers. These are the points you need to communicate clearly to your clients. It's about framing the conversation around the robust support, market insights, and dedicated effort your team provides, which are all part of the package they invest in when they choose you. It's about value. What value do they actually believe they'll get for in exchange for the investment?

If a client is overly focused on the lowest price, gently help them bring the bigger picture back into focus: the long-term gains from a well-executed deal and the legacy they are building with it. Share examples of how your strategic approach has added significant value for your clients, perhaps turning potential losses into gains through savvy negotiations and timely closings. Make it clear that the cost may be a touch higher than some brokers, the service and outcomes you deliver are unmatched.

And as you wrap up the conversation, remember your initial mindset analogy— strategically communicate why they walked into the "Mercedes dealership" of real estate in the first place. It's about exceptional quality, not just cost saving. Reiterate your commitment to not let the payment structures stand in the way of their success but also highlight that the expertise and resources you'll leverage for a successful outcome has a value that exceeds to the cost. After all, they have invested significant time and capital into this asset and they only get to sell it one time. Building lasting legacies and preserving wealth isn't the place anyone wants to cut corners.

Opening Dialogue

Client: "I can get another broker to do this for a much lower price. Why should I pay more?"

Broker Mindset "know your value!"

You: "That's a fair question. "I completely understand where you're coming from, and it's smart to evaluate all your options. But let's unpack that conversation you had with the other broker a bit — just to make sure we're considering the full picture, not just the numbers.

1. Why do you think the agent said they'd do it for that price?

2. Why was it important to share that info when they did?

   I've found that in some instances agents may fall back on being the lowest price option when they are reaching beyond the scope of their track record.

3. Would it be safe to assume that you have concerns outside of just the lowest price option that drives you decision making process?

   My goal is to help you make an informed decision — based on value and outcomes. The truth is that the right representation should *protect* and enhance your bottom line.

Developing the Value Proposition

As we dive deeper into this dialogue, remember, that you're not just paying for a service; you're investing in expertise and outcomes that preserve wealth and build a legacy.

Here are some breadcrumbs that can be woven into the discussion.

Expertise and Track Record

"Just as Mercedes is known for its engineering excellence, our firm is renowned for its expertise in handling complex commercial deals that maximize investor returns."

Quality of Service

"Consider the attention to detail, the luxurious experience of driving a Mercedes. Similarly, our comprehensive service suite ensures that every aspect of your deal is handled with precision and care."

Long-Term Benefits

"A Mercedes holds its value. In real estate, choosing the right representation can significantly increase the final sale price and replacement property impacting the long-term value."

Addressing the Fe6e Directly

"Mr. Seller, selecting the right representative for the sale of your property is a very important business decision. While the cost is a factor to consider, it should not be the sole basis for this choice. Our focus is maximizing the value received at closing and significantly increasing the probability of your success.

"We don't merely list your property and wait. We take a proactive approach to every sale. Our method involves strategic marketing, in-depth market research, and skilled negotiations, all tailored to attract well qualified investors and achieve superior outcomes. We actively manage every detail of the sales process, from vetting potential buyers to navigating complex negotiations and overseeing the escrow timeline, ensuring a smooth and efficient transaction.

"I assure you, we will not let the cost stand in the way of your success. We view it as an investment in achieving the best possible outcome for your property. That approach has consistently led to enhanced value for our clients.

"We manage the entire sales process meticulously. This includes rigorously screening all investors differentiating serious prospects from tire kickers, navigating multiple offers to secure the best possible deal, carefully overseeing due diligence, escrow timeline through the final closing. Our involvement ensures that every aspect of the sale is aligned with your best interests to guarantee a timely and successful closing

Each response articulates the value of your representation by detailing the extensive efforts involved in managing the sales process effectively. It underscores the benefits of choosing a full-service approach over a potentially less thorough option.

Conclusion: The Path Forward

As I reflect on those early days, the blizzard outside mirrored the flurry of activity and learning inside. Both were formidable, yet both were profoundly transformative, steering me toward a career where every challenge was an opportunity waiting to be seized.

Workshop Title: Full-Court Press—Navigating Real Estate Negotiations Like a Pro

This dynamic workshop transforms objection handling in real estate into an interactive, sports-themed experience. Participants will engage in role-play scenarios that mimic the high-stakes environment of key sports moments, focusing on strategic responses and teamwork.

Objective: Empower real estate professionals to tackle objections headon with precision and confidence, akin to a well-coordinated basketball team executing a full-court press.

Workshop Components:

1. **Pregame Warm-Up:**

   O A quick introduction to the fundamentals of objection handling.

   O Overview of common objections encountered in real estate transactions.

2. **Drafting the Team:**

   O Participants are divided into teams, symbolizing different positions in a basketball team (Guard, Forward, Center) representing various roles in real estate negotiations (Broker, Buyer, Seller).

3. **Tip-Off and Role-Plays:**

   O Teams face off in scripted scenarios that reflect typical negotiation challenges in real estate.

○ Scenarios are drawn from a playbook of common real estate situations involving pricing, terms, and property concerns.

4. **Halftime Review:**

   ○ Midsession analysis is where teams regroup to refine strategies and discuss what tactics are working or need adjustment.

5. **Second Half—Strategy Implementation:**

   ○ Teams implement refined strategies in a second round of role plays, applying feedback and new techniques.

   ○ Emphasis on quick thinking and adaptability, mirroring a basketball team adjusting to the opposing team's strategies.

6. **Postgame Analysis:**

   ○ Teams gather to discuss outcomes and key takeaways from the role plays.

   ○ Facilitators provide feedback on performance, highlighting effective negotiation tactics and areas for improvement.

7. **Overtime—Handling High-Pressure Situations:**

   ○ A rapid-fire round where participants handle unexpected objections and complex scenarios to simulate the pressure of a closing-minute game scenario.

8. **Victory Lap—Reflect and Celebrate:**

   ○ Conclusion with reflections on lessons learned, emphasizing continuous improvement and teamwork.

   ○ Participants share how they can apply the strategies in their real-world interactions.

Training Materials Provided:

- ❍ A playbook of scenarios and objections.

- ❍ Response tips and strategies cards.

- ❍ Access to a digital toolkit on chargingthestorm.com for continued learning and practice.

Important Compliance Reminder – Do Not Call Registry

Before making any outreach calls, **you must verify whether the number is listed on the National Do Not Call Registry**. Federal law requires all telemarketers—including real estate agents engaged in prospecting—to scrub calling lists against the Registry and to **follow all restrictions under the Telephone Consumer Protection Act (TCPA)**.

Violations can result in **significant penalties**, including fines of **up to $51,744 per call**.

Agents should review the official rules and access the Registry through the Federal Trade Commission at: **https://www.donotcall.gov**

Always consult your brokerage's policies and your state's regulations, which may include additional requirements or penalties.

CHAPTER 7

Offensive Strategies for Winning the Game: The Cold Call Playbook

*Never let the fear of striking out keep you from
playing the game.*
—**Babe Ruth**

DOES COLD CALLING WORK ANYMORE?

I've been calling for hours, and no listings, no sales...

Anyone crack the code?

What's working for you in today's market?

Scrolling through social media often exposes you to a myriad of opinions about the efficacy of cold calling. Common sentiments like, "I've been calling for two hours and haven't got a new listing; I guess cold calling doesn't work anymore," pop up regularly, sparking debates filled with various suggestions.

Contrary to the popular outcry against cold calling, I find these moments on social media to be illuminating—they showcase a widespread reluctance to engage in what can be a foundational practice for success in real estate. It's not about whether cold calling works; it's about how you make it work. When someone buys leads, what's their next step? To call them, of course. This brings us to the crux of the matter: Who are you calling, what are you saying, and how persistent are you in your efforts?

Euro Step Playbook

Let's dive in: The office is buzzing with the typical morning energy as agents trickle in, coffee in hand, ready to seize the day. At one corner of the open-plan office, Jessica, Michael, and Sam set up their makeshift role-play arena—a trio of desks pushed together, littered with notepads, pens, and highlighted scripts that resemble game plans more than property listings.

Michael: (clapping his hands together enthusiastically) "Alright, team, let's kick off with the Euro Step today. Jess, you're up first. You're on a call with a hesitant buyer who's considering pulling out because of market volatility. Go!"

Jessica: (picking up her phone, pressing it to her ear, and speaking confidently) "Good morning, Mark. I understand your concerns regarding the current market fluctuations. However, this actually presents a unique opportunity for us. Prices are adjusting, which means there's potential to negotiate a deal that could really work in your favor. Let's meet at the property this afternoon; I'd love to walk you through the adjustments we can leverage."

Sam: (acting as the buyer, hesitating) "I don't know, Jessica. I read a *Wall Street Journal* article last night that made me think twice about investing right now."

Jessica: (nodding thoughtfully, even though Sam can't see her) "Absolutely, staying informed is crucial. Why don't you forward me that article? Let's analyze it together. I'll bring some local market analytics that might offer a broader perspective. How about we Zoom at three p.m. to discuss this in detail?"

Michael: (jumps in, mimicking a challenging client) "Jessica, why should we act now and not wait for the market to stabilize?"

Jessica: (without missing a beat) "Great question! The thing with waiting is, that while we anticipate market stabilization, the prime properties—like the one we're discussing—often get snapped up. Also, the below market rents can significantly impact your long-term investment. Let's at least secure a tentative agreement that safeguards your interests while doing due diligence and keeping our options open."

Sam: (smiling, impressed) "Nice! Smooth Euro Step there, Jess. acknowledging objections, and moving forward with confidence."

Michael: "Alright, my turn. Sam, you're my seller, worried about listing now due to recent property tax hikes."

Sam: (switching roles, now acting concerned) "Michael, these new tax rates are going to scare off buyers. Maybe we should hold off listing until next year."

Michael: "I understand that tax hikes are a concern, but delaying might not be in your best interest. We have a growing list of buyers who are looking into this area specifically for its long-term growth potential. Property values are still on the rise here. Let's discuss how we can position your property as a smart buy despite the property tax increase. **Now that the exact amount is known, it may becomes easier for an investor to plan. Often, it's the uncertainty—not the number itself—that creates hesitation.**

I'm planning to visit some interested clients this weekend—how about we schedule a quick walk-through with them? It might give us a better feel of the market response."

The session continues with each agent taking turns, challenging each other with tough scenarios, refining their approach. This daily practice not only sharpens their skills but also builds a team spirit that is palpable throughout their interactions, making them a force in the commercial real estate market.

Five-Second Rule

As the clock struck nine a.m., the hum of activity began to permeate the office. In the breakroom, the scent of freshly brewed coffee filled the air, setting the stage for a morning of high stakes and higher ambitions. Sam, Jordan, and Casey—the trio of top-producing agents at Sky's the Limit Commercial—gathered around the coffee machine, each filling their mugs with the dark, aromatic liquid that promised a much-needed jolt of energy.

They huddled close, their faces lit with a mix of determination and friendly competition. "Alright, team," Sam proposed, his voice low but firm, "let's hit it hard today. Two hours of power calls before lunch. The goal? Eleven contacts and three appointments each. Whoever hits the mark first gets lunch on the others." Nods of agreement followed, each agent mentally gearing up for the challenge.

With mugs in hand, they made their way to their desks, setting their phones on 'Do Not Disturb' to shut out any distractions. The office buzzed with the sound of other agents starting their day, but for Sam, Micheal, and Jessica, the world narrowed down to their lists of leads and the phones in front of them.

Michael kicked off with a steady pace, his voice smooth and persuasive, "Have you considered how the new development on Michigan Ave, could impact your property value? ... Yes, that's awesome, I thought you might be interested. Let's meet to discuss this in person." He scribbled down an appointment time just as Sam landed his first meeting.

Sam was a master of quick rapport, diving right into his calls with a mix of professionalism and charm. "I'll be attending the investor soiree this Thursday. I can bring you updates on market trends and potential opportunities. How about we meet Friday morning to go over what I find?"

Jessica, not to be outdone, dialed with precision, her calls crisp and to the point. "We're working with an investment group actively seeking properties in your area. There's a window of opportunity for you to benefit from this. Can we discuss this over coffee tomorrow morning? I believe this will be a productive discussion."

The morning progressed swiftly, with each call building momentum. They practiced the five-second rule religiously: good call or bad, they took a deep breath, shook off any lingering frustration or excitement, and moved on to the next number within five seconds. Their focus was unyielding, driven not just by the desire to win the lunch bet but by their professional ethos to excel and deliver results.

By noon, each had not only met but exceeded their goals, proving yet again why they were considered the elite within their office. They regrouped in the breakroom, their expressions a mix of fatigue and satisfaction. Laughter and lighthearted banter filled the air as they recounted the morning's highs and lows. The camaraderie was a testament to their shared commitment and mutual respect.

Today, like every day, they demonstrated the power of dedication and the importance of setting clear, achievable goals. As they headed out to lunch, victorious and ready to tackle the afternoon with renewed vigor, the office couldn't help but take note. These agents were not just colleagues; they were a formidable force in the world of real estate, setting the bar high for all who aspired to make their mark.

Two-and-Two Playbook

Jessica and her team members, Sam and Michael, had quickly adapted to a rigorous schedule in commercial real estate, a discipline they humorously dubbed the "two and two." This meant two hours of strategic phone calls before lunch and another two after, ensuring they were always proactive and engaged with potential clients and leads.

This method has proven effective in keeping the team connected with the pulse of the market, allowing them to respond swiftly to opportunities. Despite the challenge of balancing multiple client needs, their dedication to this structured approach paid dividends, leading to several successful transactions and fostering a robust network of industry contacts. The "two and two" not only optimized their daily productivity but also instilled a sense of discipline that echoed throughout their professional activities, setting a high standard within the team for performance and consistency.

The "two-and-two" strategy that Jessica had adopted was simple but effective, entailing two hours of focused calling before lunch and another two hours immediately afterward. This routine not only structured her day effectively but also maximized her outreach to potential clients.

One morning, Jessica dialed the number of a new lead. As the phone rang, she reviewed her notes: the lead, Sam, was a local property owner who hadn't engaged much in the market recently. When Sam answered, Jessica greeted him warmly and quickly sparked a conversation about current market trends and potential opportunities.

"Have you considered how the new development at Millers Creek could impact your property values or rents?" Jessica inquired, tapping into Sam's interest.

Sam, caught off guard by the relevance of the topic, admitted he hadn't really thought about it. Sensing an opening, Jessica mentioned, "I'm planning to attend the upcoming investor soiree, where this will be discussed in detail. How about I bring back some information for you?"

This approach showed Sam that Jessica was proactive and thoughtful, qualities he appreciated in a professional relationship.

"We're also working with an investment group actively seeking new deals," Jessica continued, steering the conversation toward actionable opportunities. "I believe there's a potential match with your portfolio. Would you be open to a meeting to explore this further?"

Sam agreed, intrigued by the tailored approach Jessica was taking.

Later that day, Jessica prepared for her next call with Michael, another potential client. Michael had shown interest in expanding his investments but was hesitant about new market entries.

Jessica started the call with an update on market dynamics, "Michael, with the shifts in the commercial sector, it's a prime time to consider diversifying your investments."

Recognizing the need to build more trust, she added, "I'd love to meet you at the property to see how your current project is progressing. When's the next time you'll be there?"

Michael was impressed with Jessica's initiative and scheduled a walkthrough for the following week.

She'd successfully worked up an appetite, secured several meetings and laid the groundwork for potential deals. This demonstrated the effectiveness of her "two-and-two" calling strategy coupled with her personalized approach.

Michael shared a memorable anecdote over lunch, recounting his early days in commercial real estate. He was just starting, tasked with making cold calls about new listings. One day, he reached a seasoned investor who abruptly dismissed the property Michael was promoting with a sharp rebuke and hung up. Rather than being deterred, Michael saw an opportunity in this initial rejection.

He researched the investor, discovering his role as the president of a local property owners' organization. Recognizing the potential for a valuable connection, Michael decided to reach out again, but with a revised approach that respected the investor's vast experience.

The follow-up call went like this: "Hello Bill, this is Michael from STL Commercial. After our last conversation, I took your feedback to heart. I understand the property has its challenges, and I respect your expertise in navigating such investments. Could we meet at the property to discuss its potential and the insights you might have? Your perspective could be invaluable, whether or not you find this deal appealing."

To his surprise, Bill agreed to meet. This wasn't just a property showing; it was an opportunity to build a bridge. That meeting marked the beginning of a fruitful relationship that blossomed into numerous transactions and invaluable industry insights.

Michael learned the importance of perseverance in commercial real estate. In the "boiler room" atmosphere of relentless cold calling, he adopted the "five-second rule"—taking only a brief moment before moving on to the next call, whether the previous one was discouraging or promising. He dedicated hours each day to making and following up on calls, laying the groundwork for lasting professional relationships. Ten years later, many from those early calls remained active partners.

This story highlights the enduring value of cold calling in real estate. It's not merely about enduring the grind but embracing it, using strategy, persistence, and relationship-building to turn initial resistance into rewarding partnerships. Michael's approach illustrates how effective communication and respect for potential clients' expertise can transform a routine call into a significant opportunity, fostering dialogue and understanding that leads to long-term collaborations.

Running the Bases: Securing a Commercial Real Estate Listing

Tony, a seasoned commercial real estate broker, had been eyeing the potential listing of a notable office complex downtown. The owner, Mr. George Langley, was known to be contemplating selling some of his investment properties, and Tony saw an opportunity.

First Base: The Spark of Interest

The journey began with a cold call. Tony had done his homework and knew George had a significant portfolio, but he wasn't sure which properties might be on the market. Picking up the phone, Tony dialed

George's number, his heart racing with the familiar mix of adrenaline and anticipation. When George answered, Tony introduced himself briefly and shifted quickly to gauge interest.

"Good morning, George. I've been following your work with the downtown office complex, and I couldn't help but reach out. How's my timing with discussing potential strategies for your properties?"

There was a brief pause on the other end before George chuckled. "Well, I've been thinking about selling the complex. Your timing might just be right, Tony."

That acknowledgment was all Tony needed. He had reached first base:

the investor had raised his hand and shown willingness to sell.

Second Base: Securing the Assignment

After the initial call, Tony proposed a face-to-face meeting to discuss the property in greater detail. George agreed, and they met at a local coffee shop the following week. This meeting was Tony's chance to steal second base, showcasing why he was the right broker for the job.

As they sat across from each other, Tony laid out his preliminary analysis of the market and how it impacted properties like George's. He walked George through his strategic approach and past successes, building confidence and rapport.

"George, based on current market dynamics, your property has tremendous potential. I'd love to help you capitalize on this opportunity. How about we take a tour of the complex together? I'd like to understand your vision and expectations in greater detail."

George nodded, impressed by Tony's preparation and insight. They scheduled a tour for the following day, moving Tony securely to second base.

Third Base: Deep Engagement

During the tour, Tony's expertise shone. He discussed potential upgrades, marketing strategies, and the financial intricacies of representing such a property. They delved deep into George's goals for the sale and what he hoped to achieve with the proceeds.

By the end of their walk-through, Tony presented a customized sales strategy, aligning it with George's financial and personal aspirations. They discussed potential buyers, marketing tactics, and timelines. Tony's attentive approach turned their professional interaction into a partnership, advancing him to third base.

Home Plate: Closing the Deal

With confidence in Tony's capabilities solidified, they returned to George's office to discuss the final details. Tony laid out the listing agreement, explaining each clause and how they impacted George throughout the sale.

"George, I'm here not just to sell your property but to ensure the process aligns perfectly with your financial goals. Let's finalize this and get your property on the market with the best possible terms."

George, feeling fully supported and confident in Tony's expertise, signed the agreement. Tony had rounded the home base, secured the listing, and cemented a relationship that would likely yield more transactions in the future.

Running the Bases: A Commercial Real Estate Broker's Playbook

First Base: Initial Contact

- **Objective**: Identify the intent to sell.

- **Action:** Engage in a conversation with the property owner about their interest in selling a specific property or portfolio. This is the initial contact where the investor must explicitly express an interest in selling.

- **Key Point:** You reach first base when the owner says, "I want to sell."

Second Base: Securing the Assignment

- **Objective:** Position yourself as the ideal agent for the listing.

- **Action:** Transition from general discussion to asking for the assignment. This often involves setting up a more formal meeting, such as a Zoom call or in-person discussion, to delve deeper into the specifics of the asset.

- **Key Point:** You steal second base by discussing why you are the best choice for the job and potentially touring the property to gather and exchange detailed information.

Third Base: Deep Engagement

- **Objective:** Deepen the engagement with the potential seller.

- **Action:** Present a thorough analysis of the asset. This step involves detailed discussions about potential outcomes, the selling process,

○ the owner's decision-making process, and the next steps if they decide to sell.

○ **Key Point:** You reach third base by demonstrating your understanding of the asset and aligning your sales strategy with the seller's goals. This might involve multiple interactions where you explore their financial goals, potential reinvestment strategies, and the implications of selling.

Home Plate: Closing the Deal

○ **Objective:** Execute the listing agreement.

○ **Action:** Finalize the discussion by securing the listing agreement. This includes finalizing the terms of the sale, discussing how they will use the proceeds from the sale, and formalizing your role as their broker.

○ **Key Point:** You round home plate when the listing agreement is signed, effectively making you the broker of record and initiating the sales process.

The "Running the Bases" strategy provides a structured approach to converting a lead into a client in commercial real estate. By following these steps, a broker can systematically approach potential listings, ensuring they maintain momentum throughout the conversation and effectively address the needs and goals of the property owner. This strategy not only helps in securing the listing but also in building a lasting relationship that could lead to more opportunities in the future.

From Social Media Scrolls to Securing Listings

In the fast-paced world of commercial real estate, the journey from initial outreach to securing a property listing involves more than just persuasive pitches; it requires strategic relationship-building, deep market knowledge, and a deep understanding of client needs. This chapter explored the transformational approach of moving beyond traditional transactional interactions to creating meaningful connections that drive success in the industry.

Navigating Modern Challenges:

The narrative began with a reflection on the misleading perceptions often found in social media posts about the ineffectiveness of cold calling. These platforms frequently highlight frustration and seek quick fixes, overlooking the foundational sales activities that build lasting business relationships. Contrary to popular sentiment, cold calling remains a vital strategy for real estate professionals, serving as a crucial touchpoint for uncovering and nurturing potential leads.

The Art of Cold Calling:

We delved into the mechanics of cold calling, emphasizing that true engagement begins with handling objections, not avoiding them. A successful call isn't about avoiding resistance but engaging with it. Resistance signals engagement from potential clients, offering an opportunity to address concerns and showcase value. The narrative introduced the "Euro Step" technique in calls, highlighting the importance of anticipation, agreement, and strategic questioning to navigate and manage objections effectively.

Running the Bases Strategy:

The "Running the Bases" strategy illustrated a structured approach to securing listings, likened to advancing bases in a baseball game. This method involves:

- **First Base:** Identifying a potential seller and confirming their interest.

- **Second Base:** Establishing credibility and outlining value through preliminary meetings and discussions. This leads to an exchange of information. The owner may share critical details about the property, their vision, and motivations. The broker may share market intelligence, marketing strategies, and deal stories.

- **Third Base:** Engaging deeply with the client to align strategies with their goals and showcasing how to bring these strategies to fruition. The broker presents a property-specific proposal, discussing any objections, demonstrating why they are the right person for the job, and asking for the assignment.

- **Home Plate:** Winning the assignment by finalizing the agreement with a clear understanding and mutual agreement on terms and expectations.

Each base is designed to understand where the broker is on the path to securing a listing. They are methodically, moving deals forward and strengthening the broker-client relationship, ensuring that each party feels understood, respected, and confident in the path forward.

The bases serve as your GPS in the deal continuum. In your pipeline report, a broker may be on, for instance, first base with three clients and third base with four others. This playbook is designed to guide practitioners toward successful outcomes and solidify their roles as trusted advisers in the commercial real estate sector.

Mastering the Art of the Call: The Broker's Winning Strategy

The act of picking up the phone and reaching out to property owners is not just a task—it's the highest leverage activity you can engage in to accelerate your career and income. This chapter is dedicated to transforming how you perceive and execute phone calls, turning them into a strategic powerhouse for your business.

Plan to Succeed

The axiom "fail to plan, plan to fail" holds particularly true in the world of commercial brokering. Top earners in this field don't just work hard—they work smart. This means dedicating specific times for making calls, a method known as the 'Two and Two' approach: two hours of calling before lunch and two after. This structured approach helps ensure consistent, focused outreach without the distractions that can derail productivity.

Earning Potential

Commercial brokers who strategically manage their call schedules aren't just hoping for success; they are setting the stage for earning six to seven figure incomes annually. Scheduling your day with the precision of a CEO ensures that you treat your brokerage activities not just as a job but as a thriving business.

Offer Value First

Effective calling is about providing value on every call. Instead of the generic "Are you interested in selling?" approach, elevate your conversations by sharing insightful, timely information that property owners find beneficial. Discuss recent legislative changes, upcoming real estate conferences, neighborhood developments, or even perform a rent study to offer comparative insights into local market rents.

Building Relationships

The essence of successful calling is to make "deposits" into relationships before making "withdrawals." This metaphorical banking approach means offering value and building trust before you ever ask for a business commitment. Invite owners to events, provide updates on relevant market trends, or simply ask for their opinions on industry developments.

Discipline and Consistency

Discipline is nonnegotiable. Set your phone to 'Do Not Disturb' during call blocks to avoid interruptions. Aim for bursts of twenty uninterrupted calls, known as the "20-Call Burst strategy." This method has been backed by decades of sales strategy science, proving that concentrated, focused calling periods yield the best results.

Routine Establishes Expectations

Establish a routine that not only keeps you disciplined but also sets expectations with your colleagues and clients about your availability. For instance, if you are unreachable between certain hours for calls, people will learn to wait or schedule time appropriately, reducing interruptions and increasing productivity.

Leveraging Personal Connections

Each owner within your target market should know who you are. Whether you're just starting or are a seasoned broker, setting a goal to meet face-to-face with one hundred property owners can significantly boost your visibility and credibility in the market. For those looking to elevate their presence, begin the year with a commitment to secure one hundred owner meetings. This aggressive networking strategy ensures that your name becomes synonymous with industry expertise and reliability.

This journey from social media misconceptions to the detailed execution of a sales strategy underscores a fundamental truth in real estate: success is built on the foundation of persistent effort, skilled communication, and the ability to turn challenges into opportunities. By embracing these principles, real estate professionals can rise above the noise, exceed client expectations, and achieve lasting success in the competitive arena of commercial real estate.

In this industry, every objection is an opportunity, and every call could be the one that defines your career. The commitment to excellence, preparation, and client-focused strategy is what separates top-tier brokers from the rest as we navigate through ever-evolving market cycles.

Workshop: In the Paint—Power Play Negotiation Drills for the Win

Objective: Sharpen negotiation and objection-handling skills through a dynamic, sports-themed role-playing workshop, drawing parallels between athletic training and real estate transactions.

Duration:90 minutes

Materials Needed:

- Scenario descriptions, formatted as "Game Plays"

- Role descriptions, detailed as "Player Positions"

- Timer

- Feedback forms

- Notebooks and pens for participants

Optional Materials: Scenario and role cards from ChargingTheStorm. com, presented as Play Cards for enhanced session dynamics

Setup: Arrange the room to resemble a team huddle area, with space for each group to interact like a sports team strategizing during a timeout.

Participants: Divide participants into teams of three to four, ensuring everyone gets a chance to participate actively.

Workshop Outline:

1. **Team Huddle: Kickoff Meeting (10 minutes)**

   - **Coach's Pep Talk:** Introduce the workshop's goals, emphasizing the intersection of sports strategies and real estate negotiations.

   - **Understanding the Game:** Explain the role-playing method, the sports analogy for each negotiation tactic, and participant expectations.

2. **Training Drills: Learning the Plays (10 minutes)**

   - **Strategy Session:** Briefly go over key negotiation strategies like the "Euro Step" and "Running the Bases," using sports terminology to describe each step.

   - **Distribute Game Plans:** Provide teams with scenarios.

3. **Playing the Field: Role-Playing Scenarios (45 minutes)**

   - **First Quarter: Cold Call Defense**

     - **Play:** Participants use the "Euro Step" to tackle objections during a cold call, mimicking a basketball player's agile maneuver to avoid defense and score.

     - **Goal:** Handle objections efficiently to keep the conversation moving toward a property discussion.

   - **Second Quarter: Advancing the Ball ("Running the Bases")**

     - **Play:** Simulate the transition from expressing interest in selling (first base) to securing a listing agreement (scoring a run).

- **Goal:** Effectively communicate and negotiate to progress from initial contact to final agreement, just like advancing bases in a baseball game.

4. **Halftime: Review and Revise (15 minutes)**

   - **Team Feedback:** After each play, teams provide feedback, focusing on technique, execution, and sportsmanship.

   - **Sideline Review:** Participants jot down personal reflections and adjustments they need to make, akin to a halftime adjustment in sports.

5. **Postgame Analysis: Regular Practice and Game-Day Preparation (10 minutes)**

   - **Ongoing Training:** Emphasize the importance of continual practice sessions with team members to adapt to real-life scenarios and refine negotiation tactics.

   - **Implementing New Plays:** Encourage teams to bring actual situations they face into practice sessions, keeping their skills sharp and applicable to their real estate "games."

Final Whistle:

Highlight the parallels between successful athletes and successful real estate professionals: both require dedication, adaptability, and the relentless pursuit of excellence. Encourage participants to view each client interaction as a game where preparation, skill, and strategy lead to winning outcomes. Invite them to "keep their head in the game" by engaging in regular training and staying focused on their professional growth and client success.

CHAPTER 8

The Training Camp: Building a Solid Foundation in Commercial Investments

*Leaders aren't born, they are made. And they are made just
like anything else, through hard work.*
—Vince Lombardi

Years later, after numerous successful deals and a growing reputation, Sarah cemented her position as a prominent figure in the commercial real estate market. Her journey from a luxury residential agent to a powerhouse in commercial brokerage was marked by perseverance, strategic acumen, and a relentless drive to learn and adapt. Her name was now synonymous with lucrative deals, and her latest accomplishment—a record-breaking transaction that was the talk of the city—had just made the headlines of a major commercial real estate publication.

Vincent Marlowe, one of Sarah's early mentors and a respected figure in the industry, came across the article detailing her success. Impressed and proud, Vincent immediately reached out to congratulate her. Their conversation brimmed with the warmth of shared history and mutual respect. During the call, Vincent mentioned he was unexpectedly called out of town but had a commitment that couldn't be postponed—a boot camp he conducted for up-and-coming agents, designed to immerse them in the intricacies of commercial real estate.

"Sarah, I've been called to handle an urgent matter and unfortunately, I'll miss tomorrow's session of my boot camp," Vincent explained. "It's an essential part of the course where we dive into the language of commercial real estate. You know, all the jargon that can sound like a foreign language to the uninitiated."

Sarah, understanding the importance of the session and feeling a surge of gratitude for all that Vincent had taught her, didn't hesitate. "Of course, Vincent. I'd be honored to step in for you. It'll be like coming full circle," she replied.

The next day, Sarah stood in front of a room filled with eager young agents at Vincent's boot camp. The walls were adorned with charts and diagrams explaining various real estate metrics, and the atmosphere was charged with anticipation. Sarah began her session with a brief introduction, sharing her journey and emphasizing the importance of understanding the foundational elements of commercial real estate.

"As we delve into today's topic, we'll explore key terms that are not just vocabulary but tools that help us evaluate and strategize investments,"

She clicked to the next slide, which displayed the term *Cap Rate*. "Let's start with cap rate or capitalization rate. Think of it as the pulse of a property's financial health. It's the rate of return on a real estate investment property based on the income that the property is expected to generate."

Sarah glanced around the room. "Let's put this into a practical scenario. Imagine you're considering buying an office building priced at $7 million, with an annual net operating income of $600,000. Anyone want to guess the cap rate?" A few hands shot up, and after a brief calculation by a student, she nodded. "Exactly, about 8.57 percent. It shows us the yield of the property as if it was bought in cash."

She walked the agents through examples, illustrating how cap rates are used to estimate the investor's potential return on a property, comparing it with other investment opportunities. "Understanding the cap rate helps us communicate the value and potential of a property to investors and aligns our strategies with market expectations," she explained.

Moving to the next slide, Sarah introduced net operating income (NOI). "This is what you have left after all operating expenses are paid but before any financing costs. If your building earns $1 million in rent and incurs $400,000 in operating expenses, your NOI is $600,000."

To make it interactive, Sarah had prepared a mini exercise. "Let's break into small groups. Here's your task: You're given a property with $1 million in potential rental income, a 5 percent economic vacancy rate, and $450,000 in operating expenses. Calculate the NOI and discuss it among your group."

As the groups busied themselves, Sarah prepared for the next term: Economic vs. Physical Vacancy. "Physical vacancy is when units are empty. Economic vacancy, however, is when units might be filled, but the income isn't being realized due to nonpayment. If a building is fully occupied but half aren't paying, the physical vacancy is 0 percent, but the economic vacancy is 50 percent."

As Sarah transitioned into the next topic of the class, she introduced a concept that often changes how investors view real estate—Levered vs. Unlevered Returns. Grabbing a marker, she walked toward the whiteboard.

"Let's break it down," she said, sketching a basic example for everyone to see. "Unlevered returns, or returns without debt, are the simplest to understand. If an investor buys a $1 million property with a 9 percent capitalization rate, they'll earn $90,000 in net operating income the first year. Simple, right? Just a straightforward all-cash purchase."

The class nodded as they followed along, but Jerry, a broker from Tallahassee, leaned forward with a frown.

"Now, let's introduce leverage into the equation," Sarah continued, drawing a second diagram. "Instead of paying $1 million cash, let's say the investor partners with a bank and only puts down 25 percent—$250,000. The rest—$750,000—comes from a mortgage, amortized over thirty years at a 6 percent interest rate."

She quickly wrote down the mortgage terms on the whiteboard, explaining the math. "The annual debt service would be $53,964. So, now your net operating income of $90,000 is reduced by that mortgage payment, leaving you with $36,036."

Jerry's frown deepened. "Wait," he interrupted, "so the investor is only making $36,036 instead of the full $90,000?"

Sarah smiled. "Yes, you're right—at a glance, it does seem that way. But let's dig a bit deeper. What's the return on the investment? You've only invested $250,000."

Jerry pulled out his phone, tapping through the calculations. His eyes widened. "14.45 percent—instead of 9 percent!"

The room buzzed with excitement. Sarah could see the lightbulbs going off. Just then, Susan from Newark stood up and exclaimed, "So, the investor still has $750,000 in the bank to use for other deals!"

"Exactly!" Sarah turned back to the whiteboard, drawing a portfolio scenario. "Let's say the investor repeats this process with three more properties, each with the same structure—$250,000 down for each $1 million property. Now, instead of making $90,000 from a single all-cash investment, they're making $36,036 *four* times, for a total of $144,144."

She paused to let that sink in, turning to the class. "That's the power of leverage. The investor diversified their portfolio, spread out the risk, and still has the same initial million dollars working—except now they've quadrupled their returns."

Sarah wiped the board clean, then circled back to a crucial point. "Leveraged investing allows you to make your capital work harder for you, but it also comes with responsibility. The beauty of this strategy is that it amplifies your returns, but it's also important to be cautious— because leveraging also amplifies your losses if things go south."

Sarah took a breath and turned back to face the room. "Real estate is a long game. The key is understanding when to use leverage, how much to use, and making sure the risk is calculated. But for those who master it, the rewards can be significant."

As the afternoon break neared, Sarah reintroduced the concept of internal rate of return (IRR), a topic she knew would challenge even the more experienced brokers and investors in the room.

"Now that we've covered levered returns and cash flow," she began, "it's time to go a bit deeper. IRR doesn't just look at the cash flow in the present—it considers the time value of money. This means it calculates the overall profitability of an investment over its entire lifespan, factoring in operating income, potential refinancing, and even the sale of the asset down the road."

She paused, allowing the class to settle into their seats after lunch. Sarah knew this was going to be a bit more technical, but it was essential to understanding long-term real estate investments.

"I've set up a simulation on the course website for you to work through," she continued, "where you'll evaluate an investment using terms like *cap rate, NOI, levered returns,* and finally, *IRR.*"

With a click of her mouse, she displayed the simulation details on the overhead projector. The property they'd analyze was a multifamily building and the scenario had them tracking returns over six years with improvements and strategic refinancing.

"Let's walk through the first few years of returns before you start," Sarah said, as she picked up a marker and began sketching out the numbers. "In year one, the investor puts down a $250,000 down payment on a property with a $90,000 NOI. After debt service, they're left with $36,036 in cash flow. That's a 14.45 percent return on the initial investment."

She quickly wrote the percentage on the board, and a few students nodded in recognition.

"Now, let's say that by year two, the investor has improved the property's management, reduced expenses, and raised rents—so the net cashflow is $42,000 after debt service. That brings the return up to 16.8 percent." Sarah paused to let the class digest the figures.

"And by year three, they've continued to optimize operations, pushing the return up to 17.5 percent. But, in year four, they decide to reinvest some of that income into capital improvements—updating the building's common areas, adding amenities, and modernizing the units. So, in year four, the return dips slightly to 17 percent."

As she explained this dip, Sarah circled the numbers on the whiteboard.

"Here's where IRR comes into play," she said, tapping the whiteboard for emphasis. "We're not just looking at the cash flow in isolation; we're factoring in every year's return. So even though year four's return dips slightly due to reinvestment, the improvements lead to an increase in demand and rents, pushing the return to 20 percent in year five and 22 percent in year six."

At this point, the class was following along eagerly, typing notes on their laptops.

"Now, let's say that halfway through this period, in year three, the investor decides to refinance and cash out $200,000 from the property's equity. This gives them liquidity while still maintaining the investment. Finally, at the end of year six, they sell the building and walk away with an additional $300,000 from the closing table."

Sarah then turned to the class. "Now, it's not just about the cash flow in any given year—it's about how this investment performs over the entire period. That's what IRR helps you measure. By factoring in the fluctuating cash flows, the refinance, and the final sale, we can see the true long-term return on the initial investment."

She clicked a few buttons on her laptop, displaying a graph of the hypothetical returns over six years on the overhead screen.

"The IRR calculation would consider all these cash flows. While each year gives us a snapshot, the IRR looks at the full journey. In this case, assuming these cash flows, the investor's IRR might end up somewhere between 18 percent and 20 percent over the six-year period."

As the students logged into the simulation to try their hand at calculating the IRR for different scenarios, Sarah closed her marker and offered a final thought.

"Remember," she said, "these aren't just numbers. They're tools that help you understand not only the immediate value of a property but also its long-term wealth generation. The key to smart investing is understanding how to maximize your returns not just now, but in the future."

The room buzzed with excitement as the students dug into their simulations. Sarah smiled to herself—this was the moment when they would see the true power of real estate investing.

After the simulation, the class took a short break. When they returned, the room quickly filled— notebooks open, eyes fixed on her, ready for whatever came next. Sarah felt that familiar mix of excitement and responsibility rise in her once again.

Sarah sensed that the students were getting comfortable with the basics of IRR, but she wanted to push them further into more advanced territory. After all, she knew the value of understanding the internal rate of return (IRR) wasn't just in analyzing existing returns—it was in planning and creating a strategic roadmap before an investor even put in an offer.

She stood up from her chair and went back to the whiteboard. "Now, savvy investors—and the brokers who work with them—aren't just thinking about the first year's return or even just the cap rate. They're mapping out the entire investment life cycle. You want to look at the potential for refinancing, recapitalization, and planned exit strategies."

Sarah uncapped the marker and began outlining a six-year scenario on the board.

"Let's dive deeper into what a savvy investor would consider before even writing an offer. Let's say you, as the commercial broker, present a full IRR analysis to the investor at the start. This analysis isn't just about the first couple of years of returns; it's about the entire hold period. Let's take our same example—a six-year hold period."

The class leaned in. They were following, but Sarah knew she had to make the details shine to really drive the point home.

"Here's where things get interesting," she continued. "By year three, the investor has managed the property well and sees an opportunity to refinance. They cash out $200,000 from the equity built up in the property."

She circled the number on the whiteboard, underlining it twice for emphasis.

"This means that out of the original $250,000 down payment, they've now pulled out $200,000—which they can reinvest either in further improvements to the property or into an entirely new deal. So, at this point, the investor only has $50,000 left in the property." Sarah paused to let the significance sink in.

"Now think about what that does to the cash-on-cash return," she said, glancing around the room. "In year one, when they had $250,000 in the deal, they were making $36,036 in cash flow after debt service. But now, with only $50,000 left in the property, that same $36,036 cash flow is delivering a 72 percent cash-on-cash return."

There were audible gasps from the students, and Sarah smiled. She knew that many of them were just starting to grasp the power of leveraging returns.

"But we're not done yet," she said, waving her hand. "Here's where your planning becomes critical. As a broker, your IRR analysis should include a planned exit strategy. Let's say that, based on the market conditions and property performance, you initially expected to hold the property for seven to ten years. However, because the investor was ahead of schedule—they hit their seven-year numbers by year five—they decided to sell in year six."

She drew a quick graph on the board, showing the accelerating returns over the six years.

"Here's what happens," she explained. "If you, as the broker, do a good job of analyzing market trends, you can advise your client to sell earlier, when the property's value has appreciated faster than anticipated. In this case, they walk away with an additional $300,000 at closing from the sale, after already pulling out $200,000 in year three."

Sarah turned back to the students. "So, now the investor has a total of $500,000 back in their pocket after originally investing just $250,000. And that doesn't even factor in the cash flow they've earned over the hold period."

She pointed to the numbers, illustrating the sheer power of a well-planned investment strategy.

"The IRR on this deal takes into account all these factors—the cash flows, the refinance, and the final sale. It gives the investor a true sense of the profitability of the deal over time. And, as the broker, you've helped them plan for this from the beginning. That's what separates a great broker from just an average one."

Sarah looked around the room and saw nods of understanding. She knew they were starting to grasp the bigger picture.

"Remember," she said, as the students began preparing for their next simulation, "a deal isn't just about the cap rate or the cash-on-cash return. It's about mapping out the entire investment period, planning for when to refinance, and having a strategic exit in mind. That's how you help your clients not just buy properties but build wealth."

She motioned for the students to turn back to their screens.

"The simulation you're about to start incorporates everything we've discussed—cap rates, cash flow, refinances, and eventual sale. Your goal is to maximize the IRR for a six-year hold period. Think like the savvy investors I've described. And remember, the best brokers give their clients a roadmap before the first offer is even written."

With that, the students began their simulations, more confident in their understanding of IRR and the long-term strategies that truly make commercial real estate a wealth-building tool.

Asset Classes

Sarah stood at the front of the room, clicking the projector onto a slide titled "Asset Classes: The Foundation of Commercial Real Estate." As the class quieted down, she began, "In commercial real estate, understanding asset classes is critical because each type of property operates with its own set of dynamics, financial metrics, and investment strategies. Today, we'll break these down to see what makes each asset class tick and why specialization can be your key to success."

She clicked forward to a slide on multifamily properties, a common entry point for many investors. "Multifamily includes everything from market-rate and luxury housing to affordable housing and student accommodation. Each serves a different segment of the population and requires its own set of operational strategies. The key to making multifamily work is understanding your market. Will the majority of your residents be millennials in urban areas? Or are you tenants suburban families? Each of these strategies requires different underwriting, rent growth expectations and capital expenditures."

Sarah continued, shifting the conversation to senior housing, a hot topic given the demographic shifts in the US. "Senior housing is a sub-asset class within multifamily but operates entirely differently. We're talking about independent living, assisted living, and memory care facilities. These investments require an understanding of both the healthcare and real estate markets. Think about it this way: while student housing might face challenges like low enrollment or a shift to online learning, senior housing is booming because ten thousand people turn sixty-five every day in America. The demand is undeniable."

As the slide moved to the hospitality sector, she noted the broad scope of properties involved. "Hospitality is another dynamic asset class. It ranges from hotels and motels to specialized destinations like glamping sites and golf resorts. Running a golf resort requires a completely different operational model than managing a city hotel. You're not just booking rooms—you're managing memberships, services, amenities, and a client experience that keeps guests coming back."

Sarah paused to engage the class. "Let's have a discussion. Why might specialization in a particular asset class be more effective than being a generalist?" Hands shot up, and one student mentioned how knowing the ins and outs of a particular market or asset class allowed brokers to go deeper and create lasting relationships. Sarah nodded, "Exactly. Specialization allows you to become an expert in your field. Let's say you specialize in hotels—after a while, you could know every operator in your region and eventually even expand nationally. This deep knowledge becomes invaluable, especially when there are over $22 billion in hospitality sales in a year. If you could capture even 10 percent of that market, you're looking at significant volume."

She emphasized the importance of focus, sharing examples of niche brokers excelling in specialty markets. "Take the story of a broker who focused exclusively on schools. They listed nineteen schools in a single city, and when other municipalities saw the success, they listed even more. Now, this broker is the go-to person for school transactions. There are brokers out there specializing in churches, funeral homes, and even car dealerships. The key takeaway here is that by narrowing your focus, you can build deeper relationships and become the expert people turn to when they need specialized advice."

Moving on, Sarah highlighted the seven major asset classes in commercial real estate:

Multifamily, Hospitality, Healthcare, Retail, Office, Industrial, and Specialty

She broke them down further, explaining the nuance of each. "For example, in healthcare, you're not just looking at hospitals. Think about nursing homes, urgent care facilities, and medical office buildings. Retail isn't just strip malls—it's also big-box stores, experiential retail, and e-commerce distribution centers. Industrial could be anything from manufacturing plants to last-mile delivery warehouses."

One of the students raised a question about specialization, "Wouldn't narrowing your focus reduce your potential client base?"

Sarah smiled and responded, "On the contrary, it helps you grow deeper relationships and establish a foothold in a lucrative niche. Let's take hospitality again. If you specialize in it, you'll soon find that many hotel owners don't just own one hotel—they have portfolios. Once you become their go-to adviser, you've opened the door to multiple transactions."

As she wrapped up the discussion, Sarah set the class up for their next practical exercise. "Now, I want you to break into small groups and pick an asset class. It could be multifamily, office, or even a niche like funeral homes or car dealerships. Analyze a hypothetical property within that class. Consider the cap rates, operating expenses, and potential leveraged returns. Use everything we've discussed to determine whether the investment makes sense."

She concluded with a final thought. "Remember, specialization isn't about limiting your potential—it's about going deep, creating value, and becoming the go-to expert in your market. That's how you win in commercial real estate."

The class buzzed with excitement as they began the exercise, eager to apply their new knowledge to real-world scenarios.

As the agents busied themselves with the exercise, Sarah walked around, providing guidance and answering questions. Her ability to demystify complex terms and scenarios not only enlightened the new agents but also cemented her status as a knowledgeable and approachable figure in the commercial real estate community.

As the class wrapped up, the agents were buzzing with newfound knowledge and confidence, ready to tackle their challenges in the market.

This session not only enhanced their understanding but also inspired them to approach commercial real estate with a strategic and analytical mindset.

The class was interactive, with Sarah encouraging questions and leading discussions that helped demystify these complex terms. She used real-life scenarios and current market data to make the concepts relatable and easier to grasp.

"As commercial brokers, our role extends beyond buying and selling; we are advisers, strategists, and sometimes, translators of complex data for our clients," Sarah concluded. "Mastering this language is not just about making deals; it's about crafting opportunities that align with our client's financial goals and market realities."

Sarah felt a sense of accomplishment. She had not only shared knowledge but had engaged her students in a way that made these complex terms accessible and exciting. She knew Vincent would have been proud to see them so energized and ready to tackle their own challenges in the market.

Her session not only covered the technical terms but also imparted a broader understanding of how these terms play a crucial role in building and preserving wealth through commercial real estate investments. The agents left the room equipped with knowledge and inspired by Sarah's expertise and clarity, ready to tackle their own challenges in the market.

Vincent returned to glowing reviews of Sarah's session, reinforcing the decision to invite her to lead. This experience fortified her reputation not only as a successful broker but also as a mentor and educator, echoing Vincent's impact on her career. Their continued collaboration, marked by shared values and mutual respect, set a standard for mentorship and growth in the commercial real estate industry.

As the last student filed out with enthusiastic thanks, Sarah checked her watch, her mind already shifting gears to her upcoming engagement. She smiled to herself, feeling a surge of anticipation and satisfaction from the day's successful lecture. Now, she was set to embark on her journey to Chicago, where a new challenge awaited her.

Workshop: The Real Estate Championship—From Cap Rates to IRR and Asset Classes

Objective: In this sports-themed workshop, participants will develop a deep understanding of the key concepts that drive commercial real estate success, including cap rates, IRR, and asset classes. They'll also learn how to apply these concepts in real-world scenarios, all while having fun and tapping into their competitive spirit!

Workshop Outline:

1. **Warm-Up: Understanding Cap Rates**

   ○ **Theme:** *The Scouting Report*

   Every winning team starts with a solid scouting report. In commercial real estate, cap rates are like a scouting report for properties, showing you the expected return based on the current performance.

   ○ **Activity:**

   ◉ Participants will break into two teams. Each team is assigned a hypothetical property (e.g., an apartment building, a retail space, or a hotel). Teams must analyze the property using different cap rates (4 percent, 6 percent, 8 percent) and calculate the property's value based on a given NOI (net operating income).

   ◉ *For example:* If the NOI is \$100,000, teams will determine how different cap rates affect the property's value.

   ○ ① **Debrief:**

- Discuss how a lower cap rate signifies a more expensive (and potentially less risky) property, while a higher cap rate reflects more risk and potentially higher rewards.

- Relate it to sports: Cap rates are like player stats—sometimes you want a high scorer (higher risk), and sometimes you need a reliable defender (lower risk).

2. **The Game Plan: Leveraging Returns**

- **Theme:** *The Offensive Strategy*

  A successful offense is about maximizing opportunities. In real estate, leveraging returns is like calling plays that amplify your team's potential for scoring. A great offense doesn't just settle for small plays—it takes strategic risks.

- **Activity:**

  - Set up a mock investment scenario where each group has a million dollars to invest. One team must "play it safe" with an all-cash purchase at a 9 percent cap rate, while the other team uses leverage (a mortgage at 6 percent) to spread their investment across multiple properties.

  - Teams will calculate the difference between levered and unlevered returns, seeing firsthand how leveraging increases their overall return on investment (ROI).

- **Debrief:**

  - Use a whiteboard or scoreboard to show how leveraging allows the "offensive" team to spread their risk and increase their overall returns. Like in sports, a balanced offensive strategy often outperforms relying on a single player or play.

○ Emphasize that while leveraging boosts returns, it also comes with additional risks—just like an aggressive offensive play might leave your team open to a counterattack.

3. **The Long Game: Internal Rate of Return (IRR)**

○ **Theme:** *The Championship Season*

Winning teams don't just aim to win individual games—they aim for championships. IRR is like planning a championship season, considering not just the immediate returns but the overall success across the investment period.

○ **Activity:**

○ Teams will be given a six-year investment scenario, with each year providing varying levels of return based on operational performance and market conditions. Teams will need to calculate the IRR for their investment, factoring in refinancing in year three and a sale in year six.

○ *For example:* Team A invests $250,000 into a property that produces $36,000 in year one. By year six, the team refinances and pulls out $200,000 while still receiving cash flow and eventually selling the property for a profit.

○ **Debrief:**

○ Discuss how IRR reflects the true performance of the team's "season" and not just individual "games" (years). Just as in sports, it's about maintaining a strong performance over time to ensure long-term success.

- Relate IRR to sports teams aiming for sustainable championship runs, rather than one-off wins.

4. **Asset Classes: Picking Your Position**

○ **Theme:** *Position Specialization*

In sports, every player has a position where they excel—whether it's quarterback, point guard, or goalie. Similarly, in commercial real estate, asset classes are like positions, and successful brokers and investors often specialize in a particular class.

○ **Activity:**

- Break the group into small "teams" representing different asset classes (multifamily, retail, hospitality, etc.). Each team must make a case for why their asset class is the MVP (most valuable position) by highlighting its unique benefits and challenges.

- Teams should analyze a hypothetical property in their assigned asset class using cap rates, NOI, and potential leveraged returns. They will present their findings and why they believe their asset class offers the best investment opportunities.

○ **Debrief:**

- Discuss how specialization allows investors and brokers to "play their position" effectively. In sports, mastering your role is key to contributing to the team's overall success.

Likewise, specializing in an asset class allows you to go deep, build expertise, and win more deals.

- ○ Wrap up by emphasizing that while specialization is valuable, understanding all asset classes provides a broader field of play.

5. **The Postgame Analysis: Comparing Investment Strategies**

   - ○ **Theme:** *The Highlight Reel*

   Every team reviews game tape to see what went right and what could be improved. In real estate, reviewing different strategies (cap rates, levered vs. unlevered returns, IRR) helps investors refine their approach for future deals.

   - ○ **Activity:**

     - ○ Each team will present a short "highlight reel" of their investment decisions, focusing on how they used cap rates, leverage, and asset class selection to create the best returns. The team with the highest cumulative ROI (using a combination of cap rates, IRR, and leveraged returns) wins the workshop "championship."

   - ○ **Debrief:**

     - ○ Discuss how each team's approach led to different results and how small changes in strategy could lead to big differences in return—just like tweaking a game plan can change the outcome of a championship game.

6. **Closing Drill: Penalty Shootout (Q&A)**

   - ○ **Theme:** *The Final Shootout*

Just like penalty shootouts in soccer or free throws in basketball, sometimes it's the small details that decide the game. In this rapid-fire Q&A session, participants will have a chance to ask quick questions and clarify any doubts about cap rates, IRR, or asset classes.

Wrap-Up: Victory Lap

As the workshop concludes, encourage participants to take a "victory lap" by sharing one key takeaway that they will apply to their real estate practice. Whether it's focusing more on leveraged returns, specializing in an asset class, or refining their IRR calculations, this "victory lap" sets them up to win in the real estate championship.

This sports-themed workshop keeps the energy high while ensuring participants gain a deep understanding of key real estate concepts, making it both fun and educational!

CHAPTER 9

Master Class: Extra Innings—Complex Deal Structures

The sky was a canvas of twilight hues as Sarah's plane touched down at Chicago Midway Airport, a bustling hub that lived up to its reputation as the busiest square mile in America. With the city lights beckoning, she hailed a cab, the adrenaline of the upcoming master class replacing any fatigue from the flight.

Arriving at her hotel, Sarah quickly freshened up, her mind buzzing with the strategies and concepts she was about to dive into. Mr. Tony Hardy, the speaker for the master class, was not only a renowned figure in commercial real estate but also a bridge between her beginnings and her future in the industry. His story, mirroring her transition from residential to commercial real estate, had always inspired her.

The next morning, Sarah took her seat in a room filled with ambitious professionals eager to learn from one of the best. Mr. Hardy began the session with a warm, engaging introduction, outlining the complex landscape of advanced real estate deal structuring. The focus of the first day was on dynamic and somewhat niche strategies that could transform the way these professionals approached real estate investments.

Master Class: Strategic Maneuvers in Real Estate—The Reverse 1031 Exchange

Tony Hardy's master class was in full swing at a conference room in a downtown Chicago hotel, filled with eager brokers from various backgrounds, ready to elevate their careers with sophisticated investment strategies. The room buzzed with the focused energy of professionals sharing best practices, exchanging ideas, and learning from one of the best.

Tony: "Welcome, everyone. Today, we're diving deep into the mechanics of the reverse 1031 exchange, a powerful strategy for those looking to capitalize on market timings without the pressure of immediately selling their existing properties."

Flashback to a Deal Story—William's Path to Tax-Deferred Growth: Tony clicked to a slide showing a serene strip mall, beautifully renovated and bustling with activity.

"Let's talk about William, a seasoned investor who transformed a simple retail strip center he purchased for $1.5 million into a $3 million gem through strategic improvements. When it came time to escalate his investments, he opted for a 1031 exchange to defer the hefty capital gains tax."

Step-by-Step Breakdown:

1. **Understanding the Basics:** "A 1031 exchange lets you defer capital gains tax by reinvesting the proceeds into a like-kind property," Tony explained. "William could dodge a $450,000 tax hit, using that money to fuel further investments."

2. **Finding a Suitable Replacement:** William aimed to reinvest his $1.5 million in equity into a $6 million retail center, thus scaling his operations significantly.

3. **Engaging a Qualified Intermediary (QI):** "A QI acts as a neutral third party to oversee the process, holding funds and ensuring compliance with tax laws," Tony detailed as he showed the flow of transactions through diagrams.

4. **Identification and Closing Periods:** Tony discussed the critical timing—forty-five days to identify potential properties and 180 days to close on one, demonstrating William's strategic decisions during these periods.

5. **Avoiding Constructive Receipt:** "William never touched the sale proceeds; the QI did, ensuring the tax deferment remained intact," Tony emphasized the discipline required in such exchanges.

Interactive Session—Navigating a Reverse 1031 Exchange with Sarah: Tony shifted gears to introduce Chloe's deal scenario, engaging the class more interactively.

"Imagine you're Chloe. You've found a perfect $3.5 million apartment complex but haven't sold your existing asset yet. A reverse exchange allows you to grab the new property first, betting on selling the old one within the stringent IRS timelines."

Steps Unfolded:

1. **Engaging an Exchange Accommodation Titleholder (EAT):** "Chloe worked with an EAT to hold the title temporarily, a crucial step that differs markedly from the standard exchange."

2. **Funding and Acquisition:** "She used a mix of loans and cash to close on the new property acquisition, starting her 180-day countdown to sell the old one."

3. **Identifying the Old Property:** Within forty-five days post-acquisition, Chloe designated her original property for sale, aligning with the reverse exchange rules.

4. **Closing the Sale and Finalizing the Exchange:** "Chloe hustled to sell her original building for $2 million, directing the proceeds through her QI to complete the exchange."

Class Engagement: Tony then posed challenges to the class: "How would you handle the pressure of the ticking clock in a reverse exchange? What strategies would you employ to ensure a smooth sale of the original property?"

Breakout Sessions: Participants split into groups, role-playing both Chloe's and William's scenarios, with Tony walking around providing insights and answering questions.

Closing Remarks: "As you can see, mastering these exchanges can significantly enhance your portfolio and defer taxes, driving substantial growth. Think of these strategies as part of your real estate playbook, essential maneuvers to navigate the complex investment landscape."

The session wrapped up with robust discussions, note-taking, and network-building, as attendees prepared to implement these advanced strategies in their own burgeoning real estate careers.

The class then transitioned and covered the 1033 exchange, highlighting its use in scenarios involving property losses due to natural disasters, offering a unique perspective on asset replacement strategies. Each topic was broken down with precision, making complex regulations accessible and understandable.

721 Exchange

As Tony's master class delved into the intricate details of the 720 exchange, a hand shot up from the middle of the room, drawing all eyes to a slightly nervous yet eager participant. It was Jarred from Iowa, a man whose career in real estate echoed the undulating tracks of a roller coaster—highs of quick deals followed by drawn-out months of silence. Jarred, clad in a sharp suit that suggested a swag often seen in seasoned brokers, cleared his throat to break the silence.

"Good morning, everyone. I'm Jarred," he started, his voice gaining confidence with each word. "Like many of you, I'm here to smooth out the rough patches in my career and get a handle on more consistent success. I think understanding these complex exchange mechanisms is key to that."

He glanced around the room, making sure he had the undivided attention of his peers, and began sharing his story: "Last year, I facilitated a deal that could have benefited greatly from a 720 exchange, but due to my lack of understanding at the time, we missed a critical opportunity. My client, a local investor, had sold a commercial property with substantial appreciation but faced a hefty capital gains tax."

Jarred paused, ensuring the technicalities of his story resonated with the audience.

"We were looking at reinvestment options when I stumbled upon a potential exchange. However, without the nuanced knowledge of how a 720 exchange works, we proceeded with a more straightforward approach. The client ended up paying more in taxes than necessary, which, as you can imagine, didn't sit well with him or with my self-esteem as his broker."

The room filled with empathetic nods; many had been in similar situations, knowing all too well the sting of missed opportunities due to gaps in their knowledge.

"The 720 exchange," Tony interjected, stepping beside Jarred to lend supportive expertise, "is a specialized financial strategy allowing investors to defer capital gains taxes by reinvesting the proceeds from a sold property into a new property under specific conditions. It's about timing, precise structuring, and, crucially, understanding the fiscal landscape to maximize benefits."

Jarred, grateful for the succinct clarification, added, "And that's exactly why I'm here. To not only learn these strategies but to apply them. To turn what was a roller coaster into a more predictable path through thorough knowledge and application of these exchanges."

The room erupted into a thoughtful murmur, as other participants pondered their own experiences and the new insights being shared.

Tony nodded approvingly, "Now, let's simulate a 720 exchange scenario, does anyone have a deal story to share we're they navigated a 720 exchange?" Kelly, sitting front and center, a commercial agent from Nashville, indicated that she had a deal story to share.

"Good morning, everyone," Kelly began, her voice filled with the confidence of someone who had navigated complex waters. "Today, I want to talk about a deal that not only changed my client's portfolio but also broadened my understanding of the power of 721 exchanges."

Step 1: Exploring the 721 Exchange

"Let's start with Thomas, a longtime client of mine who owned a strip mall valued at $3.5 million. The property had appreciated significantly, and while it was a solid asset, Thomas was interested in diversifying his investments without incurring a hefty capital gains tax," Kelly explained.

She paused, ensuring the concept sunk in, then continued, "Understanding the 721 exchange was critical here—it allows property owners to contribute their asset into a partnership in exchange for an interest in that partnership, deferring the capital gains."

Step 2: Sourcing the Perfect Opportunity

"With Thomas's goals in mind, I tapped into my network and eventually identified a partnership that was acquiring a portfolio of restaurants with leases guaranteed by a top-tier, publicly traded group. This aligned perfectly with his desire for stable, long-term investments."

The audience listened intently, noting how Kelly's market savvy and connections facilitated a crucial step in the exchange.

Step 3: Property Contribution and Partnership Formation

"After some diligent negotiations and due diligence, Thomas agreed to contribute his property to the partnership, gaining a 30 percent ownership interest based on the fair market value of his mall," Kelly detailed, illustrating the strategic maneuvering involved in setting up such a partnership.

Step 4: Tax Deferral and Passive Ownership

"By contributing his strip mall, Thomas not only deferred the capital gains tax on its $2.5 million appreciation but also transformed his active management role to a more passive one. This was significant, as it allowed him to focus on broader investment opportunities while relying on the partnership's management team."

Step 5: Reaping the Rewards

"The partnership's portfolio performed exceptionally, providing Thomas with steady cash flow and appreciating in value. When the time came to sell, his share of the profit was substantial, and with the capital gains realized, he reinvested through a new 1031 exchange," Kelly concluded, showcasing the cyclical nature of successful real estate investments.

As she finished her story, Kelly emphasized, "This example underscores the tactical application of a 721 exchange and also demonstrates the importance of having a trusted network of professionals—including tax advisers and attorneys—to ensure everything aligns with regulatory and financial requirements."

"Thank you, Kelly, for sharing, and thank you, everyone," Jarred exclaimed, his initial nervousness replaced by a resolute confidence. "Today's discussion goes beyond just knowing; it's about applying and succeeding. I'm ready to tackle my own challenges in the market with a new set of tools."

As the participants applauded, Tony gave a nod of respect to Jarred, acknowledging his journey from uncertainty to empowerment—a journey that many in the room were inspired to replicate.

Tony pushed the clicker to the next slide.

In the midst of applause, a seasoned figure, Sarah, stood and said I'll take this slide, and steered the discussion toward a topic that resonates with every savvy investor aiming to amplify their returns: Cost Segregation. As she introduced the concept, the classroom transformed into a lively hub of learning, where each detail dissected opened new avenues for tax optimization.

Introduction to Cost Segregation

Sarah's poised voice filled the room, "Cost segregation is your gateway to maximizing tax savings. It's not just about seeing the numbers; it's about understanding every component of your property and how it contributes to accelerated depreciation."

The room buzzed with the energy of realization as Sarah continued, "Imagine you've just purchased a property to renovate. Before you even begin the demolition, you collaborate with a cost segregation specialist. Together, you assess the value of components like lighting, carpets, and cabinets. This isn't just busywork—it's a strategic step to unearth potential tax savings that many overlook."

Patel's Success Story: A Real-World Application

Eager to ground the theory in reality, Sarah introduced Patel's story. "Patel, an astute investor, recently acquired a hotel for $15 million. Aware of the impending tax liabilities, he sought to minimize his burden and improve cash flow through cost segregation."

She detailed Patel's process, from the initial consultation with a cost segregation team to the detailed analysis and inspection of his hotel. "The team meticulously evaluated every component of the hotel. From the carpeting to the plumbing, every part was scrutinized to determine its eligibility for faster depreciation."

The Impact of Cost Segregation

"By identifying $3.5 million in assets eligible for five-year depreciation, and $1.5 million for fifteen-year depreciation, Patel's strategic move to implement cost segregation shaved a significant figure from his tax bill,"

Sarah elucidated, highlighting the direct benefit on Patel's finances. The class listened intently, making mental notes of the process and its lucrative outcome.

Conclusion: The Strategic Edge of Cost Segregation

Concluding her segment, Sarah emphasized, "Cost segregation isn't just about saving on taxes—it's about strategic asset management. For Patel, it meant freeing up cash that was immediately reinvested into enhancing his property, directly translating to higher returns and guest satisfaction."

She encouraged the class, "Whether you're dealing with a hotel, a retail space, or an office building, understanding and utilizing cost segregation can significantly impact your investment's profitability. It works because everything that you plan to throw away, like the cabinets, the light fixtures for example may have some sort of value that if done properly could be realized through the use of cost segregation."

Interactive Workshop Component

Tony flipped to the next slide, to solidify the learning, Tony and Sarah introduced an interactive component. "Now, let's put theory into practice. I want you to form small groups and take a hypothetical property. Perform a basic cost segregation analysis using the criteria we've discussed. Think about what components might qualify for faster depreciation and estimate the potential tax savings."

The room transformed into a hive of activity, with brokers crunching numbers and debating the finer points of asset classification. It was a practical drill that not only enhanced their understanding but also prepared them to apply these insights in real-world scenarios.

As the workshop session wrapped up, the aroma of delicious delicacies se filled the air. Sarah's session on cost segregation resonated, providing the brokers with a powerful tool to enhance their client offerings and optimize investment returns. Her ability to demystify complex tax strategies and translate them into actionable insights was a testament to the depth of expertise that seasoned brokers like her brought to the field.

As the working lunch commenced, attendees mingled amid a buffet of fresh farm-to-table offerings: carved roast beef, an array of locally sourced vegetables, and artisan breads, with lemon tart and coffee to finish. As they settled into their seats, the room buzzed with anticipation for the next session on Delaware Statutory Trusts (DSTs).

Presentation Begins: Introduction to Delaware Statutory Trusts

Michael, an esteemed commercial broker known for his innovative investment strategies, took the podium. With a clear and engaging tone, he began to unfold the concept of the DST, projecting slides that complemented his narrative.

The Case Study of Tracy: A Real-World Application of DSTs

"Let's discuss how DSTs can significantly alter an investor's approach to property management and investment diversification," Michael began, introducing the case study of Tracy, a seasoned investor looking toward retirement.

"Tracy had recently sold a rental property for $1 million. Faced with the potential for hefty capital gains taxes and eager to simplify her portfolio management, she considered a DST. This tool would allow her to invest in high-quality real estate without the day-to-day management hassles."

Michael detailed how, toward the end of her forty-five-day identification period for a 1031 exchange, Tracy explored DSTs as a viable alternative to traditional property acquisitions. He explained the DST's structure, offering Tracy fractional ownership in a diversified portfolio managed by seasoned professionals.

Delving Into the Details: Investment Strategy and Management

"Tracy chose a DST holding a portfolio of Class A self-storage facilities across several states, managed by a renowned REIT. By investing $500,000 into this DST, she not only fulfilled her 1031 exchange requirements but also secured a passive income stream from a diversified asset base." Michael highlighted the benefits Tracy enjoyed:

1. **Passive Ownership**: The day-to-day operations and property management were handled by the REIT, allowing Tracy to focus on her other interests and retirement planning.

2. **Regular Distributions**: Returns from the trust were directly deposited into her account, providing a steady income flow.

3. **Simplified Tax Reporting**: The DST sponsor managed all tax documentation, significantly simplifying Tracy's tax filings.

4. **Estate Planning Benefits**: The investment was structured to pass easily to her heirs, providing them with ongoing income or the option to liquidate as per their financial goals.

Engagement with the Audience: Q&A
and Interactive Discussion

As Michael concluded Tracy's case study, he opened the floor for questions. Attendees were keen to understand how they could identify suitable DST sponsors and the specifics of entering such investments.

One participant asked, "How does one vet and choose a DST sponsor effectively?"

Michael responded, "It's important to begin by evaluating the sponsor's track record, the quality of the underlying real estate, and the transparency of their operations. Always consult with tax and legal advisers to ensure the DST fits your overall investment strategy."

Conclusion of the Session: Wrapping
Up with Key Takeaways

As the session wrapped up, Michael emphasized the strategic importance of DSTs in modern real estate investment portfolios, especially for those seeking to reduce active management roles while still capitalizing on real estate opportunities.

The attendees left the session with a comprehensive understanding of DSTs, equipped with knowledge to explore this investment structure further, reflecting on Tracy's success story as a practical model of passive real estate investment enhanced by astute professional guidance.

The workshop not only illuminated the mechanics of DSTs but also fostered a collaborative learning environment, encouraging participants to consider new horizons in their real estate careers.

In the next session, Tony introduced William, an agent in the masterclass, who was eager to share his real-life experience with Opportunity Zone investments. He began by recounting how a retail strip center in his neighborhood had become an eyesore after remaining vacant for years. Tired of seeing it waste away, William decided to take matters into his own hands. He explored ways to raise capital and came across the Opportunity Zone program.

Opportunity Zones, William explained, were created under the Tax Cuts and Jobs Act of 2017 to incentivize investment in economically distressed areas. The idea behind it is to spur economic growth and create jobs by offering tax advantages to investors who commit to improving properties in these designated zones. For investors like William, the primary appeal is the ability to defer and potentially reduce capital gains taxes by investing through a qualified opportunity fund (QOF). William raised capital through one of these funds, bought the property, and began the revitalization process, bringing new jobs and businesses into the neighborhood.

William further explained how the tax benefits work: if an investor like him holds the investment for at least ten years, they can sell the property without paying any capital gains taxes on the appreciation—something William is particularly excited about when considering selling the retail center in the coming years.

Through his initiative, William not only improved his community but also created a highly advantageous investment for himself. The Opportunity Zone allowed him to make long-term improvements while planning for a tax-efficient exit strategy. The class was impressed with his story, and Tony emphasized how Opportunity Zones represent a powerful tool for investors who want to combine community impact with favorable financial returns .

Closing Thoughts: Embracing Complexity and Collaboration in Commercial Real Estate

As we delve into the specialized topics of DST, 1031, 721, and 1033 exchanges, it becomes evident that the landscape of commercial real estate is both vast and complex. Each of these areas represents a depth of knowledge and specialization that can fill volumes, and each underscores the critical need for expert guidance in navigating such nuanced terrains.

The Foreign Investment in Real Property Tax Act (FIRPTA), for instance, introduces additional layers of complexity, especially for international investors. This, along with the concept of 'boot' in property exchanges, highlights potential tax implications that must be carefully managed to avoid costly pitfalls. In a 1031 exchange, the term "boot" refers to any portion of the transaction that does not qualify for tax deferral under the rules of the exchange. Boot can be in the form of cash, mortgage relief, or any other property received by the investor that is not like-kind to the property being exchanged. Essentially, boot is the non-like-kind value received in an exchange.

Here's how it works:

1. **Cash Boot**: This occurs when you receive cash during the exchange. For instance, if you sell a property and receive more cash from the sale than the amount you reinvest in the new property, the extra cash is considered boot and is taxable.

2. **Mortgage Boot**: This happens when there is a decrease in mortgage liability from the relinquished property to the replacement property. If you relieve more debt than you assume on the new property, the difference is treated as income received, hence taxable as boot.

The presence of a boot in a transaction doesn't invalidate the 1031 exchange, but it does require the investor to pay capital gains taxes on that portion of the exchange. To fully defer all capital gains taxes, an investor should aim to reinvest all equity from the relinquished property into like-kind property and take on at least as much debt on the new property as was on the old one, avoiding the receipt of the boot.

We've barely scratched the surface of what's possible in this journey through the multifaceted world of commercial real estate, Real estate professionals— whether brokers, agents, or new entrants to the market— must recognize the importance of leveraging specialized knowledge and the expertise of seasoned professionals.

I encourage you not to view commercial brokerage through a lens of competition that isolates, but rather as a field rich with opportunity for collaboration. The perception that this sector is cutthroat can often obscure the potential for partnerships that foster growth and success.

This book is not just a collection of insights and guidelines; it's an invitation is paved with relationships—partnerships that not only enhance our capabilities but also enrich our experiences in this dynamic field.

As the first day wrapped up, Sarah felt a deep sense of achievement and anticipation. The knowledge she was gaining here was not just theoretical but immediately applicable, capable of elevating her practice to new heights. Tomorrow promised even more insights, and as she prepared for the evening, she was already planning how to integrate these strategies into her client offerings, ensuring that her journey in commercial real estate continued to be as successful and impactful as her mentor, Mr. Marlow, had envisioned.

Workshop Title: Game Plan—Mastering the Field of Commercial Real Estate"

Overview: This engaging workshop draws inspiration from the dynamics of team sports to explore advanced commercial real estate concepts. Participants will engage in interactive learning, role-playing scenarios, and strategic planning exercises that mirror a sports coach's approach to a winning season.

Part 1: Pregame Warm-Up (Introduction)

- **Objective:** Introduce participants to the workshop's goals and the parallels between sports strategies and commercial real estate tactics.

- **Activity:** Quick icebreaker where each participant shares their experience level and what 'position' they play in their real estate "team," i.e., newbie, seasoned agent, a specialist in a certain asset class, rainmaker, team leader, or independent agent.

Part 2: First Half—Offensive Plays (Learning Key Concepts)

- **Objective:** Teach participants about different types of exchanges and investment vehicles in commercial real estate.

- **Activities:**

1. **Reverse 1031 Exchange Relay:** Participants split into teams to quickly arrange the correct order of steps in a reverse 1031 exchange, racing against each other.

2. **1033 Exchange Huddle:** Small group discussions on how to strategically use a 1033 exchange post–natural disaster, sharing insights and potential challenges.

3. **Delaware Statutory Trust (DST) Playbook:** Interactive presentation on the DST, followed by a quiz formatted like a sports trivia game.

Part 3: Halftime Review (Discussion and Reflection)

- ○ **Objective:** Reflect on the learning from the first half and prepare for more complex topics.

- ○ **Activity:** Teams gather to discuss the key takeaways from each session and prepare questions or strategies they might use in hypothetical scenarios.

Part 4: Second Half—Defensive Strategies (Deep Dive into Complex Strategies)

- ○ **Objective:** Delve deeper into sophisticated investment strategies like Opportunity Zone Funds and the 720 exchange.

- ○ **Activities:**

1. **Opportunity Zone Kick Off:** Teams create a mock investment pitch for an Opportunity Zone project, focusing on both the financial benefits and community impacts.

2. **720 Exchange Defense:** Role-play a negotiation scenario where participants must defend their decision to use a 720 exchange to skeptical clients or partners.

Part 5: Overtime—Applying What You've Learned (Application and Strategy)

- O **Objective:** Apply the concepts learned to real-world scenarios and develop a personal action plan.

- O **Activities:**

  1. **Mock Investment Draft:** Participants draft their ideal investment strategy using knowledge from the workshop, competing to convince a panel of "senior brokers" (workshop facilitators) why their strategy should be funded.

  2. **Networking Huddle:** Casual mingling session where participants can discuss potential collaborations or share leads based on the strategies discussed.

Postworkshop Review:

- O **Objective:** Ensure retention of knowledge and encourage ongoing development.

- O **Activity:** Send out a "playbook" summary of the workshop, including key points, additional resources, and a 'game film' (recording of the session) for further review.

This format not only makes learning about complex commercial real estate strategies engaging and fun but also emphasizes teamwork, strategic thinking, and real-world application, much like preparing for and executing a sports game plan.

CHAPTER 10

Navigating the Field: Strategic Plays in Commercial Real Estate

The price of success is hard work, dedication to the job at hand, and the determination that whether we win or lose, we have applied the best of ourselves to the task at hand.
—Vince Lombardi

At Tony Hardy's commercial mastery session on day two, a bright and early start had attendees gathering for the one-on-one spot coaching sessions, a special feature where Tony offered personalized guidance. Among the attendees was Jarred, a dynamic young broker from Iowa, whose career trajectory resembled a roller coaster—exhilarating highs followed by puzzling lows.

As Jarred sat across from Tony, he shared his unique journey in real estate. Despite holding a brokerage license, Jarred confessed that his real passion lay in the investment side of the industry. Most of the properties he had dealt with were his own acquisitions and dispositions, and he was now eager to scale up to commercial investing. "I'm here to find the missing piece that can stabilize my career," Jarred explained earnestly, seeking to smooth out the peaks and troughs of his professional life.

Tony, ever the astute mentor, probed deeper, discovering that Jarred owned several condominiums free of any mortgages—a significant asset base that was underutilized. "You've got a solid foundation with those condos, Jarred. Let's talk about how you can leverage them to break into commercial real estate," Tony suggested, his eyes twinkling with the thrill of potential.

Kickoff Consultation: Savvy Investment Strategies and Leveraging Equity

Tony began by outlining a strategic approach that could transform Jarred's existing assets into a springboard for larger investments. "Real estate is as much about timing and strategic exits as it is about acquisitions. Let's consider your condos. You bought them over a decade ago, correct?" Tony asked, to which Jarred nodded.

"Okay, imagine this scenario," Tony continued. "Your rental incomes have doubled, and the market value of each condo has significantly increased. You're now sitting on a substantial amount of equity. It's like having a gold mine but only selling a nugget at a time."

Jarred listened intently as Tony painted a picture of potential growth. "Instead of managing ten condos, think about how you could reinvest that equity into, say, a single commercial property—a triple net lease property with a stable, long-term tenant like a national brand. This move could drastically reduce your management headaches and provide consistent, long-term returns."

First Down: Condo Conversion to Cash Flow

Tony explained the concept of triple net leases, where tenants manage property expenses, taxes, and maintenance, providing landlords with more predictable net incomes. "Imagine owning a property leased to a company like Trader Joe's, Chipotle, or AutoZone. You get the reliability of a strong tenant plus the freedom from day-to-day property management."

He also highlighted the financial mechanics, "With the equity from your condos, you could leverage into a larger commercial property. It's about using the assets you have to get the assets you need for future growth and stability."

Advanced Investment Strategies: Mastering Equity and Returns

As Jarred sat, notebook open, Tony began to unravel the complexities of real estate investment metrics with an emphasis on understanding return on equity (ROE) versus return on initial investment (ROI).

"Jarred, think of your equity as an employee," Tony started. "Right now, your condos have accumulated significant equity, which isn't working as hard as it could be. Your current ROI is great, based on your initial outlay, but the ROE, the return on the current value of your investment, tells a different story."

Tony sketched a simple diagram:

1. **Initial Investment**: "You invested $100,000 per condo, with rents at $1,000 each. That's a 12 percent cap rate initially."

2. **Equity Growth**: "Fast forward, and each condo is now worth $250,000 with rents at $2,000. Despite a fantastic ROI, your ROE based on current market value is underperforming. It's time to put that equity to work."

3. **Exploring New Financial Horizons with Your Equity**

"Let's crunch some numbers to illustrate what's possible," Tony began, tapping into Jarred's newfound interest in elevating his real estate career. "With $2.5 million in equity from your condos and leveraging that at a practical 75 percent loan-to-value (LTV), you're looking at a staggering $10 million in purchasing power. This isn't just a step up; it's a strategic leap."

Tony paused, ensuring Jarred was keeping pace with the calculations. "This pivotal moment can redefine your portfolio, transitioning you from wealth creation to wealth preservation. Initially, your journey was about climbing to that first million, which you've impressively achieved. Now, let's strategize on how those dollars can work smarter." He continued, "By reallocating your equity into a higher-tier investment, such as a well located commercial property, you not only diversify your holdings but also drastically reduce the intensity of your day-to-day management tasks. Picture this: instead of juggling multiple residential units, you could oversee a single larger-scale commercial asset under a triple net lease, where the tenant manages one hundred percent of the operational responsibilities."

Tony leaned in, his voice firm yet encouraging, "You've moved from a six-figure to a seven-figure investor by adapting and evolving. To break into the eight-figure realm, it's about making calculated, bold moves. This isn't just about buying bigger properties; it's about smarter, more strategic investments that align with your long-term financial goals. You're at a crossroads in your career, and this path you're considering—it's not just achievable, it's a clear route to a more secure and substantial portfolio." "Embrace this moment," Tony concluded, "because it's these decisions that will define the next phase of your investment journey. Let's map out a plan that transitions you effectively from active management to enjoying the fruits of passive income, propelling you into a future where your investments work for you, allowing you more freedom and stability."

Midfield Maneuvers: Escalating Returns Through Strategic Leverage

Switching gears, Tony introduced the concept of landlord responsibilities in different types of real estate investments.

"Managing ten condos means dealing with ten sets of tenants, maintenance, and unit turnover. It's active management. Now, compare that to owning a commercial property under a triple net lease, where the tenant handles most responsibilities. It's a passive ownership model that can give you more freedom and potentially, a higher quality of life."

Market Opportunities: From Condos to Commercial Power Plays

Tony pushed a few buttons on his computer screen and shared his monitor with Jarred. On the screen is a list of potential commercial investments, tailored to leverage Jarred's accrued equity: complete with photos, financial performance, and many pertinent details. The list included:

1. **Kroger**: "A twenty-five-year lease generating $550,000 in NOI, priced at $9 million. A stable, long-term investment."

2. **Walgreens**: "Recently built, offering a $420,000 NOI for $5.65 million. Solid tenant with a robust track record."

3. **Chase Bank and Chipotle**: "Both offer solid leases with zero landlord responsibilities. Chipotle, especially, is a growth-oriented tenant with predictable revenue streams."

4. **Amazon Go Store and Verizon Wireless**: "Emerging retail technology with high potential in urban centers."

5. **Rounding out the list**: A FedEx distribution Center, CVS, and a CosMc's.

Practical Exercise: Calculating Potential Transitions

Tony guided Jarred through a practical exercise, calculating the potential shift from his current condos to one of these commercial properties.

Closing Strategy: Return on Equity Reinvestment

"As your properties appreciate and your mortgage debts decrease, your equity grows but isn't necessarily producing income relative to its potential," Tony explained. "Reinvesting this equity into higher-value properties with triple net leases can dramatically increase your cash flow and reduce your active management responsibilities."

From Condos to Commercial Mastery

Tony guided Jarred through an interactive case study to make the lesson stick. They reviewed potential properties on the market, discussed financing structures, and analyzed return on investments using Jarred's actual equity figures.

Jarred felt a renewed sense of direction as the coaching session wrapped up. The strategy laid out by Tony provided a clear pathway to stabilize and grow his investments. He was not just attending another conference but gaining a mentor and a practical roadmap to transform his real estate career.

This personalized coaching session was not just a highlight of the day but a pivotal moment for Jarred. It underscored the value of understanding market dynamics, leveraging existing assets, and the strategic foresight needed to thrive in commercial real estate. Jarred left the session energized, ready to take on the commercial market with new tools and a robust strategy.

Jarred, inspired by the session, realized that the mastery of these financial strategies could stabilize his fluctuating career and set him on a path of consistent growth and profitability.

Game Changer: Diversifying into Commercial Real Estate

As attendees walked into the hotel conference room on the second day of commercial mastery classes, they were greeted by the inviting scent of freshly baked pastries. These delightful treats, provided by local bakery owner Marcel Dupont, added a touch of culinary excellence to the morning. Marcel, renowned for his exceptional skills and a celebrated city caterer, had recently ventured into the bakery business following a fruitful collaboration with Tony. This delightful start to the day promised another session filled with insightful learning and networking.

The story unfolded as Marcel shared with the class. "Before opening my bakery, I was catering corporate events across the city, serving everything from delicate pastries to savory bites," he began. At one such event, Tony, impressed by the quality of the desserts, approached Marcel. "Where's your shop? I'd love to grab some treats for a Bears game watch at my friend Josh's place," Tony had asked, only to learn that Marcel didn't have a physical location yet.

Marcel explained how his attempts to find a suitable location had been stifled by the complexities of real estate terms and negotiations. "Every time I called on a leasing sign, I ended up more confused about triple net leases, buildout costs, and other terms I didn't fully understand," Marcel recounted.

Seeing an opportunity to assist, Tony leveraged his extensive network and knowledge of local real estate. "I knew of a bakery set up in Hyde Park where the owner was ready to retire. It was a perfect match—no buildout costs and a well-established customer base," Tony told the class, highlighting the importance of understanding client needs and the local market.

Tony brokered a meeting between Marcel and the retiring bakery owner, carefully navigating the terms of the lease assumption. "We ensured Marcel could step into a gross lease where he wouldn't have to worry about additional costs for the roof, parking lot, or building exterior—common areas typically covered under such agreements," Tony explained.

Marcel's transition to his new location was seamless. He retained the bakery's original staff, fostering good will and continuity with the existing customer base. With seven years remaining on the lease and a low monthly cost, Marcel could focus entirely on baking and growing his business without the burden of property management concerns.

As Marcel concluded his story, he expressed his gratitude toward Tony. "Without Tony's guidance, I might still be navigating leasing terminology instead of running a successful bakery. Now, I have a thriving spot in Hyde Park, a supportive community, and a clear understanding of my lease terms—all thanks to a chance meeting at a catering event."

The class was captivated by Marcel's story, which not only illustrated the practical challenges of commercial real estate but also highlighted how pivotal the right broker can be in navigating these waters. Tony used this real-life example to segue into today's topic—understanding lease structures and their impact on both landlords and tenants in commercial real estate.

"Let's dissect what Marcel just shared," Tony proposed. "This scenario underscores the importance of lease terms like 'gross lease' which can significantly influence operational responsibilities and financial planning for business owners."

We see Marcel, a talented chef, and baker who leveraged Tony's expertise to transition from a mobile catering service to owning a successful bakery in a prime location. This story not only highlights the importance of strategic location and lease negotiations but also illustrates the mutual benefits of long-term commercial relationships.

As Tony delved deeper into the nuances of triple net, double net, and gross leases, he explained how these structures affect control over expenses and risk distribution between landlords and tenants. He emphasized the strategic choice of lease type based on business needs and market conditions, linking back to Marcel's story as a practical example of these concepts in action.

The session then transitioned into a broader discussion on major commercial real estate asset classes, including self-storage facilities, data storage, and solar farms, touching upon their unique characteristics and implications for investors. Tony aimed to equip the class with the knowledge to not only choose appropriate properties for investment but also to understand the intricacies of managing these assets effectively.

As the day progressed, Tony's masterful blending of real-world stories with technical knowledge not only enriched the learning experience but also inspired the participants to explore the multifaceted world of commercial real estate with confidence and curiosity.

Asset Classes and Lease Structures

In today's session of the commercial mastery class, Tony Hardy shifts the focus to an essential foundation of commercial real estate: understanding asset classes and lease structures. As the classroom buzzes with anticipation, Tony begins by reviewing the major "food groups" of commercial real estate asset classes that they discussed in yesterday's session. He then dove into some additional nuances of different lease types.

"We often talk about the diverse world of commercial real estate, but today, let's simplify it by focusing on lease structures—a fundamental aspect that every commercial real estate professional must master. Understanding the types of leases is crucial for both positioning your offerings and managing expectations," he continues.

"First, let's talk about triple net leases, often seen in retail and stand-alone properties. Here, the tenant is responsible for all costs associated with the building, including property taxes, insurance, and maintenance. It's like handing over the keys and saying, 'You take care of it!' "

"Double net leases are similar but typically exclude structural repairs, which remain the landlord's responsibility. And then there are gross leases, where the tenant pays a flat fee, and the landlord covers everything else—these are common in office spaces."

As Tony outlines these structures, he introduces the concepts of base terms and renewal options. "Each lease has an initial term, say ten or fifteen years, with options to renew. These options are critical—they give tenants the ability to continue their tenancy under predefined conditions." At this moment, a skeptical student named Emily raises her hand. She's been following along but has a couple of pressing concerns. "What happens if a tenant decides not to exercise a renewal option, or worse if a store goes out of business? Aren't these scenarios risky for the property owner?"

Tony nods appreciatively at Emily's questions, recognizing this as a teachable moment for the class. "Excellent questions, Emily. Not exercising a renewal happens from time to time and isn't always a sign of trouble. For example, a tenant might not renew if they're expanding and need more space or if they're restructuring their business. In such cases, if the property is in a prime location with high traffic and a strong community presence, finding a new tenant is often manageable. This is where you, as skilled brokers trained in this master class, come into play."

"However, if a tenant goes out of business, that's a different scenario. This risk is part of commercial real estate investing, but it's manageable. For instance, properties in prime locations are rarely vacant for long, especially if they serve a staple community need. Plus, properties with high-profile or creditworthy tenants like national chains are less likely to face sudden vacancies without fulfilling their lease obligations."

"To mitigate these risks," Tony adds, turning toward a slide showing various property types, "investors often choose properties with strong fundamentals and in growth areas. They also diversify their holdings across different asset classes and geographic locations to spread risk."

As the class progresses, Tony uses real-world examples to illustrate how understanding these elements—asset classes, lease types, and tenant dynamics—can empower real estate professionals to build successful, resilient portfolios. Through interactive discussions and case studies, he ensures that even skeptics like Emily leave the room equipped with the knowledge to navigate the complexities of commercial real estate.

Amid the master class, Tony Hardy brought clarity to a nuanced topic that often perplexes even seasoned investors: the difference between a tenant not renewing a lease and a tenant going out of business, particularly when it involves high-credit entities like national chains.

"Let's address a common concern," Tony began, redirecting the room's focus with a scenario that resonated with many in the audience. "Imagine you have a tenant like Walgreens in your commercial property. What happens if they decide to close that location? It's an important question because the answer affects how we perceive risk and manage our properties."

He paused to ensure he had everyone's attention. "Walgreens, a company founded in 1901, hasn't missed a payment to anyone for anything since its inception, despite the evolving retail landscape and pressures from online competitors like Amazon. This resilience is underpinned by their high credit rating, which reassures landlords that even if a store closes, Walgreens remains obligated to fulfill its lease terms."

Tony detailed further, "If a publicly traded company closes a store, they continue to pay rent for the duration of their lease agreement. This is because these companies usually secure long-term leases to maintain their strategic locations. And should they choose to vacate early, as we've seen with some large banks, they often offer the landlord a buyout, which can be quite lucrative."

He then contrasted this scenario with a nonrenewal situation. "Now, if a tenant decides not to renew a lease, that's a different dynamic. It doesn't necessarily reflect the financial health of the tenant but rather their strategic business decisions or market conditions. For instance, a tenant may seek to relocate to a more profitable area or reduce their physical footprint. Here, the challenge for you as a landlord is to find a new tenant, which can be an opportunity to negotiate better terms or upgrade the tenant mix."

"However," Tony added, switching to a more strategic tone, "it's important to choose properties in prime locations—those with high traffic counts and strong demographic support. Such properties are easier to release if a tenant moves out. For example, a location vacated by Walgreens could be quickly filled by another high-value tenant like CVS or Dollar Tree, often with minimal downtime." Also, lease renewals don't just happen you know years in advance when they are. Also, tenants typically need to give the property owner a year or so of advanced notice on whether they intend to renew. So, the property owner can begin showing the property a looking for an ideal tenant well in advance of the lease expiration.

Tony wrapped up his point by emphasizing the importance of understanding these scenarios in depth. "As commercial brokers and investors, distinguishing between these situations helps you build resilience into your investment strategies. You prepare not just for the expected but also for the unexpected, ensuring your investments continue to generate returns regardless of individual tenant decisions."

By framing these explanations within real-world examples and demonstrating the proactive steps one can take, Tony ensured that his fellow commercial brokers left with a practical understanding of how to manage and mitigate risks associated with tenant transitions in commercial real estate. This deep dive not only clarified common confusions but also showcased the layers of strategic thinking required to succeed in this field.

When discussing renewal strategies and tenant negotiations, Tony used a recent example to illustrate a complex yet common scenario in commercial real estate. He presented the case of a Kroger grocery store to highlight how proactive management, and strategic foresight can lead to favorable long-term commitments from tenants.

The Red Zone: Sealing the Deal with Kroger's Legacy Lease

Tony began by recounting a real-world example that highlighted the complexities of lease renewals, tenant negotiations, and long-term property management.

The discussion opened with a scenario that real estate professionals may face at some point in their careers—handling a legacy tenant like Kroger, a grocery store that's been part of the community for over two decades. "Imagine a tenant that's been with you for twenty-three years," Tony explained. "Now, they're nearing the last two years of their final fiveyear renewal option, but their operations are starting to show their age. Their systems are outdated, and they're faced with the need for major renovations just to remain competitive."

As Tony laid out the situation, the class quickly picked up on the delicate balancing act required in such negotiations. On one hand, Kroger had a long-standing presence, a loyal customer base, and decades of investment in the community. Yet, on the other hand, their hesitancy to renew their lease was tied to the growing pressure to upgrade their systems and compete with an incoming competitor nearby. Tony elaborated, "This is the point where a landlord must think beyond the immediate cash flow concerns and focus on the future. Without Kroger, the anchor tenant, not only could several months of rental income be lost, but the challenge of filling such a prominent space in a shifting retail environment becomes harder. You might end up dealing with extensive construction periods, tenant improvement allowances, and costly concessions to attract the right fit."

Tony paused to let the gravity of that sink in. "For us, this is where the opportunity came in. The property owner didn't just need a quick solution; they needed expert guidance to navigate what could become a risky situation. Initially, we were brought in to start scouting for a replacement tenant, but after reviewing the bigger picture, we saw the potential of negotiating with Kroger. The first step was initiating a conversation with them, to understand their concerns and see if there was a win-win solution."

The commercial brokers leaned in, sensing the tension and complexity of the scenario. Tony continued, "Our deeper discussions revealed that Kroger had concerns about the cost of revitalizing the store and maintaining its competitiveness. They were also weighing whether it made sense to move to a new location altogether. This forced us to get creative—how do you ensure the tenant feels secure, while also safeguarding the property's long-term value?"

As Tony continued the story, he emphasized the critical turning point in the negotiations. "For Kroger, their biggest concern wasn't just about staying put—it was about ensuring their investment in renovations made sense long term. When a tenant has been in a space for over two decades, they've already built brand loyalty and customer traffic. So, the real question became, 'Do we reinvest here or start fresh somewhere else?' "

The class listened intently as Tony explained how the landlord faced a difficult decision as well. The grocer had the option to purchase a nearby plot and build a brand-new store, which would have left the landlord with a massive vacancy to fill. "It's one of those make-or-break moments for property owners. If Kroger had left, not only would the landlord have been stuck with a large vacancy but finding a new anchor tenant in the current market, with a competitor nearby, would have been challenging."

Tony detailed how the two parties negotiated carefully to ensure both their interests aligned. "The landlord understood that he needed to act strategically. They offered a solution that would benefit Kroger's business while securing long-term occupancy: one year of free rent, spread out over two years of rent at fifty percent payment per month, followed by a twenty-year renewal term. This gave Kroger the incentive to invest in renovations and stay competitive while ensuring the landlord's property maintained its value."

Tony paused to make sure the class absorbed the importance of this deal. "This wasn't just about short-term gains. The twenty-year lease agreement also included annual rent increases and two consecutive ten-year renewal options. This wasn't just a renewal—it was a move to lock in Kroger for potentially forty more years, solidifying the property owner's long-term investment and significantly boosting the property's value."

The class murmured in appreciation as Tony summed up the strategy. "What I want you all to take away from this is that commercial real estate is as much about filling vacancies as it's about crafting deals that create stability, future-proof your investments, and set you and the clients you represent up for long-term success."

With the groundwork laid, Tony was ready to dive deeper into the nuances of this lease negotiation, illustrating how understanding both tenant and landlord perspectives can lead to a deal that benefits everyone involved.

Tony paced the room as the class eagerly waited for the next insight. He knew this was the final stretch—the moment to bring everything together and leave a lasting impression.

"This deal was about legacy, not just survival," Tony emphasized. "For Kroger, it was about more than just staying competitive in a changing market. They saw the potential of reinvesting in a community where they had already built deep roots. For the landlord, a forty-year commitment wasn't just about collecting rent. It was about setting up his family for longterm financial security, ensuring this property remained a cornerstone of their wealth."

Tony glanced at the whiteboard where he had sketched out key elements of the negotiation: the free rent incentive, the extended lease term, and the annual rent escalations. "These are more than just numbers on a contract—they're strategic moves that will ripple through this family's financial future for decades."

The class was silent, absorbing the weight of the decisions. Tony added, "In commercial real estate, you're not just dealing with properties— you're dealing with futures. Every lease renewal and every negotiation are opportunities to build or lose momentum. It's about anticipating market shifts, understanding the needs of your client, and positioning them and their assets to remain successful long term."

He looked around the room, making eye contact with each participant. "Now think about your own deals. Are you just looking to close a transaction, or are you thinking two, three, or even four steps ahead? That's the mindset you need to cultivate to truly master this business."

Wrapping up, Tony concluded, "This Kroger deal wasn't just a win for the landlord—it was a win for the entire community. Keeping a well-known, long-standing tenant in place meant stability for local jobs and services. It's a perfect example of how smart real estate strategies can create ripple effects beyond just profit margins."

As Tony finished, the class erupted into applause. They had not only learned the mechanics of deal-making but had been inspired by the broader implications of their work. Tony's master class had successfully shown them that commercial real estate wasn't just about filling spaces— it was about shaping futures and building legacies.

Workshop: Full-Court Press—Mastering Lease Negotiations

Welcome to the final workshop of Tony's master class, where we'll dive into the full-court press of lease negotiations. Just like a basketball team that applies constant pressure, you need to stay sharp and adaptable throughout each stage of the negotiation process. Let's take the lessons from Marcel's story and Kroger's negotiation and translate them into actionable strategies.

Warm-Up: Setting the Playbook

Before we jump into the full-court strategy, we need to stretch our negotiation muscles and get familiar with the *basics*:

- Landlord (Team Captain): Wants long-term stability, market-rate rents, and to protect the asset's value.

- Tenant (Franchise Player): Needs favorable lease terms, potential buildouts, and security in their space to grow their business.

- Broker/Adviser (Head Coach): Balances the needs of both teams, keeps everyone in the game, and helps drive the win-win.

Now that we've set up the teams, it's time to look at the court.

First Quarter: Dribble and Dangle (Understanding the Situation)

Just like in basketball, you need to move the ball to gauge your options and explore the other side's weaknesses. Start by understanding what each team is working with.

Workshop Exercise 1:

- Team Landlord: Your goal is to retain a legacy tenant like Kroger for the long term, but you're facing challenges such as competitors moving into the area and the tenant's need for renovations.

- Team Tenant: You have a long history in the community and need assurance from the landlord that they'll assist in revitalizing the space to maintain competitiveness.

- Each team will strategize how to approach the negotiation, considering their strengths and weaknesses. We'll regroup and discuss both sides' opening positions.

Second Quarter: Fast Break (Making the First Move)

This is where the game starts to pick up speed. Each team makes its first move. For the tenant, that could be asking for rent concessions or buildout allowances. For the landlord, it could mean leveraging the tenant's established presence and the competitive market to offer terms that benefit both parties.

Workshop Exercise 2:

- Team Tenant: Create a list of tasks based on your current position (e.g., rent abatements, capital for renovations).

- Team Landlord: Determine what concessions you can make while still protecting your investment. How do you keep your tenant happy without losing out?

Teams will reconvene to present their initial offers. We'll focus on how each team handles objections and works through their opening strategies.

Third Quarter: Half-Court Trap (Defending Your Position)

This is where the negotiation heats up, and both teams dig in. The landlord team is trying to maintain cash flow and prevent vacancy, while the tenant team is pressing for better terms to stay competitive in the long run. This is where tactical defense comes into play.

Workshop Exercise 3:

- Team Tenant: Come up with creative defenses for your requests (e.g., a new competitor moving in, the cost of renovation).

- Team Landlord: Push back strategically by emphasizing the value of a long-term renewal and the current market conditions.

Both teams will defend their positions and refine their negotiation strategies. We'll analyze how each side adapts and responds to pressure.

Fourth Quarter: Full-Court Press (Closing the Deal)

It's crunch time. The clock is winding down, and both sides need to make their final moves. Just like in basketball, this is when you apply the full-court press, pushing hard for the best outcome while keeping the game fair.

Workshop Exercise 4:

- Team Tenant: Decide if the final terms are acceptable. Are you willing to commit to a twenty-year lease with rent escalation for renovation support?

- Team Landlord: Finalize your offer. What incentives can you provide to ensure a long-term deal, like Kroger's twenty-year commitment, without compromising future market value?

This is the final quarter—teams will reach a final agreement or continue negotiating until they find common ground. We'll review each team's negotiation tactics and how they managed to seal the deal.

Postgame Wrap-Up: Legacy Plays

In the end, every negotiation is about building a legacy—whether you're helping the landlord secure long-term financial stability, or the tenant create a thriving business in a competitive market.

In Tony's case with Kroger, the negotiation wasn't just about getting the best deal today; it was about creating a win-win scenario that would benefit both sides for decades. Now it's your turn to create your legacy play by mastering the nuances of lease negotiations.

Quick-Fire Q&A:

- ○ What were the key takeaways from today's workshop?

- ○ How do different negotiation strategies (like rent abatements or long-term leases) impact both parties in the long run?

- ○ How will you apply these lessons to your deals?

This Full-Court Press—Mastering Lease Negotiations workshop will help you apply practical skills to real-world scenarios, just like the pros in commercial real estate. Now get out there and make those deals count!

CHAPTER 11

Capital Plays: A Masterclass in Multifamily Mastery

You miss 100% of the shots you don't take.
—Wayne Gretzky

Keynote Speech by Dr. Evelyn Hart, Chief Economist at Sky's the Limit Wealth Advisory

As the gentle hum of conversation settled and the last clicks of coffee cups being set down faded, the room's focus shifted to the stage. The morning sunlight filtered through the expansive windows of the Newport Beach conference hall, casting a warm glow that seemed to underline the optimism of the gathering.

Dr. Evelyn Hart stepped up to the podium, her presence commanding the attention of everyone in the room, including Tony, Jarred, Sarah, and Emily. With a clear view of the Pacific Ocean as her backdrop, Dr. Hart began her discourse on the current state of the multifamily market in the US, weaving in crucial terminology that every commercial real estate professional should grasp.

"Good morning, esteemed colleagues and future leaders of real estate," Dr. Hart began, her voice firm yet inviting. "Today, we dive into the multifamily market, a segment that has shown remarkable resilience and dynamism over the past quarters."

Understanding the Multifamily Landscape

"The US multifamily market has continued its strong rebound in demand as of the second quarter, absorbing 168,000 units—the highest number post-pandemic number on record. This resurgence is underpinned by stable economic growth and a deceleration in the transition of renter households to homeownership, which has tightened the available unit pool."

Dr. Hart paused to ensure the absorption of the information, her eyes scanning the room for engagement.

Vacancy Rates and Rent Growth Dynamics

"Despite the addition of 186,000 new units in the last quarter, we've seen the smallest supply-demand gap in over two years. This has resulted in a steady vacancy rate of 7.7 percent, marking a significant period of stability not observed in nearly three years."

She clicked on a graph displaying the trends on a large screen behind her. "Notice here," she pointed, "how the national vacancy rate has risen by 325 basis points in the last four years. Concurrently, year-over-year rent growth has decelerated sharply from 9.2 percent to just 2.1 percent."

Segment-Specific Trends

"Focusing on property grades, the luxury segment—or as we categorize, A and B class properties—has experienced the weakest growth at only 0.2 percent. This trend underscores a broader market recalibration. Conversely, C-class apartments have posted the highest growth rates at 2.1 percent."

Dr. Hart transitioned smoothly into regional variations. "In the Midwest and Northeast, moderate supply additions have fostered a balanced sector, exhibiting favorable rent growth. However, the Sunbelt tells a different story. Post-pandemic development surges have led to oversupply, dampening rent increases in many of these markets."

Projections and Future Outlook

"As we look toward the remainder of the year, expect a decline in new deliveries, with only 329,000 units projected—a stark contrast to last year's figures. This contraction in supply, if coupled with sustained demand, could herald a period of market stabilization and recovery as we move into the new year."

Dr. Hart concluded, "The multifamily market, with its nuanced dynamics and regional disparities, offers both challenges and opportunities. For those looking to expand or shift their portfolios, understanding these trends isn't just beneficial—it's essential."

As the audience absorbed the wealth of information, the room buzzed with the energy of newfound knowledge and the anticipation of discussions that would shape future strategies. Tony, Jarred, Sarah, and Emily exchanged looks of approval and curiosity, each mentally noting the insights that would inform their next big moves in the world of commercial real estate.

Finalizing the Play: From Contract to Closing in Commercial Real Estate

The Call from Atlanta

It was a bright morning in Newport Beach, California. Megan was seated at a roundtable discussion, surrounded by top commercial real estate professionals from across the country. She had just finished her second cup of coffee when her phone buzzed. She glanced at the screen—an incoming call from Jason, a young agent, making a bold move from residential to commercial, whom she'd been mentoring for the past six months back in Atlanta.

Excusing herself from the conversation, she stepped out onto the balcony overlooking the ocean and answered.

Megan, smiling as she answers the phone: "Jason, what's up? I didn't expect to hear from you today. How's everything going?"

Jason, sounding excited but a little nervous: "Megan! You won't believe it—I landed my first deal! Twelve units, a midcentury building in a good part of town. The LOI was signed yesterday, and I'm moving toward the contract stage. But… I could use a little guidance before I dive into the next steps. Could you peek at the T-12s and rent roll? I want to make sure I'm doing everything right."

Megan smiled, proud of the progress Jason had made in such a short time. She had been mentoring him since he transitioned into commercial real estate, and now, it seemed, his hard work was starting to pay off.

Megan: "That's fantastic, Jason! Congratulations. Send over the documents, and I'll take a look. Tell me a bit more—how did the LOI negotiation go?"

The LOI Story

Jason leaned back in his chair at his Atlanta office, gathering his thoughts as he recounted how the deal came together.

Jason: "Well, the buyer's team had been eyeing the building for a while, and once they saw the property go live, they reached out. After a few back-and-forth conversations, we agreed on the key terms—purchase price, financing, and due diligence timelines. I drafted the LOI, and we got it signed quickly. They've put $20,000 down as earnest money, with twenty-one days for inspections and thirty days for financing contingencies. I've passed the LOI on to the attorneys, and they're drafting the contract now."

Megan could sense Jason's excitement through the phone, but she also knew this was where the real work began. She had been through enough deals to understand that getting the LOI signed was only the beginning of the journey.

Megan: "Nice job on getting that done so quickly. It sounds like you've covered the key points. Once the attorneys finish drafting the contract, make sure you take a careful look at the language before it goes out. Sometimes a little detail in the fine print can lead to bigger issues down the road. But so far, it sounds like you're in good shape."

Jason felt a little more confident hearing that from Megan. He had spent hours putting together the LOI, but now the weight of the full contract drafting process was looming.

Guidance to the Contract Stage

Jason took a deep breath, feeling more confident with each passing minute.

Jason: "Thanks for walking me through that, Megan. So, what should I be doing now while the attorneys draft the contract?"

Megan: "First, follow up with them to make sure everything is on track. The contract will be longer and more detailed than the LOI, so you want to be sure the key points—purchase price, financing terms, inspection periods—are captured correctly. Once it's ready, make sure the buyer signs first, then the seller. That way, you're managing the flow of the deal. As soon as the contract is executed, send it to all parties, and then you'll move into escrow."

Jason: "Got it. I'll be on top of that. And once we're in escrow?"

Megan: "Once escrow opens, that's when things will really pick up. You'll have your earnest money deposit from the buyer, and that's when the clock starts ticking for the inspections—both financial and physical. You'll want to line up the inspectors early, and I can help guide you through that process too."

Jason felt like he was gaining momentum. He had gotten through the LOI, handled the initial financial review, and now the contract was on its way.

Megan: "Remember, Jason, collaboration is key. You're not just walking the buyer and seller through the process—you're making sure every piece of the puzzle fits together for a win-win. Keep your communication clear, stay organized, and don't hesitate to ask questions along the way. You've got this!"

Narrator: "As Megan hung up, she couldn't help but feel proud of Jason's progress. He had landed his first deal, and though there was still a long road ahead, he was learning the ropes with confidence. The power of mentorship and collaboration was on full display, guiding this young agent through the complexities of commercial real estate with the support he needed to succeed. Now, with the contract phase nearly complete, the next challenge—inspections—loomed ahead, but Megan knew that Jason was ready to take it on."

Megan heads back into the conference, knowing she had set Jason on the right path, but the story of the deal was far from over. The inspections would be critical, and she would be there to guide him every step of the way.

Escrow Opens Smooth Sailing Ahead?

The contract process unfolded more smoothly than Jason had anticipated. Following Megan's advice, Jason integrated the key terms from the LOI directly into a purchase and sale agreement template he had downloaded from the local realtor's association website. By doing so, he avoided what could have been a prolonged back-and-forth between attorneys, which often drags on for weeks.

With the key elements already laid out, the attorneys quickly finalized their review, speeding up what is typically a lengthy process. The buyer, following Megan's recommendation, signed the contract first. Soon after, the seller added their signature. The moment the agreement was fully executed, Jason felt a familiar wave of excitement—it was official.

Jason on the phone with Megan: "We're officially in escrow, Megan. I just received confirmation from both parties—signed, sealed, and delivered." Megan, smiling on the other end of the line as she sits by the poolside cabanas in Newport Beach: "That's great, Jason. Now the real fun begins."

Jason: "I'm sending over the escrow timeline now. It's got all the critical dates—earnest money deposit, inspections, contingencies, the whole deal. I want to make sure it all lines up before I send it to the buyer and seller."

Megan: "Good thinking. Shoot it over, and I'll check it out."

The Escrow Timeline and Earnest Money

Megan was relaxing in a cabana, soaking in the late afternoon sun after a long day at the commercial real estate conference in Newport Beach. Her iPad sat on the table next to her, the occasional email ping cutting through the soothing sounds of the ocean waves. She picked it up, refreshed her inbox, and saw Jason's email with the subject line: *Escrow Timeline—Take a Look.*

She tapped the screen and opened the document, immediately scanning the key dates.

Megan, talking out loud to herself: "Okay, earnest money deposit due in five business days, check. The financial inspection period ends after twenty-one days, physical inspection by day twenty-five. Looks good so far."

She thumbed through the timeline carefully, making sure that every contingency and deadline was accounted for. Jason had done well—he had captured all the critical milestones and outlined the steps clearly for both buyer and seller.

Just as she finished reading through the timeline, her iPad pinged again— this time an email from Jason with an attachment titled: *Financials and Rent Roll—Seller Just Sent These Over.*

Megan chuckled and took a sip of her iced tea.

Megan, calling Jason: "Hey, I got the escrow timeline. It looks solid. I'm about to dive into the financials now."

Jason, picking up immediately: "Awesome. I wanted to make sure everything lined up before we started inspections. I've already sent a copy of the timeline to the buyer and seller for review, but I'd love your eyes on these rent rolls and T-12s."

Scene: Financials and First Look at the Rent Roll

Megan leaned back in her cabana chair, her iPad on her lap, as she pulled up the rent roll Jason had sent. The more she scanned the numbers, the clearer the opportunity became. Jason had mentioned there was some loss-to-lease potential, but now that Megan had the official numbers, she saw an even bigger opportunity waiting to be unlocked.

Megan, speaking to herself as she reviews the document: "Alright, rents are ranging between $690 and $750, but it's pretty clear the building is under-rented overall. Let's start with the basics. The average rent is around $721 per unit, but based on market research, similar units in this area should be renting for closer to $850."

She paused, running the math quickly in her head.

Megan: "That's a $129 per unit loss-to-lease, multiplied by twelve units over twelve months. That's $18,576 in potential rental income the owner is missing out on annually."

111 S State Street

Unit #	Tenant Name	Unit Mix	SQ FT	Rent	Market Rent	Balace/Creit		Security Deposial	Move In Date	Lease Expiration
111 # 1	Albert A.	1BRM	600	$715	$800	$	-	$650	43 Months	6 months
	2 Brad B.	1BRM LRG	750	$700	$900	$	(200.00)	$0	5 Months	7 Months
	3 Charlse C.	1BRM	600	$715	$800	$	-	$625	13 months	11 Months
	4 David D.	1BRM	600	$700	$800	$	-	$696	36 Months	Mo/Mo
	5 Edward E.	1BRM	600	$750	$800	$	-	$0	3 Months	9 Months
	6 Frank F.	1BRM LRG	750	$750	$900	$	-	$750	25 Months	9 months
	7 Gary B.	1BRM LRG	750	$750	$900	$	-	$750	69 months	6 Months
	8 Hiedi H.	1BRM	600	$715	$800	$	-	$700	4 Months	8 Months
	9 Juanita J.	1BRM	600	$705	$800	$	-	$625	17 Months	7 months
	10 Keisha K.	1BRM LRG	750	$690	$900	$	715.00	$0	23 Months	mo/Mo
	11 Lori L.	1BRM LRG	750	$750	$900	$	1,500.00		13 Months	11 Months
	12 Mary M.	1BRM LRG	750	$715	$900	$	-	$715	2 Months	M0/Mo
Total			8100	$8,655	$10,200					
Average			675	$721	$850					

Megan immediately saw the significance of this figure. Closing that gap would provide an immediate boost to the property's net operating income

(NOI), and with a 6.5 percent cap rate, it would unlock a considerable amount of value.

Megan: "That $18,576 in additional rent would translate to a $285,784 increase in property value. Not bad for just adjusting the rents over time."

As she continued to examine the rent roll, she noticed some specific discrepancies between identical units, and that's where she knew Jason could start his conversation with the buyer.

Megan: "Let's look at Unit 3, a one-bedroom that's currently renting for $715. The same size unit, Unit 9, is only rented for $705. And the most significant gap is in Unit 10, a larger one-bedroom that's pulling in $690, while several other identical units in the building are getting $750. That's the first step—bringing the rents within the building up to a consistent level."

She typed a few notes to include in her follow-up email to Jason, detailing the steps he should take next.

Megan: "Step one is closing the rent gap within the building itself—getting those lower-rented units up to match the highest rents already being achieved. That alone will bring in some extra income. Step two, over time, will be bringing all the units up to market rent. By carefully phasing in those rent increases as leases renew, the buyer can realize significant value in just the first few years of ownership."

As she clicked over to the T-12, she planned how to explain the strategy to Jason in a way that would be clear for the buyer to understand. Megan knew this wasn't just about numbers on a page—it was about crafting a vision of the property's future and showing the buyer how it could unlock its full potential.

Jason's Check-In

Back in his Atlanta office, Jason was pacing, waiting for Megan's call. He knew there was opportunity in those rent rolls, but he wanted to make sure he was seeing things correctly. When his phone rang, he picked it up immediately.

Jason: "Megan! What did you think?"

Megan: "Hey, Jason. I just went through the rent rolls, and there's definitely some untapped potential here."

Jason could hear Megan's excitement through the phone. He scribbled notes furiously.

Jason: "That's huge. And that boosts the NOI, right?"

Megan: "Exactly."

Jason smiled, seeing the path forward.

Jason: "Got it. First, get everyone in the building paying similar rents, then work toward market rates over time."

Megan: "Exactly. I'll send you an email with a breakdown of my findings, and you can share that with the buyer. They'll be able to see how closing the gap will boost their returns right away and, over time, position them for even higher returns. You're already looking at adding around $285,000 in value, and that's before any other improvements."

Narrator: "With Megan's guidance, Jason could now explain the full scope of the deal to the buyer. It wasn't just about the immediate value—they were looking at a strategy that would unlock even more potential over time. Megan's approach to commercial real estate mastery wasn't just about finding hidden value; it was about shaping a vision that both buyers and sellers could believe in."

Jason heads back to his office, ready to send Megan's findings to the buyer. The groundwork is set, and with Megan's coaching, the deal is starting to come together in a way that promises real value for both sides.

Trailing twelve-month statement T-12

111 S State Street	Aug-23	23-Sep	23-Oct	23-Nov	23-Dec	24-Jan	24-Feb	24-Mar	24-Apr	24-May	24-Jun	24-Jul	
Income													
Actual Rent Collected	$ 8,100.00	$ 7,045.00	$ 7,045.00	$ 8,435.00	$ 7,745.00	$ 7,055.00	$ 7,745.00	$ 8,100.00	$ 7,745.00	$ 7,000.00	$ 9,090.00	$ 7,770.00	$ 92,875
Loss to lease *													
Other Income	$ 320.00	$ 320.00	$ 320.00	$ 320.00	$ 320.00	$ 320.00	$ 320.00	$ 320.00	$ 320.00	$ 320.00	$ 320.00	$ 320.00	$ 3,840
Late Fees		$ 100.00				$ 20.00				$ 20.00			$ 140
Total Income													$ 96,855
Uncotrollable Expenes													
Property Tax		$ 4,567.00						$ 5,237.49					
Insurance	$ 418.91	$ 418.91	$ 418.91	$ 418.91	$ 418.91	$ 418.91	$ 418.91	$ 418.91	$ 418.91	$ 418.91	$ 418.91	$ 418.91	5,027
Electric	$ 50.20	$ 45.00	$ 54.00	$ 76.00	$ 68.00	$ 88.00	$ 50.20	$ 44.00	$ 50.20	$ 36.00	$ 50.20	$ 56.00	668
Gas Heat	$ 262.00	$ 262.00	$ 262.00	$ 262.00	$ 262.00	$ 262.00	$ 262.00	$ 262.00	$ 262.00	$ 262.00	$ 262.00	$ 262.00	3,144
Water & Sewer	$ 220.00	$ 220.00	$ 220.00	$ 220.00	$ 220.00	$ 1,150.00	$ 1,150.00	$ 220.00	$ 220.00	$ 220.00	$ 220.00	$ 220.00	4,500
Trash Removal	$ 98.00	$ 98.00	$ 98.00	$ 98.00	$ 98.00	$ 98.00	$ 98.00	$ 98.00	$ 98.00	$ 98.00	$ 98.00	$ 98.00	1,176
													14,515
Controlable Expenses													
Janitor	$ 300	$ 300	$ 300	$ 300	$ 300	$ 300	$ 300	$ 300	$ 300	$ 300	$ 300	$ 300	3,600
landascping	$ 200.0	$ 200.0	$ 200.0	$ 200.0	$ 200.0	$ 200.0	$ 200.0	$ 200.0	$ 200.0	$ 200.0	$ 200.0	$ 200.0	2,400
Snow Removal	0	0	0	0	150	300	300	0	0	0	0	0	750
Management 5%	$ 405.00	$ 352.25	$ 352.25	$ 421.75	$ 387.25	$ 352.75	$ 387.25	$ 405.00	$ 387.25	$ 350.00	$ 454.50	$ 388.50	4,644
Total Expenses													25,908
Operations & Admin													
Legal				1500	0	0	0	0	900	0	0	0	2,400
Leasing Commissions	0	0	0	0	750	0	0	0	0	0	0	750	1,500
Plumbing Repairs	0	0	0	0	0	2500	500	0	0	0	0	0	3,000
Electrical Repairs	0	0	0	0	0	0	0	0	0	0	0	0	-
General Maintenance	120	120	400	400	500	500	120	320	456	565	676	234	4,411
Total Operations													11,311
Net Operating Income													45,121

$19,872 in loss to lease not included in the t-12

The T-12 Detective Work: Uncovering the Water-Bill Spike

Megan had just finished reviewing the rent roll when she turned to the T-12. As she scanned through the monthly expenses, something jumped out at her immediately—the water bill had spiked dramatically in January and February. Typically, the water bill averaged around $220 per month, but during those two months, it had shot up to $1,150.

Megan, thinking aloud: "That's quite a jump. What happened here?"

She quickly cross-referenced the expenses and saw a plumbing repair around the same time. Without missing a beat, she picked up the phone and called Jason to discuss.

Megan: "Hey, Jason. I just went through the T-12, and I noticed something odd with the water bill—$1,150 in January and February, way above the average twenty dollars. I also saw a plumbing repair in that same period. Did the seller mention anything?"

Jason: "Funny you should ask. I gave the owner a call this morning, and he explained that the water pump malfunctioned during those months. It was taking longer for hot water to reach the apartments, so the tenants were running the showers and sinks much longer before the water heated up. After replacing the pump, the water bill returned to normal in March."

Megan smiled. This was exactly the type of issue that could be flagged during due diligence, and Jason was already ahead of it.

Megan: "Perfect. That makes sense now. You can normalize those costs moving forward, which means the spike was just a one-off issue. I'll adjust that in the financials. That $1,150 bill isn't a regular expense, so we'll add back around $4,000 to the NOI."

Jason jotted down the notes, feeling more confident about how the deal was shaping up.

The Physical Inspection and Closing the Deal

With the financials in good shape, it was time to dive into the physical inspection. Jason arranged for the buyer's team to do a walk-through, focusing on the condition of the units and the plumbing issue that had caused the water spike. The new water pump was on their checklist, and when they confirmed its installation, everything was in order.

Inspector, checking the mechanical room: "New pump looks good. This should prevent any future issues with hot water delays."

Jason was relieved to hear the confirmation. As the inspection wrapped up without any major red flags, it was clear that the deal was moving smoothly toward the finish line.

Excitement at the Closing Table

The deal had come together faster than anyone had expected. From the LOI to the contract drafting, from the deep dive into the financials to the physical inspection—Jason had navigated every step with precision, thanks to Megan's guidance.

Now, the closing day had arrived. Jason sat across from the buyer and seller, both looking eager to finalize the transaction. The attorneys exchanged final documents, and the tension in the room was palpable as everyone waited for the last signatures.

Attorney, with a nod: "Everything is in order. All we need is the signatures."

The buyer signed first, then the seller. When the final signature was made, the room seemed to exhale all at once.

Jason, unable to hold back a grin: "We did it. The deal's closed."

Megan was on FaceTime, watching from Newport Beach. Although the conference had ended, she'd decided to extend her stay, cheering Jason on remotely.

Megan: "Jason, you absolutely nailed it. Congratulations! You've just closed your first commercial deal."

The buyer shook Jason's hand, already talking about plans to raise rents and improve the NOI over the next few years. They were thrilled with the deal, knowing they were entering into a property that had hidden value waiting to be unlocked.

Buyer: "That water pump issue had me worried, but everything checked out in the end. And with your help, we've got a clear plan to get those rents up to market."

Jason: "Exactly. You've got over $285,000 in additional value just from closing the rent gap and normalizing the water expenses. And with the NOI improving over the first few years, the internal rate of return is only going to get better."

Megan smiled, watching her mentee celebrate his first big win. "Jason, you've taken all the right steps here. From flagging the rent roll discrepancies to digging into the T-12 and navigating the inspection, you handled it all like a pro. This is just the beginning—there are more deals ahead."

The Power of Mentorship and Collaboration

As Jason walked out of the closing office, the weight of what had just happened began to settle in. He had successfully navigated his first commercial real estate deal, and he had Megan's mentorship to thank for it. The lessons she taught him—from understanding the financials to managing the physical inspections—had carried him through.

Back in Newport Beach, Megan reflected on the journey, knowing that Jason's success was a testament to the power of mentorship and collaboration. She had coached him through each challenge, guiding him remotely, yet empowering him to make the right decisions at every turn.

Narrator: "In the world of commercial real estate, deals like this aren't just about numbers—they're about relationships, knowledge, and collaboration. For Jason, it was the start of a promising career, and for Megan, it was another reminder of the impact a great mentor can have. Together, they had turned a complex deal into a win-win for everyone involved. As they looked ahead, both knew that the lessons learned on this deal would carry forward, shaping the future of their careers."

Jason gets into his car, smiling. The deal is done, the future is bright, and his career in commercial real estate has officially taken off.

Summary and Conclusion: Key Lessons from LOI to Closing

1. **Streamlining the LOI Process:** The first step in any commercial real estate deal is getting a solid letter of intent (LOI) in place. Jason's early success came from quickly drafting a clear LOI with key terms like the purchase price, financing contingencies, and inspection periods. By including a prefilled purchase and sale agreement alongside the LOI, he and Megan were able to cut down on attorney review time, moving the deal forward much faster than expected. **Lesson:** Being proactive and prepared at the LOI stage sets the tone for the entire transaction.

2. **Understanding the Rent Roll and Loss-to-Lease:** Jason and Megan's deep dive into the rent roll uncovered significant loss-tolease potential. By identifying undermarket rents, they saw how a $129-per-unit rent gap, multiplied across the building, added up to $18,576 in lost income annually. Correcting this through gradual rent increases could unlock over $285,000 in property value. **Lesson:** Understanding how to analyze rent rolls and close loss-to-lease gaps is crucial for boosting a property's net operating income (NOI) and increasing its value.

3. **Mastering the T-12 and Expense Analysis:** A key moment in the deal came when Megan spotted a sharp spike in water and sewer costs on the trailing twelve-month (T-12) financial statement. By calling the seller and learning about a temporary issue with a malfunctioning water pump, Jason was able to adjust the numbers and normalize expenses, adding $4,000 back to the NOI. This one-off expense correction increased the property's value by another $60,000. **Lesson:** Pay close attention to financial anomalies in the T-12. Normalizing unusual expenses can add significant value to a deal.

4. **Navigating Physical and Financial Inspections:** The physical inspection confirmed the installation of the new water pump, which had initially caused concern due to the water bill spike. With the financials in order and no major red flags from the physical inspection, the deal moved smoothly toward closing. **Lesson:** Both the physical and financial inspections are critical steps. Thorough due diligence protects the buyer from unexpected issues and ensures that the property's value is accurately reflected.

5. **The Importance of Mentorship and Collaboration:** Throughout the entire process, Megan's mentorship played a pivotal role in guiding Jason through his first commercial deal. From helping him spot rent roll discrepancies to walking him through the T-12 and inspection phases, Megan's advice ensured that every part of the transaction was handled smoothly. **Lesson:** Mentorship and collaboration are invaluable in commercial real estate, especially for newer agents navigating complex transactions for the first time.

Conclusion: This chapter highlighted the journey from the initial LOI to closing, showing how careful attention to financials, inspections, and strategic rent adjustments can unlock significant value in a commercial real estate deal. Jason's first deal was a success, not just because of the property's potential, but because of his ability to collaborate with experienced mentors like Megan. The lessons learned here are critical for anyone looking to master the world of commercial real estate—success comes from attention to detail, proactive planning, and the power of teamwork. As this chapter closes, Jason's career is just beginning, with many more deals and opportunities ahead.

Workshop: The Deal Playbook—How to Navigate Commercial Real Estate from LOI to Closing

Welcome to the "Deal Playbook" workshop! Today, we're going to walk through the key steps that transform a commercial real estate deal from an initial letter of intent (LOI) to a successful closing. Just like in sports, real estate success is all about preparation, strategy, and teamwork. Get ready to train hard and master the playbook to win in the world of commercial real estate!

1st Quarter: The Kickoff—Drafting the LOI

Play: Setting the Terms for Success

Objective: Get the LOI signed and set the foundation for the deal.

Coach's Notes: Think of the LOI as the opening kickoff in football—it sets the stage for the entire game. A clear and concise LOI covers the major terms: purchase price, contingencies, inspection periods, and financing. If you prepare and communicate the LOI effectively, you'll hit the ground running and avoid unnecessary delays.

Key Play: Be proactive! Like in a fast break, move swiftly by drafting a prefilled purchase and sale agreement alongside the LOI. This gives both parties something concrete to work from and cuts down on attorney back-and-forth.

Drill: Pair up with a teammate and practice writing an LOI based on a sample property. Include key terms like price, financing contingencies, and inspection timelines. Discuss other terms that could be drafted into the LOI. You'll get immediate feedback to improve your drafting skills.

2nd Quarter: Running the Numbers—Tackling the Rent Roll

Play: Closing the Gap

Objective: Identify loss-to-lease and potential rent increases to boost property value.

Coach's Notes: Once the LOI is signed, it's time to run the play—analyze the rent roll like a quarterback reading the defense. Look for loss-to-lease by comparing current rents to market rates. If the average rent in the building is $721, but market rent is $850, you've spotted a gap—just like finding a hole in the defense.

Key Play: Small adjustments can lead to big results. By closing that $129 gap per unit, you could add nearly $20,000 in additional income and unlock $285,784 in property value. It's a game changer.

Drill: Analyze a sample rent roll and identify any loss-to-lease. Calculate the potential increase in income and property value using a cap rate. Work as a team to find the most underperforming units, just like running a practice drill to expose weaknesses in the defense.

Halftime: Mentorship Huddle—The Power of Teamwork

Play: Lean on Your Coaches

Objective: Learn the importance of mentorship and collaboration.

Coach's Notes: Just like in any sport, you need a good coach to help you win the game. In commercial real estate, mentorship can be the difference between success and failure. Whether you're the rookie agent (Jason) or the veteran mentor (Megan), it's all about working together to navigate tough situations.

Key Play: Be coachable. No matter how much experience you have, there's always room to grow. Surround yourself with mentors who can guide you through the tougher parts of the deal.

Drill: Role-play a mentor-mentee scenario. Have the mentee bring a challenge—such as rent roll analysis, T-12 questions, or inspection concerns—and see how the mentor provides guidance. Reflect on how mentorship can elevate your game.

3rd Quarter: The T-12 Play—Defending Against Financial Anomalies

Play: Normalizing Expenses for a Win

Objective: Analyze the T-12 and uncover financial inconsistencies.

Coach's Notes: The T-12 (trailing twelve-month financial statement) is like watching game footage—it shows you how the property has performed over time. Look for spikes in expenses, like a sudden jump in water bills. In Jason's case, the water bill spiked from $20 to $1,150, but a closer look revealed that it was a one-off issue caused by a malfunctioning water pump. After fixing it, the expenses normalized.

Key Play: Find the outliers and normalize expenses. By identifying the one-time water bill spike, Jason added $4,000 back to the NOI, which increased the property value by $60,000. Sometimes, it's the little plays that win the game.

Drill: Break into teams and review a sample T-12. Spot any financial anomalies and discuss what might have caused them. Work together to normalize the expenses and calculate how much extra value you can add.

4th Quarter: The Final Drive—Inspection and Closing

Play: Sealing the Deal

Objective: Navigate the physical and financial inspections smoothly and close the deal.

Coach's Notes: You're almost at the goal line—don't fumble! The inspections are your last major hurdle before closing. Make sure everything checks out physically (like Jason confirming the new water pump) and financially (reviewing leases, expenses, and market potential). If you play this right, you're heading to the closing table for a win.

Key Play: Confirm everything. Have the inspectors check the condition of the property, confirm repairs (like the water pump), and ensure the financials match what was promised. Once you've cleared these hurdles, move quickly to close the deal.

Drill: Simulate the inspection process. Have one team role-play as inspectors, while the other team represents the buyer's agent. Go through a mock inspection checklist and identify any red flags that could impact the deal. Discuss how to resolve issues before closing.

The Final Whistle: Closing the Deal

Play: Celebrating the Victory

Objective: Successfully navigate the closing and reflect on lessons learned.

Coach's Notes: You made it to the closing table! All your hard work from drafting the LOI to running the numbers, normalizing expenses, and managing inspections has paid off. Jason's deal, for example, added nearly $300,000 in immediate value, with even more potential over the coming years. Now it's time to celebrate the victory and prepare for the next deal!

Key Play: Never stop learning. Every deal you close brings new lessons, and those lessons will make you a better agent. Celebrate your wins, but always stay hungry for the next challenge.

Drill: Have the group share one key lesson they learned from the workshop that they will apply to their next deal. Discuss how they plan to incorporate these skills into their real estate practice moving forward.

Conclusion: The Deal Playbook—Your Path to Mastery

Just like in sports, mastering commercial real estate takes practice, preparation, and a great team behind you. By following the plays we've outlined today—from drafting the LOI, running the numbers, normalizing expenses, and navigating inspections—you'll be well on your way to becoming a commercial real estate champion. Remember, each deal is a learning experience, and with the right mentorship and teamwork, you'll be celebrating many more victories down the line.

This workshop is designed to be engaging, with practical drills and lessons built in to help new agents grasp the key steps in commercial real estate deals. Feel free to adapt it further based on your training style!

CHAPTER: 12

Strategic Team Building for Optimal Investment Outcomes

The strength of the team is each individual member. The strength of each member is the team.
—Phil Jackson

Laurant's Arrival: A Disastrous First Look

The sun beat down on the tarmac as Laurant's private jet touched down in Columbus, Ohio. For most, the idea of leaving behind the coastal beauty of Calabazas Sorth—an exclusive suburb of San Jose where the rolling hills and vineyards gave way to sprawling estates— might be daunting. With homes averaging around $3 million, Laurant's quiet life in California was one of luxury and seclusion, far from the grind of his real estate investments. But today, he wasn't headed back to his sprawling estate or his villa in the South of France, nestled on the stunning peninsula of Saint-Jean-Cap-Ferrat. Instead, he found himself in the Midwest, preparing to roll up his sleeves.

As his town car pulled into the 238-unit garden-style community he now owned, Laurant felt a sinking feeling in his gut. The swimming pool water was green, algae clinging to the surface like a bad omen. The oncegrand clubhouse was now a shell of its former self, strewn with empty beer cans on the pool table and broken furniture. It resembled a frat house more than a place where tenants could gather and relax.

And then came the worst sight of all—the maintenance staff, nonchalantly loading sacks of quarters from the coin laundry into the back of their pickup truck, like it was business as usual. Laurant watched from his car in disbelief. If that wasn't bad enough, a tenant stormed into the leasing office, yelling, "Who am I supposed to make my rent check out to this month?"

Laurant, to himself: "Mon Dieu…no wonder the collections are under 50 percent while occupancy is at 95 percent. What have I walked into?"

The landscaping was overgrown, with grass standing nearly six inches tall, and notices from the city lay piled up, reminding Laurant of multiple building code violations he now had to contend with. The investor he had trusted—someone he had met at a prestigious real estate conference months prior—had given up entirely, leaving Laurant with this mess.

He had flown in expecting a quick inspection, but he knew, deep down, that he'd be staying in Columbus far longer than planned. His return flight to the luxury of California's hillsides would have to wait.

Lunch at the Sports Bar: Strategizing the Turnaround

Two weeks later, Laurant sat across from Sarah at a local sports bar in downtown Columbus. The walls were lined with large screens showing football games, and as fate would have it, his favorite team was playing. Laurant, typically silent when it came to hands-on management, had been in town longer than expected—weeks now, dealing with the mess he had inherited.

Sarah, a sharp and seasoned commercial broker, was the key to turning things around. They sat in a corner booth, and the noise of cheering fans faded into the background as Sarah listened intently to Laurant's story.

Laurant, with a sigh: "I was hoping I'd be back in Calabazas by now. I've spent the last month dealing with everything—from pillaging maintenance staff to tenants not knowing who to pay rent to. I've been putting out fires nonstop. This isn't what I signed up for." Sarah leaned in, her focus unwavering.

Sarah: "It sounds like a nightmare. But Laurant, I'm telling you, this is fixable. If you sign up with me, we'll navigate through this mess. It's going to take time and effort, but you won't be alone. I've got the right team we can bring in to clean this up, and it starts with getting the right people in place."

Laurant nodded. Sarah's reputation preceded her. She wasn't just another broker—she was known for assembling high-performing teams and turning around distressed properties. Her work in Kentucky had proven that much, where she had taken a property in disarray and brought it back to life, increasing its value by over $4 million in just nine months. He needed that kind of magic now.

Sarah: "Let me be honest with you. If we went to market today, based on the 'as is' value of this property and all the challenges you're facing, we'd be lucky to get $7 million. But with the right strategy, I can help you push that number much higher. It's going to take hard work, but it's doable."

Laurant sipped his drink, his mind racing. The idea of taking a massive loss on the property was too much to stomach. He had already invested time and money into trying to fix it himself, but it was clear now that he needed someone with the expertise Sarah brought to the table.

Laurant: "I thought I'd be here for a day or two, just checking in. Now I'm six weeks in, and it's clear this isn't a quick fix. What do you suggest?" Sarah smiled, her eyes gleaming with confidence.

Sarah: "Here's what we do. I'll take a small retainer to get started, and we'll bring in the team you need—starting with a new property manager. I know someone perfect for this. She's just come off working with a national REIT that sold off its local portfolio, so she's available, and she's one of the best in the business."

Laurant: "That's exactly what I need—a strong manager on the ground."

Sarah: "Next, we'll address the maintenance staff and find a reliable general contractor to get this place back in shape. Then, I'll assemble specialists to tackle your building code violations, clean up the property, and get those collections back on track."

Laurant leaned back, a weight starting to lift from his shoulders as Sarah laid out the plan. It wasn't going to be easy, but it was clear that she knew how to handle a crisis. For the first time in weeks, Laurant felt like he could breathe again.

Sarah, finishing her pitch: "If we follow through on this, Laurant, you won't just be getting out of a bad situation—you'll be coming out ahead. Let's turn this around, get it stabilized, and then position it for a profitable sale. We'll get you far beyond that $7 million, and you can go back to your estate in the South of France with a solid win under your belt." Laurant smiled. The thought of returning to the peaceful shores of Saint-Jean-Cap-Ferrat had been a distant dream ever since he arrived in Columbus. But now, with Sarah's strategy in place, it seemed like there was finally a path forward.

As Sarah and Laurant wrapped up their meeting, the football game played on in the background, but their focus was on the game plan for the months ahead. Sarah had the expertise and the connections, and Laurant had the resources. Together, they were about to turn a sinking investment into a winning venture. The team was about to come together, and the real work was just beginning.

Assembling the Dream Team: All Hands on Deck

Back at Sarah's bustling office in downtown Columbus, the team gathered for a critical strategy session. The meeting room buzzed with energy as the project was entering its next phase—cleaning up the property, stabilizing operations, and ultimately preparing it for a profitable sale. Sarah stood at the head of the table, a whiteboard behind her filled with the key goals and milestones for the next few months.

Sarah: "Alright, team, this is it. Laurant needs us to bring this property from disaster to desirable. We've got all the tools and talent right here, so let's make it happen."

She gestured to Thomas, the team's data-savvy analyst, a recent graduate from Northwestern School of Business.

Thomas, pulling up his presentation on the big screen: "I've been diving deep into the pro forma numbers, and here's what we're looking at if we can stabilize this asset and get it in top shape. Right now, we're struggling to get to $7 million, but based on the trends in this area—especially with the West Coast tech companies moving in—we're on track to push the value north of $17 million."

The team leaned in as Thomas walked through the numbers. Google, Facebook, Nestle, and others were setting up shop in Columbus, causing a spike in demand for housing. Thomas projected a path that, with rent growth in the area due to the influx of high-paying jobs, the asset could trade at $17.74 million.

Thomas: "The vacancy issue could actually be our opportunity. With these companies bringing in more workers at higher salaries, we have the chance to reposition those vacant units as high-end corporate housing. We're talking luxury amenities—keyless entries, smart home systems, fully furnished spaces."

Sarah nodded. She knew this was the angle they needed. The local market was heating up, and if they could capitalize on it, they'd be able to flip the property at a massive gain.

Sarah: "Perfect. We'll start by converting those abandoned units into luxurious corporate housing. Let's target those companies coming into town for long-term master leases at premium rates."

Rachel, the property manager Sarah had brought in from a previous REIT deal, chimed in next. She had been on the ground for the past two weeks and had already made headway with the cleanup process.

Rachel: "I've got a landscaper and a facilities manager ready to come on board. Both were displaced recently, and they're eager to get started. We can tackle the overgrown grass, get the pool back to sparkling condition, and fix up the clubhouse within days. We'll be fully operational again in no time."

Sarah knew that Rachel was the right person for the job. With her strong management background, she was the perfect person to get the complex back on track.

Sarah: "Great. Let's also bring in an attorney to help with the building code violations. We need someone to navigate that quickly, and I've got just the person for the job—Ben Carter. I've worked with him on several deals over the years, and he's a magician when it comes to dealing with city inspectors."

As the meeting progressed, Amanda, the team's transaction coordinator and legal support, stepped in with another crucial piece of news.

Amanda: "Thomas and I audited the accounting, and we found something interesting. Some of the missing funds were actually in an account Laurant had partial ownership of from a prior deal. We've already contacted the bank and recovered a significant amount of the funds."

The room erupted in applause. Recovering those funds was a huge win and allowed them to plug some financial holes immediately.

Sarah, smiling: "Good work, Amanda and Thomas. This is exactly what we needed. Now, let's get the pool back to sparkling blue, get that clubhouse cleaned up, and start the marketing for the new corporate housing units. We're going to turn this place around."

Challenges on the Ground: Turning Vacancies into Opportunities

Within days, the landscaping crew was out in full force, mowing the grass, trimming bushes, and giving the entire property a fresh, welcoming look. The pool, once green with algae, was now a shimmering blue oasis, ready for the tenants and their families to enjoy. Rachel's facilities manager had whipped the maintenance team into shape and converted the laundry to card only, ensuring that no more quarters disappeared from the laundry machines.

Meanwhile, Thomas ran the numbers and drafted a new set of proposals for tech companies in the area. The team converted the abandoned units into high-end corporate housing, complete with keyless entries, tech packages, and sleek furnishings. They were soon leased at rates well above market to companies eager to find long-term housing solutions for their employees.

Thomas, presenting to Sarah and the team: "We've already locked in master leases for twenty of the corporate units. And we're not done yet—the demand is higher than we expected. If we stay on this path, we'll hit those pro forma projections, maybe even exceed them."

Rachel wasn't without her own challenges. One night, she received a call from security that a former tenant, banned from the property, had been banging on the door of one of the corporate units. He thought his exgirlfriend had moved in with a new man, unaware that she'd relocated to a smaller unit on the opposite side of the property. Rachel quickly diffused the situation, ensuring both the corporate tenant and the former resident were handled professionally.

Scene: The Road to Market—Preparing for the Big Sale

Six months after their initial meeting at the sports bar, Laurant could barely believe the transformation. He had watched much of the progress remotely from his estate in Calabazas Sorth, calling into Zoom meetings with Sarah and the team, eager for updates.

The property was unrecognizable. Corporate leases had filled the vacant units, collections were up to 95 percent, and the building code violations had been addressed. The pool glistened under the sun, and the clubhouse, once filled with beer cans and broken furniture, had been renovated into a sleek, modern gathering space.

The team sat around the conference table, ready for the final push. Sarah stood at the head, confident and prepared.

Sarah: "Alright, team. We've done it. The property is stabilized, the market is on fire with these West Coast companies coming in, and our corporate housing units are bringing in premium rates. It's time to go to market."

Thomas pulled up the latest market comps on the screen.

Thomas: "The property is ready to list at $17.74 million. We've exceeded all projections and based on the current rent growth in this part of Columbus, I'm confident we'll hit that price—maybe even higher."

Laurant, appearing via Zoom from the sunlit veranda of his estate in Calabazas Sorth, couldn't help but smile. Six months ago, he was staring down the barrel of a failing investment, but now, thanks to Sarah and her team, they were about to bring it to market at a valuation that exceeded even his wildest expectations.

Laurant: "You've worked miracles, Sarah. I can't thank you enough. Let's get this property sold and close this chapter."

Marketing Brilliance: Bringing the Property to Market

With the property stabilized, Sarah knew the final phase of the project—bringing the asset to market—needed to be nothing short of spectacular. The team's work over the past few months had transformed Laurant's 238-unit garden-style community from a liability into a high-performing asset. Now, it was time to sell.

Taylor, the marketing director, was in his element. Known for his eyecatching visuals and attention to detail, he had been working tirelessly to ensure the property was presented in the best possible light. Armed with a top-tier camera and drone equipment, Taylor had captured the property's transformation from all angles.

Taylor, showing Sarah the aerial shots: "These drone photos are going to blow the competition out of the water. We've got shots of the pool sparkling under the sun, and I've made sure to capture the fresh landscaping and renovated clubhouse. The drone even caught the newly installed smart tech amenities in the corporate units."

Taylor wasn't just focusing on the beauty shots. He had also captured key details that out-of-state investors would want to see—close-ups of the mechanical equipment, roof conditions, and even date codes on the HVAC units.

Taylor: "This way, investors who aren't local can get a real sense of what they're buying. It's about transparency. No surprises down the road."

The virtual tour Taylor created was nothing short of a cinematic experience, allowing prospective buyers to walk through the property without ever stepping foot in Columbus. Within days of launching the marketing campaign, the team was already receiving interest from institutional investors and private equity firms across the country.

Scene: An Offer Above List Price

Day one of the campaign, and the team had already struck gold. Sarah received a call from an agent named Tony, representing a private investor out of Chicago. The offer was above the list price—$17.74 million wasn't enough for Tony's buyer. They were willing to go $500,000 above asking, bringing the total to $18.24 million.

The offer came with a serious commitment: a $1 million initial earnest money deposit that would go nonrefundable twenty-four hours after the expiration or waiver of the ten-day inspection period. Sarah could hardly believe the speed and enthusiasm with which the buyer was moving.

Sarah, to Laurant on Zoom: "Laurant, we've got an offer of $500,000 over the list, and they're putting up $1 million as nonrefundable earnest money. We're talking about a smooth path to closing as long as the inspection clears. If all goes well, that money passes straight to your account."

Laurant, calling in from his sun-soaked terrace in Calabasas Sorth, was elated. After months of worry and effort, it looked like they were finally heading for a win.

Laurant: "That's incredible, Sarah. I knew your team would deliver, but I didn't expect it to move this fast. Let's get through the inspection and lock this in."

Day Nine: The Incident

It was day nine of the inspection period, and everything seemed to be going perfectly. The buyer's inspections had been clean, and Sarah was getting ready to prepare for the next phase of the sale. But just as the team was celebrating the smooth process, disaster struck.

At three a.m., Rachel received a frantic call from security. A man was banging on one of the doors and yelling incoherently. It turned out to be the ex-boyfriend of a tenant who had moved to a smaller unit on the other side of the property. The boyfriend, who had already been barred from the property due to erratic behavior, had found out where his ex had relocated and was demanding to see her.

Rachel called the police, and within minutes they arrived on the scene. After detaining the man, they found paraphernalia in his book bag. What started as a domestic disturbance turned into something far more serious.

Rachel, on the phone with Sarah at four a.m.: "Sarah, it's bad. The police found materials in his bag that could be used to assemble a meth lab. They're going to search the unit. We need to get ahead of this."

By the next morning, Sarah knew this was about more than just the incident—it was a potential environmental nightmare. The police were preparing a statement, and the local news was ready to run a story about the discovery. The presence of meth-making materials created serious concerns about contamination in the unit and possibly the surrounding areas.

Scene: Managing the Crisis—The Call to Tony's Buyer

Sarah didn't waste any time. She gathered her team and prepared for an impromptu call with Tony and his buyer. They needed to get ahead of this situation before it hit the news. Sitting at her desk, she dialed Tony, bracing herself for the tough conversation ahead.

Tony, picking up the phone: "Hey, Sarah. We're just about ready to waive the inspection. Everything's looking good on our end." Sarah took a deep breath and got straight to the point.

Sarah: "Tony, I'm going to be completely transparent with you. We had an incident last night on the property involving a former tenant's ex-boyfriend. The police were called, and they found materials in his possession that could potentially be used to make meth. The unit is being tested for contamination as we speak, and I wanted to let you, and your buyer know before this hits the news."

There was a long pause on the other end of the line. Sarah could almost feel Tony processing the gravity of the situation.

Tony: "That's a curveball. Is this going to delay things?"

Sarah: "Here's the deal—there's a chance the environmental testing could push us past the inspection period. But I want to assure you, we're handling it. We've already brought in environmental specialists to assess the unit, and we'll have full transparency on the results."

Tony, knowing how important this deal was, agreed to relay the information to his buyer. Sarah knew she had to manage this perfectly to keep the deal on track.

The Environmental Impact: A Nuance in Commercial Real Estate

Environmental issues like this one are more than just an inconvenience—they can turn into costly liabilities if not managed properly. In commercial real estate, environmental due diligence is critical. Meth production, even attempted or small-scale, can contaminate a property, leaving behind dangerous chemicals that could require expensive remediation.

Sarah understood the complexity of the situation. It wasn't just about cleaning up the unit; it was about ensuring the entire building was safe. Even though the contamination was isolated to one unit, the environmental specialists needed to verify that no residual chemicals had spread to neighboring areas.

Over the next few days, Sarah worked tirelessly with the environmental consultants and her legal team to ensure that the property was thoroughly tested. They provided Tony's buyer with full transparency and an updated timeline, extending the due diligence period by a few days to allow for the testing results.

Sarah, *in a follow-up call with Tony:* "The good news is, we caught this early. The contamination is contained to the single unit, and the environmental team is handling the cleanup. We'll have everything documented and certified, so there will be no future liabilities for your buyer."

Going to Market: The Final Push, EPA, and OSHA Involvement

With the environmental scare behind them, the team was back on track. However, it wasn't without a few hiccups. The chemicals found on the visitor were more dangerous than initially thought. The Occupational Safety and Health Administration (OSHA) and the Environmental Protection Agency (EPA) had both gotten involved, concerned about the potential for contamination. Fortunately, the erratic ex-boyfriend had never entered the unit itself and was apprehended outside while banging on the door. But given the nature of the chemicals, the authorities weren't taking any chances.

The affected unit, along with the neighboring ones that shared walls, had to be gutted down to the light flexicore concrete materials to ensure that any potential contamination was removed. The team, however, was undeterred. The flexicore construction meant they had some natural protection, but the units still needed a full renovation to meet safety standards.

Sarah's team moved swiftly. They'd already begun renovations on the other side of the community, but this unexpected turn of events shifted their focus. The permits for the work were expedited thanks to Sarah's strong relationships with the city officials, who were more than happy to support the quick turnaround of the property. What had once been a nightmare of building code violations and tenant complaints was now a story of transformation.

Rachel, reporting back to Sarah: "The renovations are nearly done. We gutted the affected units, and the flexicore walls made it easier than expected. The city's been cooperative, and we've fast-tracked the final inspection. In a couple of days, those units will be back on the market."

A Flexicore building refers to a construction method using precast concrete slabs, often used for floors and roofs. These slabs, also known as hollowcore, are manufactured off-site and cut to size. The slabs are prestressed concrete panels that have hollow tubes running through them, which reduces weight and material costs without sacrificing structural integrity. Flexicore construction provides several benefits, such as soundproofing, fire resistance, and high load-bearing capacity, making it a durable and cost-effective option for commercial and residential buildings.

Sarah, nodding: "Great work, Rachel. Let's get these units filled as quickly as possible. We've already secured corporate tenants for half the building—let's keep the momentum going."

Earnest Money Goes Nonrefundable

As the team finalized the renovations, the buyer's inspection period expired. Tony's buyer, impressed with how quickly and transparently Sarah and her team had handled the environmental scare, decided to move forward without hesitation.

The one-million-dollar earnest money deposit went nonrefundable and passed straight into Laurant's account twenty-four hours after the inspection period. The excitement was palpable. Sarah had navigated one of the most complex deals of her career, and now it was time to close.

Laurant, dialing in from his estate in Calabasas Sorth, couldn't hide his excitement.

Laurant: "Sarah, I don't know where in the world you've been all my life, but this—this is beyond what I could've imagined. A few months ago, I was staring at disaster. Now, we're about to close at over $18 million. I can't thank you and your team enough."

Sarah, smiling through the Zoom call: "Laurant, you trusted us, and we delivered. This has been a team effort all the way through, and I can't wait to get this deal across the finish line."

Scene: Closing Day—The Big Win

The closing was set for a bright Friday morning. Sarah had gathered her team in the office to celebrate, and Laurant joined via Zoom once again from his sun-drenched estate. The paperwork was signed, and within hours, the deal was officially closed at $18.24 million—half a million dollars above the original list price.

It wasn't just the price that mattered, though. The story of how they had turned the property around was the real victory. From battling building code violations and missing rent payments to dealing with an environmental crisis and a former tenant's criminal activity, Sarah's team had navigated every twist and turn. They had stabilized the asset, improved collections, and turned vacancies into high-end corporate housing—all within a matter of months.

Tony, speaking on behalf of the buyer: "Your team's transparency and quick action after the environmental issue really stood out. This wasn't just a smooth deal—it was an example of how to do business the right way. We're excited to take over the property and build on what you've done."

Laurant, visibly moved, raised a glass of champagne during the Zoom call.

Laurant: "To Sarah and her team—you've all done the impossible. This is a win not just for me, but for everyone involved. Thank you."

Scene: The Celebration—Southern France

As a token of his appreciation, Laurant invited Sarah and her entire team to his estate in the South of France. Located on the breathtaking peninsula of Saint-Jean-Cap-Ferrat, his vineyard-covered property overlooked the Mediterranean, offering sweeping views of the sparkling blue waters. The estate, a stone's throw from Monaco, had been in Laurant's family for generations.

Sarah and her team arrived at the estate for a ten-day stay, ready to unwind after months of hard work. The air was warm, the scent of lavender and rosemary wafting through the gentle breeze as they stepped onto the estate grounds. Laurant, dressed in a relaxed linen suit, greeted them with a warm smile.

Laurant: "Welcome to Saint-Jean-Cap-Ferrat! You've earned this. Please, make yourselves at home." Over the next few days, the team enjoyed the finer things life had to offer. They sipped wine from Laurant's vineyard, watching the sun set over the Mediterranean, the sky ablaze with oranges and pinks. Mornings were spent strolling through the lush vineyards, and afternoons were dedicated to exploring the unique activities of the peninsula—luxury yacht excursions, scenic hikes, and even private tours of some of the world's most beautiful villas.

On one of the days, Laurant arranged for a private dinner in the estate's courtyard. Long wooden tables were set under twinkling lights, and the sound of the waves crashing against the rocky coastline provided a serene backdrop. The wine flowed, the food was decadent, and the conversation was lighthearted. It was a well-earned celebration after months of hard work and dedication.

Sarah, raising her glass: "To the team—none of this would have been possible without each and every one of you. From navigating the environmental crisis to transforming the property, this was a true team effort. And to Laurant—thank you for trusting us and for hosting us here in paradise."

Laurant raised his glass in return, smiling.

Laurant: "To the best team I've ever worked with. You've set the bar high, and I'm proud to call each of you partners. Santé!"

Scene: Looking Ahead

As the trip came to a close, Sarah and her team reflected on the incredible journey they had just completed. From turning around a struggling investment to celebrating in one of the most beautiful places on earth, it was a testament to what could be achieved when a team comes together with the right strategy and dedication.

The trip to Saint-Jean-Cap-Ferrat wasn't just a celebration—it was a reminder of the importance of teamwork, perseverance, and strategic thinking in commercial real estate. The lessons learned from this deal would carry them forward into their next projects, ready to tackle whatever challenges lay ahead.

Narrator: This wasn't just a deal—it was a transformation. Laurant's troubled asset had been turned into a high-performing property, sold above asking price, and Sarah's team had cemented their place as top-tier commercial real estate professionals. The experience was a masterclass in navigating environmental issues, property management, and marketing—all while building lasting relationships that would pave the way for future successes.

Summary: Turning a Struggling Asset into a MultimillionDollar Win

This chapter captures a complex real estate transformation led by Sarah and her dedicated team. What started as a distressed 238-unit property in Columbus, Ohio, filled with code violations, tenant issues, and environmental crises, ended with a stunning sale above the asking price. Here are the key takeaways:

1. **Assembling the Right Team:** Sarah's team comprised top talent across disciplines:

   ○ **Rachel, the property manager**, brought in the right maintenance staff and contractors to clean up and stabilize operations.

   ○ **Taylor, the marketing director**, produced stunning drone photography, virtual tours, and an impeccable marketing brochure to attract buyers.

   ○ **Thomas, the analyst**, highlighted market trends, projecting future value based on rent growth and corporate housing demand, making a compelling case for investors.

   ○ **Amanda, the transaction coordinator and legal support**, worked behind the scenes to recover missing funds and ensure that permits and inspections were expedited. This strategic collaboration, supported by Sarah's leadership, transformed the property's trajectory.

2. **Handling Environmental Challenges:** The team faced a significant environmental issue when a former tenant's exboyfriend was found with meth-making materials. This incident required coordination with the EPA and OSHA to ensure thorough cleanup. The property's flexicore construction allowed for a rapid renovation, which was expedited with help from city officials. This swift response preserved the deal and maintained buyer confidence.

3. **Maximizing Marketing Efforts:** The property was marketed brilliantly, with Taylor using drone footage and virtual tours to attract out-of-state investors. Sarah's connections helped secure

an offer $500,000 above list price on day one, with a $1 million
nonrefundable earnest money deposit once the inspection period
expired.

4. **Turning Vacancies into Opportunities:** Sarah's team repurposed
    vacant units into high-end corporate housing, locking in
    longterm master leases with West Coast tech companies entering
    the Columbus market. This not only filled vacancies but raised
    the overall rental income, increasing the property's value.

5. **Navigating the Sale:** Even with the environmental scare, the
    team maintained full transparency with the buyer's agent, Tony,
    ensuring trust remained intact. By addressing all issues head-on,
    they moved the deal through the closing process seamlessly.

Conclusion: A Lesson in Real Estate Mastery

This chapter showcases the power of teamwork, strategic thinking, and
perseverance in commercial real estate. Sarah and her team demonstrated
the importance of assembling the right experts, from property management
to marketing and financial analysis, to turn a struggling asset into a high
performing property.

Their ability to manage environmental concerns with speed and
professionalism, combined with their skillful repositioning of the property's
value, resulted in a profitable sale at $18.24 million—well above the initial
expectations.

Laurant's trust in Sarah's team paid off, not only in terms of financial gain
but also in creating a real estate success story. The team's postsale celebration
in the South of France was a fitting reward for their dedication, a reminder
that in commercial real estate, the right strategy and collaboration can turn
even the toughest challenges into significant wins.

Workshop: Teamwork Playbook—Scoring Big in Real Estate with Collaboration and Strategy

Welcome to "The Teamwork Playbook," a high-energy workshop designed to help you understand the power of teamwork, strategic problem-solving, and flawless execution in commercial real estate. Much like in sports, the best wins come from collaboration, not solo efforts. You're about to learn how to play your position, trust your teammates, and work together to turn challenges into opportunities.

Warm-Up: The Kickoff—Why Teamwork Wins Games

Coach's Notes: Before we dive into the plays, let's set the stage. Real estate deals can be like a high-stakes game—fast-paced, complex, and full of twists and turns. Going at it alone is like playing a team sport without teammates—you're going to burn out fast and miss key opportunities. Teamwork allows you to leverage each other's strengths, solve problems quicker, and execute at a higher level.

First Quarter: The Huddle—Assembling Your Team

Play: Position Players Win Games

Objective: Understand that you can't do everything yourself. You need specialists in key roles to tackle different aspects of a deal.

Key Lesson: In real estate, just like in football or basketball, every position matters. You can be the quarterback calling the shots, but without a strong offensive line, a running back, and receivers, you won't make it to the end zone. In commercial real estate, your team should include:

○ **Property Manager**: Your on-the-ground player, ensuring the asset runs smoothly.

○ **Marketing Director**: Like your wide receiver—catching the attention of buyers with stellar presentations.

○ **Analyst**: Your offensive coordinator, breaking down the numbers and creating the game plan.

○ **Transaction Coordinator**: The point guard distributes the ball, ensuring all moving parts come together smoothly.

○ **Attorney/Legal Team**: Your defense, protecting the deal, and keeping everything compliant.

Drill: Break into teams of five and assign each person a role from the list above. Each team will be presented with a mock real estate scenario that needs quick problem-solving. You'll have five minutes to come up with a strategy and assign tasks to your "team members." Then, present how each person's expertise will help execute the plan. The goal is to highlight the importance of each role in getting the deal done.

Second Quarter: The Game Plan—Solving Problems as a Team

Play: Stay Calm Under Pressure

Objective: Work together to tackle real estate problems by leaning on each other's strengths.

Coach's Notes: In the heat of a game, things don't always go as planned. A last-minute environmental issue or tenant crisis can feel like the other team just intercepted the ball. Instead of panicking, stay calm, call a timeout, and regroup with your team. The key is recognizing when you need help and relying on your teammates.

Drill: Present a challenge scenario where an environmental issue comes up during the inspection period (similar to the meth lab scare). As a team, brainstorm how each person can contribute to solving the problem:

- The property manager reports the issue to the city and coordinates with the contractors.

- The analyst determines the financial impact and creates a plan to adjust timelines.

- The marketing director ensures the buyer is kept informed and adapts messaging.

- The attorney steps in to manage compliance with EPA regulations.

- The transaction coordinator keeps the timeline on track and ensures communication flows smoothly.

After the discussion, each team presents their strategy to the group. The takeaway? No single person solves the problem alone—it's a collaborative effort.

Halftime: Mentorship Huddle—Lean on Your Coaches

Play: Call for Backup

Objective: Understand the importance of having a mentor or coach to guide you.

Coach's Notes: Even the best players have coaches. In real estate, mentorship is your lifeline when things get tough. It's easy to feel overwhelmed by a complex deal, but reaching out to someone with more experience can turn the game around. Just like Laurant leaned on Sarah, find a mentor who can offer guidance and help you see the big picture.

Drill: Each team will discuss who their "coach" would be if they faced a real estate challenge in real life. Whether it's a senior agent, a broker, or a trusted colleague, identify the person you'd call for advice. Share why this person is important to your success and how you could use their wisdom to solve problems faster.

Third Quarter: Execution—Making the Play When It Counts

Play: Flawless Execution = Victory

Objective: Once you've got the strategy, execution is everything.

Coach's Notes: Great strategy only works if you execute it. In commercial real estate, this means doing everything with precision: from getting the marketing materials out on time, handling the paperwork, and making sure your client feels informed and supported throughout the process. Execution is what wins games.

Drill: Each team will now revisit their strategy from the second quarter. This time, focus on execution—what are the steps you need to take to make sure everything happens flawlessly? Who's responsible for what? How do you communicate with your clients and keep them informed? Present the detailed steps you'll take to ensure smooth execution.

Fourth Quarter: The Final Drive—Closing as a Team

Play: Finish Strong Together

Objective: Bring the deal to a successful close with teamwork, communication, and celebration.

Coach's Notes: Closing the deal is the final drive down the field. Everyone needs to be on the same page, working in unison. Celebrate the small wins along the way and keep the momentum going. And when you finally score, remember—this is a team win, not a solo effort.

Drill: Simulate a closing process where the deal is almost finished, but a last-minute issue arises (like an inspection problem or funding delay). Each team needs to come up with a plan to communicate with the client, solve the issue, and get the deal across the finish line. Teams will present their final "closing play" and celebrate the collective win!

Final Whistle: Teamwork Wins Championships

Play: No Lone Wolves

Objective: Recognize that success in real estate is a team effort.

Coach's Notes: The biggest takeaway from today's workshop? You don't have to do this alone. The best deals, the biggest wins, and the most successful careers come from collaboration and teamwork. Don't be afraid to call for backup, lean on your teammates, and recognize the strengths each person brings to the table.

Conclusion: Your Team is Your Strength

- **Key Lesson:** Success in commercial real estate is about more than just your personal talent—it's about the power of your team. Each role, from marketing to management, is crucial in getting the deal done. When you work together, you'll not only solve problems more efficiently but also close deals faster and more effectively.

- **Next Steps:** As you move forward in your real estate career, remember the importance of teamwork. Build your network, trust your teammates, and don't try to be a lone wolf. The best victories come from collective effort, and with the right team behind you, you'll score big every time.

This workshop is designed to be fun and interactive while driving home the importance of teamwork, problem-solving, and execution in commercial real estate.

CHAPTER 13

The Quarterback's View—Legal Frameworks and Compliance

Talent wins games, but teamwork and intelligence win championships.
—Michael Jordan

As the sun set over Newport Beach, casting an orange glow over the luxurious patio of the swanky oceanfront venue, Sarah mingled among the crowd of brokers who had gathered for the afterparty following the real estate conference. The air buzzed with laughter, competitive banter, and the clinks of cocktail glasses. Nearby, a group of commercial brokers were playing bocce ball, casually tossing heavy balls while recounting their most memorable deals. A sponsor had decked out the beachfront venue with high-end details—white couches with blue accents, soft lanterns swaying in the breeze, and trays of gourmet appetizers making their rounds.

It was there, amid the lively atmosphere of brokers trading war stories, that Sarah spotted Mark, a familiar face from her hometown and a fellow broker she'd recently worked with on a deal that had been nothing short of a rollercoaster.

"Sarah!" Mark greeted her with a big smile, motioning her over. He'd just finished his turn at bocce and offered her a glass of champagne from the nearby bar. "I was just thinking about that deal we wrapped up a few months ago—the one that nearly fell apart half a dozen times."

"Oh, don't remind me," Sarah laughed, shaking her head. "That was a *nail-biter*, but the sellers' agent really stepped up and quarterbacked it to the goal line."

As they sipped their drinks, the conversation turned to the intricacies of that particular deal, which had tested both their patience and expertise. Sarah leaned in, recalling the series of events with an animated grin. "You remember how close we were to losing the whole thing, right? It was thirty days before closing, and the buyer's insurance company was demanding an inspection of the electrical panel. The whole process had already been dragged out by that ridiculous back-and-forth in the early negotiations."

Mark nodded in agreement, interjecting, "That was one of the longest tennis matches I've ever seen. Price back and forth, terms bouncing like a ball across the net."

"Exactly," Sarah said. "And after all that, we thought we were in the clear until the insurance company threw in their request. But Marcus— God bless him—he knew we had to address the seller's concerns without ruffling too many feathers."

Mark chuckled, adding, "Oh, right. The infamous deal fatigue. I've never seen a seller so close to pulling the plug."

The seller, Sarah recalled, was facing a critical deadline to complete a 1031 exchange and couldn't afford any more delays, yet the buyer still needed an extension to release funds from a 401K account. The entire deal was on the verge of collapsing, and Marcus, the sellers' agent, knew he had to step in carefully.

"The seller's attorney wanted to send a formal request for a nonrefundable deposit," Sarah said. "But Marcus knew that Bob—our buyer's attorney—would push back *hard*. He wasn't about to let his client risk a penny without a fight."

Mark shook his head, clearly familiar with the buyer's notoriously combative attorney. "Bob is a bulldog. He'd have torn that letter apart."

"Exactly. That's when Marcus decided to take a different route," Sarah continued. "He didn't rely on formal letters or stiff legal language. Instead, he decided to attend the buyer's insurance inspection—just him and the buyer—using the casual setting to have a direct conversation."

"Smart move," Mark nodded, tossing his bocce ball in the sand. "That personal touch can make all the difference."

"Right? During the inspection, Marcus brought it up in a relaxed but honest way. He framed it as, 'Look, we've all been through a lot with this deal, and the seller just wants to make sure we're all moving toward the finish line.' He suggested the nonrefundable deposit not as a penalty but as a good-faith gesture to keep things moving."

"And the buyer went for it?" Mark asked, raising an eyebrow.

Sarah smiled. "Not right away, but Marcus had built up enough trust that the buyer was willing to consider it. By the end of the inspection, the buyer had agreed to a partial nonrefundable deposit. It gave the seller enough confidence to grant the final extension and keep the deal alive."

Mark raised his glass. "Toast to a quarterback move if I've ever seen one."

Sarah, "To, Quarterback moves!"

As Sarah and Mark continued to recount the story, Sarah added a key detail that illustrated just how precarious things had been after the candid conversation Marcus had with the buyer.

"The next day, the buyer's attorney, Bob, practically went through the roof when he got the formal letter," Sarah explained, her tone matching the tension of the moment. "The letter asked for $50,000 of the earnest money deposit to go nonrefundable and to be released to the seller in exchange for the extension. It also clearly stated that if the deal closed on time, the $50,000 would be applied toward the purchase price, but if not, the seller would keep it."

Mark winced. "Oof, I can only imagine Bob's reaction."

"He was furious," Sarah continued, shaking her head. "He immediately started drafting a letter of objection. He was ready to fight tooth and nail, convinced that this was an unfair demand designed to trap his client."

"But then came the turning point," Sarah said, leaning in. "The buyer called Bob directly and said, 'This is what I want to do.'" "Really?" Mark asked, surprised.

"Yep," Sarah nodded. "The buyer explained that after the conversation with Marcus during the inspection, he understood the seller's perspective. He didn't want to risk losing the deal over another delay, especially since he was confident the funds were coming in soon. Once the buyer made his intentions clear, Bob had no choice but to back down."

Mark laughed, shaking his head in admiration. "That's the beauty of a good quarterback. Marcus handled it perfectly—by building trust with the buyer, he defused the entire situation before it could escalate further."

Sarah smiled, finishing the story. "Exactly. Once the buyer got Bob to pipe down, the payment was processed, the extension was granted, and the deal stayed on track. It just goes to show that sometimes, the best moves in real estate happen behind the scenes, when the broker steps in to smooth things over."

They raised their glasses again, appreciating the subtle dance that often comes with navigating high-stakes deals.

"Totally," Sarah agreed, clinking her glass against his. "And it saved the deal. We ended up closing right on time, and everyone walked away happy."

The brokers around them were now engaged in a spirited debate about the best negotiation strategies, but Sarah and Mark knew that in this business, deals were often saved by the quiet but crucial interventions that never made the headlines. They were the behind-the-scenes moments, the broker's candid conversations, the timely nudges that transformed potential deal-breakers into closed transactions.

As the night wore on, the atmosphere around them grew even more festive, but Sarah and Mark continued exchanging stories—each one reminding them that while the stakes in commercial real estate were high, it was the skillful management of relationships and well-timed plays that ultimately sealed the deal.

Due Diligence Starts Early

As the night progressed, Sarah, Mark, and a group of seasoned brokers found themselves near the bocce ball court, sharing drinks and exchanging their best "war stories" from the world of commercial real estate. Between lighthearted jokes about missed deals and tight deadlines, Sarah's face lit up when Mark asked about a particular deal that nearly went south during the due diligence phase.

"I'll never forget it," Sarah started, rolling a bocce ball down the court. "I was working on this mixed-use property that seemed promising on paper but had some sketchy financials. It was a ten-unit retail complex, but the seller's financials were all neatly rounded—like $300,000 NOI, no decimals or variations." The group chuckled knowingly, already recognizing the red flags. "Turns out, those numbers were more estimates than actual figures," she added, shaking her head. "So, I had to dig deeper. Before I even let the buyer think about committing, I requested detailed financials—bank statements, rent rolls, everything. And you wouldn't believe the difference between the estimated NOI and the real one."

Mark nodded. "Due diligence is like a pregame warm-up," he said, "it's where you separate the tire kickers from the serious players."

Zoning Laws and Building Permits

The conversation smoothly transitioned to zoning issues. Mark, tossing the next bocce ball, brought up a recent deal he had closed, which nearly got derailed by zoning complications. "I had a client who bought a failed condo project," he said. "Fifty oversized, inefficient units—completely ridiculous. He wanted to convert them to high-density apartments. The city officials were useless, though—couldn't get any clear answers."

Sarah leaned in, curious. "How'd you pull it off?"

"I got him in touch with a zoning attorney. In five minutes, the attorney figured out that we could increase the number of units to 132 without even needing special variances." Mark paused for dramatic effect. "Eighteen months later, that place was leasing out faster than we could put up the 'for rent' signs."

Sarah whistled. "Fifty to 132? Talk about a power play."

Another broker chimed in, "That's the magic of zoning. One call can take a deal from mediocre to gold."

The brokers continued swapping tales, each one more compelling than the last. Despite the laid-back atmosphere of the Newport Beach afterparty, these stories underscored the crucial importance of doing due diligence, understanding zoning laws, and working with a knowledgeable team to turn potential challenges into opportunities.

As the Newport Beach waves rolled in and out, the group huddled around the warm glow of the fire pit, roasting marshmallows and making s'mores. The crackling fire provided a cozy backdrop as brokers traded war stories. Sarah and Mark were among them, savoring the quiet moments between deals, but the night's conversation kept circling back to the inevitable challenges of commercial real estate.

Environmental Assessments: Navigating Risk Before It's Too Late

After some hearty laughter over a previous story, Mark leaned in, his voice dipping into a more serious tone. "You want to talk about a dealkiller? How about the time a potential multimillion-dollar purchase nearly imploded because of soil contamination?"

Sarah nodded knowingly. "I've seen it time and time again. Brokers think they're in the clear, and then—bam—environmental red flags pop up during due diligence. It's something you have to catch early, not in the final stretch."

Mark continued, recounting the story of how a Phase I Environmental Assessment flagged possible contamination from an old gas station next door. "We ended up needing a Phase II, and the buyer almost walked."

Sarah chimed in, explaining to the group. "Phase I is all about history. The inspector looks at the property and surrounding land, checking old gas stations, dry cleaners, or anything that might have dumped hazardous waste. If Phase I shows something suspicious, then Phase II digs deeper— literally. They test soil and water samples, and that's where delays start piling up."

"You've got to be proactive," she added, flipping her marshmallow to avoid charring it. "If you know there's an old factory next door or a dry cleaner down the street, get ahead of it. It can be the difference between a deal that closes and one that dies in escrow."

Balancing Building Codes and Safety Standards with Owner Perceptions

Pete, another broker, was next to pipe up. "Ever have a seller tell you something was 'brand new,' only to find out it's ten years old?" His frustration was met with understanding laughter from the group. It was a common tale.

Sarah smiled. "Oh, the 'brand-new furnace' trick." She explained how property owners often see something they installed as 'new,' even if it's approaching the end of its lifespan. "It's not that they're lying," she clarified, "but to them, it *feels* new because they paid for it."

"And then," she continued, "there's the whole issue of permits. I can't tell you how many times I've walked into a property, and the owner has done a complete renovation without ever getting the proper permits. That's a financial and legal time bomb."

The fire crackled as someone added more wood, sending sparks into the night sky.

Lease Review: Reading Between the Lines

By now, the marshmallows were long gone, but the stories continued. Sarah transitioned to one of her favorite examples: a quirky lease clause that nearly derailed a retail deal. "We were marketing this retail center with a well-known chicken chain as a tenant," she began. "Turns out, their lease had a clause that prohibited any other restaurant from serving chicken."

The group erupted. "Wait," Mark interrupted, "so you couldn't have, say, a Popeyes or KFC move-in?"

Sarah grinned. "Exactly. The clause eliminated 90 percent of potential competitors, but the beauty was that it also made the current tenant really valuable. They were paying for exclusivity."

As the fire crackled and the waves whispered, Sarah turned the conversation toward the importance of understanding every nuance in a lease. "You've got to read between the lines. Sometimes, those quirky clauses that seem restrictive can actually be your biggest selling points."

The night wore on with brokers sharing stories, insights, and laughs, the waves continuing to crash in the background. Sarah had seamlessly woven the evening's conversation into a mini-masterclass—one that blended real-world experience with invaluable lessons in environmental assessments, building codes, and lease clauses.

By the time the last marshmallow was roasted, everyone left the fire pit feeling a little warmer—and a lot wiser.

Building a Legal Compliance Strategy

By mastering legal frameworks and compliance, Sarah portrays the commercial real estate broker not just as a deal facilitator but as a strategic adviser and protector of client interests. This session arms brokers with the knowledge and strategies needed to navigate the legal intricacies of commercial real estate confidently.

To develop a robust legal compliance strategy, consider the following:

1. Stay informed about changes in laws and regulations that affect commercial real estate.

2. Attend legal seminars and workshops to deepen your understanding of real estate law.

3. Build relationships with experienced real estate attorneys and legal professionals.

4. Maintain open communication with local regulatory agencies to ensure compliance.

5. Develop standardized processes for due diligence and maintain detailed records.

6. Proactively identify and address potential liabilities and create contingency plans.

By positioning yourself as a knowledgeable and trusted adviser, you'll be able to navigate the complex legal landscape of commercial real estate with confidence. Remember, in commercial real estate, it isn't about trying to do everything yourself. It's about assembling the best team to get the property across the goal line. Partner with experts, pay them for their efforts, and focus on creating win-win solutions for your clients. With a strong understanding of legal frameworks and a commitment to thorough due diligence, you'll be well-equipped to quarterback successful commercial real estate transactions.

Workshop Title: The Playbook—Quarterbacking Commercial Real Estate

Welcome to the final session of *The Playbook*, where brokers are the quarterbacks, driving deals from start to finish. Today's session is all about making the right calls at the right time, navigating commercial real estate deals with precision, and leading clients to victory. Get ready for some fun, sports-themed drills and interactive exercises as we tackle everything from due diligence to retrades.

First Quarter: The Environmental Scramble

Objective: Learn how to navigate environmental assessments and avoid potential pitfalls that could derail a deal.

Play Setup: Just like a quarterback reads the defense before the snap, brokers need to anticipate environmental liabilities. We'll simulate a Phase I Environmental Assessment where each team reviews the history of a property (e.g., former gas stations, factories) and decides whether a Phase II assessment is required.

- Kickoff Drill: Review case studies (old retail centers, industrial sites) and discuss whether to proceed with additional environmental testing based on initial findings.

- Game-Day Challenge: You're the quarterback—make the call! Should you move forward with confidence, or run further inspections before closing?

Key Drill: Phase I vs. Phase II Decision: Much like a quarterback deciding whether to pass or hand off the ball, teams will decide when to stop or proceed to the next level of environmental inspection.

Second Quarter: Flag on the Play! (Building Codes & Permits)

Objective: Master the art of balancing property owner perceptions and local building codes and safety standards.

Play Setup: In football, avoiding penalties is key to winning. Similarly, brokers must avoid "penalties" in the form of noncompliance with building codes. Teams will navigate scenarios where property owners overestimate the quality of their property or forget to pull permits for renovations.

- The False Start Drill: Teams role-play as brokers gently correcting property owners who claim to have "brand-new" systems or roofs that are actually nearing their end-of-life. The challenge is maintaining rapport while guiding the seller to see reality.

- Offside or Just an Overlook? Teams are tasked with evaluating property renovations done without the necessary permits. They must avoid penalties (financial and legal complications) by bringing the property into compliance before closing.

Key Drill: Permits Scrimmage: Teams review real-life property details and flag any overlooked permits. The goal is to ensure compliance before the "closing buzzer," avoiding costly delays.

Third Quarter: Reading the Defense (Lease Review)

Objective: Learn to identify potential threats (deal-breakers) and opportunities hidden within lease agreements.

Play Setup: Just like a quarterback reads the defense to make the right play, brokers must carefully examine leases to avoid any surprises during the deal. Each team is handed a commercial lease with quirky clauses, such as exclusive rights that limit tenant competition.

○ Formation: Your team is in the red zone—close to closing the deal. Now, you need to carefully review the lease for any hidden threats that could derail the deal, such as a clause prohibiting certain tenants (e.g., the "no chicken" clause).

○ Playbook Drill: Teams strategize whether these clauses enhance or limit the property's value. Does this exclusivity increase tenant loyalty or shrink your buyer pool?

Key Drill: Lease Review Touchdown: Success is measured by your ability to adapt the lease terms to maximize your client's advantage. Teams will discuss how to tackle renewal options, restrictions, and first-right-ofrefusal clauses to secure the best deal.

Fourth Quarter: The Retrade Blitz

Objective: Learn to call a smart retrade (price reduction or credit request) based on due diligence findings without fumbling the deal.

Play Setup: In the fourth quarter, things get tense—unexpected issues may arise, and you'll have to renegotiate (retrades). Your team must decide if they're going to ask for a reduction in price or credits for unexpected repairs, or if they'll move forward as is.

○ Blitz Drill: Teams receive a case study with a last-minute issue, such as an old roof that needs replacing or a surprise environmental concern. Will your team push for a retrade or absorb the risk?

- O The Hail Mary: Teams role-play a situation where a buyer's inspector uncovers a hidden issue just days before closing. Will you secure the deal with a well-executed retrade or risk it by pushing too hard?

Key Drill: The Ronnie Drill: Review the story of Ronnie, the tough inspector who always finds something wrong. Teams strategize how to use the inspector's findings to negotiate a fair credit or price reduction without losing the deal.

Overtime: Legal Compliance and Closing

Objective: Understand that quarterbacks (brokers) don't win alone. It's all about assembling the right team and navigating the legal landscape to close deals.

Play Setup: You've made it to the end zone—now, it's time to finish strong. Teams will assemble a dream team of inspectors, attorneys, and lenders to ensure the deal crosses the finish line without penalties. Who's on your dream team and why?

- O Formation: Teams work together to create a "closing playbook," identifying key legal hurdles, zoning complications, or environmental cleanup delays.

- O Handoff Drill: Each group will simulate the final stretch of closing a deal. Teams face real-time decisions on legal compliance, handling last-minute retrades, and zoning challenges.

Key Drill: End Zone Celebration: Teams review their strategy, pinpoint key success factors, and celebrate their victories—just like scoring a gamewinning touchdown!

Wrap-Up: Locker-Room Talk

In the final huddle, teams come together to share their biggest takeaways from *The Playbook*. Brokers discuss the strategies that worked, lessons learned, and how to quarterback successful deals under pressure. Every play, from due diligence to retrades, gets you closer to the win.

Bonus Challenge: The Two-Minute Drill

In this final test, teams face a sudden-death scenario where they have two minutes to solve a commercial real estate challenge. The challenge will focus on handling lease reviews, zoning complications, and building code issues. The fastest and sharpest team wins the championship and takes home the title of "Top Quarterback."

Conclusion:

The Playbook has armed you with the knowledge and strategies to quarterback your commercial real estate deals with precision. Now, go out there and lead your clients to victory with confidence and a winning playbook!

CHAPTER 14

The Touchdown—Closing Deals and Building a Legacy

Talent wins games, but teamwork and intelligence win championships.
—Michael Jordan

On a crisp, clear day, the panoramic views from the rooftop of the twenty-five-story apartment building were breathtaking. To the north, the Chicago skyline stretched majestically, a testament to the city's architectural ambitions. To the east, the serene blue expanse of Lake Michigan mirrored the sky. It was atop this very building, towering above the neighborhood where he once lived, that Tony Hardy found himself reflecting on his journey from a young, eager college student at a career fair to a seasoned commercial real estate broker.

Tony wasn't just any broker; he was a visionary in his field, known for his meticulous attention to detail and innovative approach to investment sales. Today, he was conducting a final inspection before taking this property to market. His expert gaze scanned the building's facade as he looked down. From this vantage point, imperfections were stark against the backdrop of the city—bulges in the masonry, failing lintels—details that could easily be missed from the ground.

"The roof looks solid, about five years into its twenty-year economic lifespan," Tony noted to his colleague, marking the final checklist item with a satisfied nod. As they exited the rooftop, they passed the boiler room where the maintenance specialist was just wrapping up his assessment. "Yep, looks good," the specialist confirmed with a thumbs-up. This building, one of forty-two others built across Chicago in the 1970s, represented the era's architectural and technological advancements. If laid down, the building would stretch seventy-two yards on a football field, from the red zone at the twenty-yard line through the endzone.

Tony had chosen his starting lineup to ensure the best team was on the field for his clients, the sellers. He picked Randy Sullivan from his firm's New York office and Bryan Keller, with whom he had closed over forty deals in the past twenty-four months. Together, these three were unstoppable. They were supported by a top-notch team including a marketing expert, a transaction coordinator, an in-house professional photographer, a senior analyst pouring over the numbers and market trends, and a well-equipped and well-trained back office.

Now, standing on the brink of taking this property to market, Tony felt the weight of the moment. It had been a long journey to this point— winning the assignment amid fierce competition. "This deal," Tony began, addressing his team with a determined look, "is more than just a transaction. It's a culmination of everything we've worked for. Now, we must execute; we're backed up into our own end zone and must cross the goal line. It will not just be a win for us but a landmark in our careers."

The team listened, energized by Tony's vision. They were ready to handle everything from finalizing the listing to managing the complex negotiations that lay ahead. Each phase would require precision, from showcasing the property's potential to handling the inevitable challenges of such a significant transaction. During the inspection period, the investor hired a team of two to meticulously inspect each of the building's 6,725 windows. This detailed approach anticipated potential issues that were indeed identified. The buyer requested a credit, anticipated by Tony's initial inspections, and preemptively negotiated. Bad news doesn't kill deals, but surprises can derail them, and Tony's preparation ensured there were no surprises.

Ten months after going under contract, Tony received a call from Bryan, "Flight gear is out; we've been cleared to land. We are descending toward our runway and anticipate touchdown." This was it—the final approach to a monumental $20.6 million sale, closed just one year and two months after their rooftop assessment.

This chapter serves not just as the closing of a deal but as a testament to what can be achieved with vision, expertise, and an unwavering commitment to excellence in the world of commercial real estate. From the young African American at the career fair to the seasoned broker standing atop a legacy of high rises and high hopes, this journey is a playbook for anyone aiming to make their mark in the complex and rewarding field of commercial real estate.

From the early days as an ambitious young African American Senior at a career fair—choosing to forgo the conventional corporate career path and instead, dive into real estate working rigorous seven a.m. to seven p.m. shifts—to this moment, the path had been a testament to the power of perseverance, knowledge, and strategic acumen. Each chapter of this journey, much like each chapter of this book, *Resimercial Revolution:*

A Broker's Playbook for Commercial Real Estate Mastery, provides the guidance and vision for building a career that could scale unimaginable heights.

The Journey from Rookie to Veteran

The journey began with the basics—understanding property types, learning to assess markets, and recognizing the crucial interplay between investment goals and real estate opportunities. As Tony learned at the college fair and during his early days at Century 21, mastering these fundamentals was like laying the foundation of a high-rise. Each skill and each piece of knowledge added another floor to the towering structure of his career.

At the Newport Beach conference, surrounded by seasoned professionals and eager newcomers, the lessons shared, emphasize that in commercial real estate, one's career is built one transaction at a time. It behooves, new agents transitioning from residential to commercial sectors, to embrace the importance of patience and persistence. The complexities of commercial deals, with their larger financial implications and more extensive due diligence requirements, necessitate a meticulous approach—one that is cultivated over time and with experience.

Team Building for Optimal Outcomes

Sarah's stories on team building should resonate deeply with any commercial broker aspiring to reach new heights. In commercial real estate, success is rarely a solo endeavor. It requires a constellation of skilled professionals—from analysts and marketers to legal experts and transaction coordinators. Each member plays a pivotal role, much like players on a football field, where the quarterback can only succeed with a strong team that does the blocking and tackling supporting them.

Real Estate practitioners who know this and know this well can achieve unprecedented success; your ascent in commercial real estate is not and will not be the result of just your own doing but the result of collaborative efforts and shared expertise.

For the seasoned agents facing peaks and valleys in their transaction histories, focus on consistency and personal development. Engaging with mentors, expanding one's network, and continuously learning about new market trends and financial strategies could smooth out the rough patches. Continue to leverage the strategies outlined in the book as GPS to navigate the complex terrain of commercial deals.

The Importance of Strategic Mentorship

Mentorship had been a crucial aspect of Tony's journey. Like the early mentors at Century 21 showing him the ropes, helping him understand that every challenge was an opportunity to learn and every setback a chance to reassess and realign. For agents at any stage, finding a mentor and coach who can provide guidance, encourage when times are tough, and celebrate when deals close, is invaluable.

Closing with Vision and Precision

In closing, Tony's narrative from the rooftop was clear: the path to mastery in commercial real estate is built on a robust foundation of knowledge, supported by a team of experts, and elevated through continuous personal and professional development. Whether you are a new agent eager to make your mark or a seasoned broker aiming for consistency and breakthroughs, the plays in *Resimercial Revolution* are designed to guide you through every phase of your career.

With the skyline behind him and the future ahead, Tony turned from the vista, ready to tackle the next challenge. For him and for anyone willing to learn from his journey, the possibilities were as vast as the view from the rooftop of that twenty-five-story building.

As you close this book, consider it not as the end of your learning, but as a foundational step toward a future where you, too, can build careerdefining deals. I look forward to the opportunity to collaborate with you, to share in your journey, and to celebrate the successes that we can achieve together. Remember, the complexity of commercial real estate is not a barrier; it's a gateway to developing a profound and impactful career.

Thank you for joining me on this explorative path. Here's to building legacies and shaping communities, together.

About the Author

Tony Hardy, a prominent figure in commercial real estate, was recently featured on Fox News alongside Mike Flannery and his team to discuss the evolving dynamics of Chicago's multifamily and commercial real estate markets. In his interviews, Tony emphasized the city's remarkable resilience, noting how Chicago has continued to thrive despite the challenges brought on by the pandemic and a shifting global economy. He underscored the importance of Chicago's robust pipeline of talent, fueled by world-renowned institutions like Northwestern University and the University of Chicago, which contribute to the city's standing as a major hub for innovation and leadership.

Tony also highlighted the vast diversity of Chicago's business landscape, including over thirty Fortune 500 companies in manufacturing, logistics, and financial trading with the Chicago Board of Trade and Mercantile Exchange, and a growing tech presence with major players like Google and Chamberlain Group. Furthermore, Chicago's healthcare and life sciences leadership positions the city as a premier destination for business growth.

Throughout the conversation, Tony remained a strong advocate for property owners, steering discussions toward opportunity and sustainable growth. He tactfully addressed the importance of balanced legislation, avoiding the pitfalls of pessimism, and instead focusing on the longterm strength of the market and the importance of maintaining a positive outlook for future development in Chicago's vibrant commercial landscape.

In 2020, Tony was appointed Executive Director of Keller Williams OneChicago Commercial, overseeing their three prominent offices in O'Hare, Lincoln Park, and Lakeview. Under his leadership, the commercial division has experienced unprecedented growth. Since then, Tony has taken on an even larger role as Interim Regional Director following the retirement of his mentor and friend, Kris Keller. Tony's influence continues to expand as the Mid-American Regional Ambassador for Keller Williams Commercial, where his leadership now impacts thirtyfour offices across the region.

Tony's journey as a leader extends beyond his role at Keller Williams. His commitment to mentorship has transformed his career. Over the past three years, he has mentored a group of eleven commercial agents, meeting with them twice daily to guide their unprecedented growth. This group, made up of realtors transitioning from residential to commercial real estate, has made remarkable strides, dominating Chicago's commercial real estate market and closing record-breaking deals.

Tony's mentorship has not only benefited this group but also numerous individuals who have gone on to hold prominent leadership positions throughout the industry. His passion for sharing knowledge and empowering the next generation of real estate professionals has left an indelible mark on the industry. Through his leadership, Tony ensures that his mentees are well-equipped to navigate the complex landscape of commercial real estate, building lasting legacies of their own.

In addition to his leadership in commercial real estate, Tony's expertise is recognized on national platforms. He has written over a dozen columns for *Multi-Housing News*, one of the industry's leading publications. His featured articles, such as "The Savvy Investor's Road to Success," "A Common

Mistake Sellers Make," and "Buy, Sell or Hold: Timing the Market," offer actionable insights for both seasoned investors and those new to the field.

Tony's influence extends to his advocacy work. From 2019 to 2023, he served on the Chicago Association of Realtors Board of Directors, representing over seventeen thousand members as a voice for commercial real estate. During this time, he also chaired the Chicago Association of Realtors Commercial Forum in both 2019 and 2020, where he spearheaded the development of Commercial Contracts Pro, a resource that empowered independent agents to access top-tier commercial documents. This initiative leveled the playing field for agents in smaller offices, allowing them to compete with larger, more established commercial firms.

Tony's advocacy doesn't stop there. He serves on the Executive Committee of the Neighborhood Building Owners Alliance, a coalition that represents small and midsized property owners across eleven associations in Chicago. As the President of the South Side Community Investors Association, a position he's held since 2020, Tony champions the interests of local investors, ensuring their voices are heard in discussions about housing policy and regulatory reform. Under his leadership, the association has grown from a small group of landlords into a powerful network of over a hundred members who mentor new investors and share best practices in property management and investment strategy.

Tony's career achievements are underscored by his strong academic background. He earned his Juris Doctor from Whittier Law School and a Bachelor of Science degree in Agribusiness Economics from Southern Illinois University. His dedication to continuous learning and his ability to blend legal expertise with business acumen make him a force in the real estate industry.

Resimercial Revolution: A Broker's Playbook
for Commercial Real Estate Mastery

Tony Hardy's book, *Resimercial Revolution*, provides a roadmap for agents looking to master commercial real estate, drawing from Tony's years of experience, mentorship, and leadership. This is not just a guide—it's a playbook filled with strategies, insights, and practical tools that have helped Tony and his team achieve extraordinary results.

In this book, you'll discover how to navigate the complex commercial real estate landscape, seize opportunities, and avoid the common mistakes that many brokers and investors make. Whether you're new to real estate or looking to transition from residential to commercial, *Resimercial Revolution* offers a detailed blueprint for success. Tony's approach emphasizes teamwork, mentorship, and the power of collaboration, all of which are essential elements in today's competitive market.

Through this book, Tony invites you to join the revolution—one that blends the best of residential and commercial real estate into a new model of success. His goal is to inspire real estate agents and investors from around the world to embrace new ways of thinking, break through barriers, and achieve commercial real estate mastery.

Why Work with Tony Hardy

Tony Hardy's leadership is more than closing deals—it's about creating opportunities, building relationships, and shaping the future of real estate. His mentorship, advocacy, and industry expertise have made him a trusted name in commercial real estate, in Chicago and across the mid-American region.

With a deep commitment to fostering new talent and creating win-win situations for property owners and investors, Tony's legacy is one of empowerment. He's guided his team to remarkable success, growing them from new agents to market leaders, and his impact on the industry continues to grow through his regional leadership roles.

Whether you're reading this book to sharpen your real estate skills, seeking guidance as a new investor, or looking for a leader to help you navigate your next commercial deal, Tony Hardy's expertise is a resource you can trust. His unique approach to mentorship, combined with his strategic leadership, ensures that those who work with him are set up for long-term success.

Anthony "Tony" Hardy,

Keller Williams ONEChicago's—Commercial Division

Executive Director

Interim Regional Director

Keller Williams Realty International—KW Commercial (KWRI)

Regional Ambassador—Mid-American Ambassador

Supply Chain Manufacturing Logistics Commercial Real Estate & Development Group "sclmcre.com"

IL Market Vice President

My Assisted Living Consulting "myALFconsultant.com"

IL Market Vice President

Multifamily Investment Advisors

Managing Director

South Side Community Investors Association

President

Chicago Association of Realtors

Director 2019–2023

Commercial Forum

Chairman 2019–2021

Awards & Recognition

2024: Crexi—Platinum Broker Award 2023: Crexi—Platinum Broker Award

2023: Keller Williams ONEChicago—Quadruple Gold, Gross Commission Income

2023: Chicago Association of Realtors—Leadership Award 2019–2023

2023: Commercial Forum, a division of the Chicago Association of Realtors

Platinum—Multifamily 5+ Units, # of Transactions

Gold—Multifamily 5+ Units, Sales Volume

2022: Keller Williams ONEChicago—Platinum, Gross Commission Income

2022: Chicago Association of Realtors—Leadership Accelerator

Certificate of Completion

Platinum—Multifamily 5+ Units, # of Transactions

Platinum—Multifamily 5+ Units, Sales Volume

Platinum—Retail, Sales Volume

Gold—Retail Leasing, Gross Sq. Ft.

Gold—Retail Sales, # of Transactions

2020: Chicago Association of Realtors—Commercial

Achievement Award

Commercial Achievement Award—In recognition of outstanding contributions to the commercial real estate industry and positive leadership in our community

2018: Commercial Forum, a division of the Chicago Association of Realtors

Platinum—Multifamily 5+ Units, # of Transactions

Platinum—Multifamily 5+ Units, Sales Volume

2016: Commercial Forum, a division of the Chicago Association of Realtors

Platinum—Multifamily 5+ Units, Sales Volume

Gold—Multifamily 5+ Units, Sales Volume

2011: Marcus Millichap

Rookie of the Year Chicago/Oakbrook

Pacesetter